THE LAST CALL

Book Twenty of the Hayle Coven Novels

PATTI LARSEN

chapter one

I couldn't see my feet. Who was I kidding? Knees, either. Thing was, it was probably for the best.

Considering I'd blown up to the approximate size of a zeppelin on steroids with a healthy dose of hippopotamus thrown in for good measure, I felt certain I wouldn't recognize my own feet even if I could lay eyes on them.

Grunt.

Everything was an effort. Walking. Standing. Talking. Breathing.

And if I had to pee one more freaking time, I was going to choke someone.

Lula Kennecott's smiling face appeared over the ginormous mound of my belly, her healing magic retreating as she folded down the hem of the only dress I had left that fit me—affectionately referred to as "the pup tent"—and gently patted the nugget making my life

1

miserable.

"You're doing amazingly well," she said, nose wrinkling as she helped me up, freckles scrunching across the bridge and out over her round cheeks. Her hazel eyes sparkled with good humor as she brushed back a stray lock of brown hair, fallen loose from her ponytail.

"Thanks." My bladder protested as I sat erect. Peanut's foot or hand or something hard pressed fiercely in every which direction. Including my spine. My liver. And, I knew, any day now, he'd find a way to tap-dance on all of my major organs at once.

That would be just delightful.

Grumble.

At least I was over my embarrassment. The first time Lula wanted to have a little look-see at some very private parts of mine, I almost freaked out. Almost. Now, I was happy to whip up my skirt in the hope she would just reach in there and pull him out already.

Would have paid her whatever she wanted.

"Can you tell if he's ready yet?" Mom's question made me think of roasted chickens. Which made my mouth water. And my stomach roll. Alternating between starvation and nausea had grown old so long ago I could only sigh and bear it.

Meanwhile, my mother hovered, smiling and twitching, one hand patting my shoulder, the other stroking my hair, but on autopilot. As though it wasn't me she soothed.

Sheesh.

Lula shrugged her thin shoulders, making me want to kick her. Hard. Somewhere painful.

"He'll come when he's ready."

Don't get me wrong. Lula was awesome. I adored her down to the ground.

But right then, at that moment?

I. Hated. Her. So. Much.

"We could just take him out now, right?" I tried to stand, leaning on Mom to support me as I fought to rise from the edge of the bed. Hoping Lula's answer would be different from the last ten times I asked her.

Immediately pressed both of my hands to the small of my back as the massive weight in front tried to sever my spinal cord in three places. My vertebra groaned in protest.

And women did this multiple times?

We were cracked.

Lula's energy reached out, slid inside my back, eased the pressure until I sighed in relief and actually found I could smile after all.

She was kind of forgiven. For now.

The young healer took my hand in hers, massaging the palm with strong fingers. Energy radiated outward from her touch, soothing muscles I didn't know were tense. "We could encourage him to come early," she said, "but, as you know," nice of her to chide me with a smile on her face, "part of his proper development is his own choice of freedom. I know you don't want to risk even a tiny detail when it comes to your son's birth."

Damned witches and our stupid magical needs. Nice of them to tell me long after I was pregnant and blowing up like a balloon with too much air in it, unlike normal babies, ours had to be allowed to emerge on their own. Only under the most dangerous circumstances did witches have cesarean sections. Part of our power emergence came from the desire to be an individual, to be free.

Sucked so much. Besides, the nugget was more Sidhe than anything, right? And, from the feeling of him, as sweet and easy going as his father—

Choke.

I pushed down the flare of tears rising when I thought about my dead husband, Liam—

Reached for irritation. There it was, waiting on the sidelines. My favorite.

My salvation, most days.

"I know, I know." I grumbled as I shuffled away from Lula, heading for the door, my bare feet scuffing over the carpet. Mom and Lula followed me into the hall. Charlotte waited at the top of the stairs, already reaching for me as I neared the landing. The weregirl's firm grip on my arm and stoic expression told me she was in protectoress mode.

Who was I kidding? Four months into the Sydspansion she moved back to the house full time and her new, happy self disappeared in favor of her old, silent, and grim demeanor. The only times she laughed or smiled was when she didn't see me looking. Usually while staring at my growing belly.

Charlotte continued to guide me down the stairs while I tucked one hand under my ginormous protuberance and begged the nugget to just freaking hurry up already.

Gram sat, knees bouncing, at the kitchen table, faded blue eyes bright, a tight grin on her face. Shenka stood next to her, arms wrapped around herself, also smiling. They would have been in the room with us, if I allowed it. But after being examined countless times by the kind-hearted Lula while a gallery of anxious family tried to hover and watch, I put my foot down.

One at a time. That was it. And today was Mom's turn.

Like it was the first time any of them had seen a pregnant woman.

Galleytrot lifted his big head from the floor, red flames lighting his black eyes as his tongue lolled out the side of his mouth. "Is it time?" His big tail thudded on the ground twice, only falling still when Mom shook her head with a smile so tragic I felt like I'd failed.

Give the knocked up chick a break, would you?

Sassafras licked one paw with careful attention as he spoke. "The boy is too nice to make demands," he said. "Just like his father."

Everyone in the room held their breath. I felt them freeze, turn to stare at me with fear and worry. Like Sass bringing up (my dead husband) Liam would make the world explode. Their collective concern was so heavy I shrugged my shoulders in an effort to free myself of it. While I smiled and, with Charlotte's silent help, bent to kiss the top of Sassafras's head.

"With you, Gram and Mom feeding him power and your influence," I said, "I'll be surprised if he's not more Hayle than O'Dane."

Exhale.

How funny, my family. So protective.

I loved them for it.

And yet, the ache of Liam's loss had faded with time, mostly thanks to the little person I carried around. As Charlotte eased me into a chair, I began to worry maybe once the peanut was born my pain would return.

"The baby is perfectly fine," Lula said. "And although you're now two weeks overdue, I have to assure you such timing is completely normal for a first pregnancy."

I nodded. Heard this before, too, fell silent myself. Maybe he'd just stay in there forever. And keep me from my grief.

But no. I had to birth him, let him out. If only so I could finally be free to go after Ameline Benoit. And pay her back for making me a widow. Just before I went after Max, my supposed drach friend and gave him a piece of my mind—and magic. Then, Iepa. Light Fate.

So many people to thank for their participation in the loss of the man I loved.

I sank into my fury, feeling it tighten my body, my tension rising so swiftly I choked on a breath.

Nugget chose that exact moment to wake up and begin babbling.

Nonsense stuff. An endless stream of chatter. Muttering, giggling, cooing. Which drew Mom, Gram, Galleytrot, everyone, like a herd of nosy cats, all their power reaching for him at once.

And instantly dissolved the hate growing in my heart.

He'd started communicating after the first month, mind touches, mostly. As he developed, however, he seemed to grow mentally and emotionally much more quickly than physically.

Lula assured me this was normal, though even she seemed surprised the first time he talked to her in his silly nonsense. We had to simply chalk it up to the influence of Cian, the Sidhe soul my son carried. I was half tempted to contact Sonja O'Dane and ask Liam's mother if she experienced the same thing, but decided against it. I hadn't seen her since Liam's funeral when she slapped me in grief and blamed me for his death. Though she was my baby's grandmother, the thought of coming face-to-face with her in my condition made my whole body shudder.

Later. As unfair as it seemed. Once the baby was born.

Maybe.

The only problem with my peanut's magical activity? Every time he woke up, everyone knew about it. I almost protested my family's eagerness to embrace the baby, their need for him so powerful I felt like I carried a rock star in my stomach and I was just his groupie holding back the masses.

My son needed his space, didn't he? And I never seemed to have him to myself. But the love pouring out of him, the welcome he always greeted everyone with, grew with each contact until I had to just sit back and allow it.

Lula's mind touched mine as my crazy family interacted with my unborn son. Nope, not a groupie. An organic bassinet.

He will be remarkable, she sent, her power soft and sweet. *He already is, Syd. I think you're going to have a very powerful child on your hands. Tempered with the kindness of his father.*

I think so, too. Stupid tears. Beat it. *What if—*

Yeah. I was the Queen of Blurts.

You will be an excellent mother, Lula sent, firm and

supported with a surge of magic. *You don't have it in you to be otherwise. And with all the support*, she grinned like it was freaking funny or something, *you have around you, I know the child will never want for anything.*

He already had a collection of baby clothes and toys so big it took up most of my bedroom closet.

My egos wriggled and whispered to the baby even as Mom and the others retreated. Nugget spun sideways abruptly before going back to sleep with a contented mental sigh. The girls had been amazing, thankfully, keeping watch over him as they'd done for me, allowing me to sleep, knowing he always had a guardian with access to power watching over him. Aside from the ones outside my body, that was.

"I'll be back tomorrow." Lula stepped away, heading for the door. Waved to me. "But I'm at your call if you need anything."

I waved back in thanks, wishing my fingers didn't look like sausages attached to a slab of ham, wondering at my own vanity at a time like this. Mom turned back, beaming, hands clasped under her chin.

"Let's go for a walk, shall we?" She was convinced exercise was the key to encouraging the peanut to leave my body at last. Had read it in some baby book for normals. Despite knowing the only thing we could do was wait for him to want to come out.

Just thinking about stumping my way around the

block with my over-protective werefriend and the trail of Persian, black hound, grandmother in fuzzy socks and various other assorted coven members who popped up out of the woodwork with fake surprise on their faces made me wince.

Not to mention the fact I didn't think I'd make it without my knees giving out.

"I'm good," I said. I really didn't mean to be surly. And felt bad Mom's face fell. How they all stared at me, waiting.

Expecting me to pop. Right. Then. And. There.

Argh.

When Gram and Sassafras's magic reached out to the baby, I had enough. Shoved myself out of my chair with a groan. Shook my head when Charlotte tried to take my arm.

"I just need a few minutes alone," I said. Growled, actually. Spun—not gracefully, but I managed—toward the basement door and waddled toward it. A heavy, furry body pressed to my side, Galleytrot glaring up at me.

Fine. Whatever. I leaned on him as we descended into the darkness.

Trying not to resent every step.

chapter two

I was actually grateful for the big hound's presence when I grunted my way into the lotus position in the center of the family pentagram. Sure, I could have used magic, but I found doing so lately sometimes woke the nugget's need to try his own hand at spinning power. A very disconcerting experience from inside my womb.

Triggering his magic interfered with mine. I'd had a few giggle and groan worthy moments over the last few months when the baby tried to help—I had the distinct feeling that was his intention despite the results—turning a patch of damaged grass bright purple when I meant to encourage it to grow. Thanks to his curiosity during another instance, I almost started a new ice age when I tried to cool my coffee half a degree before drinking it. Since then I'd pretty much kept my magic use to a minimum, just in case.

My luck, if I tried to use power to sit like this, we'd end up floating off into orbit.

I patted Galleytrot's heavy shoulder as I settled, lower back twingeing all over again, just adding to my irritation.

"Thanks," I said. Actually meant it through my annoyance. "Now beat it."

He swiped my cheek with his very wet tongue before chuckling and bounding back up the stairs. I wiped at the nastiness with the sleeve of the pup tent.

So. Gross.

And yet, the baby giggled.

We'd see how much he liked being slobbered by the big hound.

My stomach churned, turned over. Settled. Damn it, everything made me feel nauseated these days. I was lucky not to have had a pukey pregnancy at the outset, but I was more than making up for it the last month or so.

You're eating too much meat, Shaylee sent.

No, my demon growled, *she's not eating enough*.

You need to drink more water, sent my vampire.

Water. Nice of her to remind me. I'd just gone to the bathroom before Lula arrived. And, wouldn't you know it? Had to go again.

I ignored my bladder as the girls grumbled their advice in the background. Drew a deep breath—as deep as I could with a bowling ball sitting on my diaphragm—and exhaled.

The Last Call

My eyes closed on their own, the powers inside me settling. Tried to, anyway. My swollen ankles made it hard to find a comfortable position, not to mention my chest was about twice its normal size and *hurt*. All tender and swollen. Nasty. I'd given up on bras about two weeks ago.

Screw that. Let them sag. I'd have Lula magic them back to perky when this was over.

Another poke from my lower back pulled a soft groan from my lips. This was it. No more freaking kids for me. But even as I had the thought, two things happened. Nugget stirred all over again, murmured, hugged me with his power. And I remembered I still had future daughters to mother.

Sigh.

Maybe a girl would be different. Though, I had to admit, I was very lucky all along, not a sniff of trouble to be had. I'd breezed through the first three months, still in my favorite jeans until the start of my second trimester. Though if one more person told me I was all baby, I was going to punch them in the face.

With all the support for the baby and myself, I really didn't have anything to complain about. Except finding myself floating over my bed in the middle of the night. Or reaching for a carton of milk in the fridge only to have it disappear the second I touched it.

Yeah.

And yet... so worth it as the baby woke from his brief

nap, his babbling quiet for once, and touched my mind like he was fully aware of who I was.

A. Maze. Ing.

I loved this part. The moments we had alone together, so few and far between with the magical interference of my family a constant companion, as constant as the beautiful boy inside me. Everything went away when his mind touched mine. My body didn't exist, my aches and pains and discomfort long gone. Only the nugget and me. And the girls, all together.

Curiosity. Contentment. A budding need to understand who he was and where. His purpose. All tied to the simmering earth power of the Sidhe.

And, for the first time, others. I hadn't felt them before, so strong was Cian's influence. But as I sat there, hugging my child with my arms and my magic, I finally felt the powers blossoming inside him.

Vampire. Witch. Demon. Creation. And yes, the blackness of sorcery.

I drew a breath of awe and sudden worry.

I was going to give birth to a maji child.

He burbled happily, his powers mingling. But no, he didn't have enough, at least not yet. The magicks I sensed were trace, bits and pieces. Reminded me of the wild magicks, the souls of the fallen drach. Slivers of power. Wound together with Cian.

Making something entirely new.

Whatever power my son had access to, I knew I had enough of my own to guide him. Just as long as I didn't screw him up in the process.

Nervous much?

We will never allow that, my vampire sent. *And neither will you.*

I actually smiled, confidence returning as the nugget stretched, pushed against me with his mind and his body.

Regardless of whether that was true, we didn't have much choice. He'd be coming out eventually and I'd just have to deal.

Maybe this new need to understand meant he was ready to be born. But was I ready to let him go? In moments like this...

Not a chance.

I hugged my belly harder, feeling tears trickle down my cheeks, those same cheeks aching from the huge grin on my face. The family reached for me at that moment, feeling my joy, and I let the coven in, all of them. Allowed them to feel my son, his sweetness and brilliance, the expanse of his magic. Showed him who they were and impressed on him how important he was to us.

And the family embraced him back, showering him with love and adoration. Excitement to see him, to feel his uniqueness and the powers he possessed.

Peanut sighed, muttered something and hugged them back before slipping back into sleep.

The family left me then, with murmurs of encouragement and leaving behind the compression of their love for me. I wiped at my tears, all irritation gone, rubbing soft circles around my expanded belly, feeling the bumps and lumps of my son through my skin.

Soon.

I looked up at the touch of demon magic, felt the veil part, the heat of Ahbi's power as my demon grandmother's spirit said hello. I embraced her with my energy as the family had held me before releasing her and focusing on my sister on the other side.

While Ahbi giggled and cooed over the sleeping nugget.

"How did your exam go?" So much anxiety mixed with anticipation in Meira's voice. I grinned at my sister through the veil where she sat on the edge of her desk, the Demonicon sky visible through the window behind her.

"Fine," I said. "No change." A hint of frustration returned as I jealously eyed Meira's tall, slender demon form, her gorgeous figure prickling my vanity. "What else is new?"

She must have sensed my annoyance because she smiled and sent me a soft hug of power. "I'm so envious," she said, cutting my own envy out from under me. "He's going to be an amazing boy, Syd."

Grumble mumble.

Grin.

Yeah.

"Did you open the gift I sent?" She leaned forward eagerly, taut, flat stomach exposed, shining black horns curving back from jet curls cascading over her shoulder and down almost to the floor. Damn it.

"I did." I caught myself still stroking my belly as I answered, wondering if mine would ever be so smooth again. "The booties are darling." Made from some kind of Demoniconian creature's fur, so soft they felt like air. "Thank you, Meems."

She smoothed the front of her gold-threaded skirt hanging low on her thin hips and bounced a little in place. "I have a whole outfit for him for winter," she said. Beamed, white teeth bright against her red-tinted skin as her amber eyes flared with fire.

"You're the best auntie." Totally meant it.

"I'll do my damnedest." She winked. "Though he has the most amazing and beautiful mother ever. So he really doesn't need me."

My lips twisted in a wry smile. "If you're into bloated and gargantuan," I said.

Meira rolled her eyes, poking a finger in my direction. "You have no idea how gorgeous and glowing you are," she said.

I suddenly felt old despite her words, way older than my twenty-two years. I'd ignored my birthday this year, choosing to focus on the peanut. But in doing so I almost forgot Meems also had a birthday, not so long ago. Shenka saved my ass with a nice present—a new pair of platform boots made of chrome, Meira's favorite. But at fourteen, she looked older than me, thanks to her time on Demonicon and the hyped up nectar Sassafras's mother hooked her on a few years ago.

Wow. Was it years?

Old. Yup yup.

Meira's smile faded as she leaned back, arms crossing over her chest, biting her bottom lip. "I wish this was just our daily social call," she said. "But I have some news."

Okay then. "I can take it," I said, even as my hormones chose just then to go wacko, a giant lump rising in my throat. Because I just knew what she was about to tell me.

And I wasn't going to like it.

Not one little bit.

"Your official invite will come from Dad," Meira said, lips turning down into an unhappy frown, "but he asked me to warn you ahead of time. So you can prepare Mom."

Damn. It. I knew it.

"He's finally picked one," Meira said, a snarl in her voice. "And the betrothal ceremony is in about a month."

One. A new wife.

Oh, hell.

chapter three

I sat there for a long time, unable to speak or stop the tears—now of sadness—rolling down my cheeks. Meira held her own silence, just the quiet of the basement, the cool darkness soothing me as much as our mutual stillness.

With a hiccup, I finally used my well-worn sleeve to swipe the moisture from my face and nodded.

"This is just the betrothal ceremony," Meira said, as if that made some kind of difference. "The wedding won't happen until later."

"Nice of Dad to wait until I can come," I said, much more harshly than I intended. But Meira just nodded. I met my sister's eyes, hesitated. Blurted, "What's she like?"

Meira rolled her amber eyes, snorted. "Weak," she said. "I think Dad went way to the left after the whole thing with Merlotsenilater ." Right. Thing #3 on the roster who'd tried to kill Meira. "But, at least she won't be a problem when it comes to power. I can work around her. She's happy just knowing she's going to be Ruler's wife."

Wife.

Gulp.

Holy hell, Dad. And yet, like me not so long ago, he really didn't have a choice, did he?

I bobbed a nod. "You must *adore* her."

My sister hissed with her own irritation. "She drives me nuts," she said. "But she has no illusions about her place, knows she's just there to give Dad a pure demon heir." We both snorted, like there was something wrong with us or something. Stupid demon politics. "At least she doesn't have an ambitious bone in her body. I have no idea how she survived this long without being dropped down to a low-level Plane. I haven't seen her fight one battle. Has this sweetness about her that grosses me out, but seems to keep everyone else from being interested." Meems tossed her hands. "Maybe that's her M.O.. No one has ever seen her as a viable target because she's so pathetic."

That did surprise me. From the sounds of things, she would have been an easy target. "Maybe she's smarter than you're giving her credit for?"

"Maybe." Meira chewed one thick, black fingernail. "Thanks a lot. Now you have me worried I've misjudged her."

I chuckled and shook my head. "You're welcome."

"Smartass." Meira flashed a smile. Went all fake giggly and wide-eyed, voice going up several notches in a mimic of an irritating bubbly pop. "You can come over and do girlie stuff with us. Won't that be family funtastic?"

Blech. We both shuddered and then laughed.

I sobered first. "You realize this is all kinds of crappy? That you're dropping this in my lap and I'll have to punish you for it later?" Mom. Yikes.

Meira's face fell. "I'm sorry," she said. "I'll come and talk to her with you."

I shook my head, sent her love. "I'm just teasing," I said. "Bad enough you have to deal with the politics and ick over there. I can handle this part. Besides, when I burst into ugly tears, everyone will just blame it on my whacked out hormones."

Meira bobbed her head. "Bad, huh?"

I rolled my eyes, feeling my throat tighten just at the thought of talking to our mother. "You have no idea." The words came out in a groan. Hell, I'd suddenly sobbed, for no apparent reason, over an egg I dropped on the floor yesterday morning. Shenka cleaned it up while Charlotte patted my back while I wept like I'd killed someone.

Yeah. Not so bad.

"I'll tell Mom." I blurted the words in an effort to

keep from crying. Too hard.

Meira sighed deeply, rising to pace a little. "Syd, I wouldn't even ask you to come if you wanted to stay home. I'm sure Dad would understand. But..."

"Meems," I took back control of my churning emotions, sending her a magical hug and a flare of demon power that actually didn't go wonky for once and managed to burn off my need to curl up and weep. "There's no way I'm letting you go through this alone." Chances were, Dad was putting things off so my sister wouldn't have to attend without me. Nice of him to include me in the heart-crushing moment. "Okay?"

She spun away, shoulders down, head bowed. Nodded once, barely visible as her body shook. When she turned back, I saw the misery on her face.

"Oh, Meems," I said, tears firing up all over again, lower lip trembling. "I'm so sorry I haven't been here for you."

She forced out a laugh, breathless, faced me full on, long curls spinning around her. "Silly," she said. "I was thinking the same thing." Her hands made short work of her tears, impatient with them. "Are you sure you don't want me there when you tell Mom? I can come over, no problem."

I thought about it. Spread both hands over my belly. Shook my head. "I'll take care of it," I said. "Somehow."

Meira hesitated. Her face crumpled a moment more

before she threw her arms around herself. And her power around me.

"I love you so much," she said.

And closed her side of the veil.

I let her go, echoing the words back at her in my mind as I hugged Ahbi before my side sealed shut and I was alone again.

Not quite. A soft paw settled on my thigh, a fat, furry Persian body snuggling up in what little space there was beside my belly.

"You don't fit anymore," I said, stroking Sassafras's tail. He pressed his cheek to my stomach, purring softly. Aimed at the nugget.

"This is just fine," he said. Looked up, amber eyes flaring with power. "Can I ask a favor?"

Um. Weird. "Anything," I said.

He closed his eyes, body vibrating with his purr. "Let me tell your mother."

Gulp.

Choke.

Sob.

I lifted him into my arms, settling him on top of the swell of my pregnant body, feeling his power taking the weight. He rubbed his cheeks against mine, paws kneading my collarbone as his tail beat a soft melody against my tummy.

"I really should do it," I said when I was able to

speak.

"No," he said. "I've been taking care of Hayle witches for a hundred and fifty years. Miriam was my baby once, Syd. Just like you. Just like your children will be to me." He licked the tears from my cheek. "My job is to be here for all of you, no matter your age. Because, to me, you're all still my little girls."

I rocked him gently, weeping again, but this time in happiness.

"Thank you, Sass," I whispered.

His purring increased, not just for the baby this time, rumbling in my chest in a beautiful song of love.

"Let me help her through this." He met my eyes again, pushed in nose almost touching mine. "Please, allow me this burden. For, to me, it is no burden at all, but my calling."

I nodded, snuffled. Managed a smile. Kissed his forehead. "I love you, Sassafras."

His body trembled. "I love you so much, Syd." One paw dropped and patted the bump of my nugget before he went on. "I promise you, as I have for every one of the Hayles I've known, good and bad, I will watch over this child. Without prejudice. And always with love." He head-butted my shoulder. "As I've done so many other Hayle witches before him. And I will never let anything happen to him."

So. Much. Love.

"He couldn't ask for a better friend," I said through more tears, a burning throat, aching to sob all over his silver fur. "A more amazing confidant. I know I couldn't have."

Sassafras's amber eyes welled with moisture as he pressed one paw to my lips.

"At least he won't give me trouble," Sass said at his most arrogant. Actually sniffed, nose rising in the air. "His father's influence will keep him nice and pliable." Another sniff. "Unlike some witches I know."

I hugged him again, laughing, crying. "We'll see," I said. "He's his mother's son too, remember."

Sass groaned. "The elements preserve us," he said. And laughed, eyes sparkling. "Oh, Syd," he whispered. "You know I wouldn't have it any other way."

Neither would I.

Sassafras helped me stand, his power supporting me, my aching legs begging me to return to the ground. Or bed. Bed would be good right about now.

No, wait. Pee first. Then a million pillows and the open window with a breeze to cool my hot cheeks.

Bliss.

Not to be. I should have known better. Because my life was all kinds of straight forward and easy, right?

I barely had time to contemplate a nap when a gaping black hole opened in front of me.

And Demetrius Strong walked through.

chᴀpᴛᴇʀ ꜰoᴜʀ

Talk about a shock to the system. I gaped at the well-dressed and impeccably groomed man standing before me with a sweet smile on his cherub face. Though his hair was still white and softly curling, Demetrius's scar was gone, skin flawless. He looked at least twenty years younger, more Mom's age than the beaten, broken nutpot I'd known.

This Demetrius appeared much more like when we'd first met. Back when he was leader of the Chosen of the Light, the sect of fanatical magic users intent on destroying all those they deemed unworthy and unclean. Not his fault, I knew now, as much as I'd hated him then. Shattered and reassembled by Liander Belaisle, Demetrius's prior life had been as a Steam Union sorcerer.

A story I still didn't have the full text of yet. But hoped to one day. Because I knew it involved Gram somehow.

For now, it was wonderful to see him in his pale gray suit coat, clean white t-shirt beneath, dark jeans. He looked like a really cool college professor or internet mogul, not a dirty street person in a torn and stained shirt I'd tried to get him to change, ratty shorts and tattered tennis shoes he tolerated when his sanity was questionable.

Hair cut. Stubble free. Beaming smile.

Blast from the past. Minus the creep factor, much to my delight. I didn't think this Demetrius Strong was interested in burning me at the stake.

He reassured me I was right when he murmured his joy, reaching out to touch my cheek, blue eyes bright with moisture. "Syd," he whispered. "How radiant."

Blushing. I suddenly felt awkward and hideous, wishing I could just take the compliment. "Thanks," I said, though uncomfortable with my physical condition, unable to hold back my smile at seeing him again. "You too."

He laughed, a sound so full of happiness the nugget woke up and immediately cooed back. Demetrius's eyes fell to my tummy, though his sorcery remained firmly in control. "Congratulations, my very dear," he said, the edge of his sorcery touching mine with a feather-light stroke, touching the baby's. Demetrius's smile widened. "Remarkable," he said. Paused as his kind eyes rose to mine again. "Might I add to my salutations my utmost condolences on your loss. Liam was a wonderful young man who did not deserve the Fate assigned him."

If it hadn't been for my shock at his coherence—despite knowing he'd regained his sanity during the battle at the stronghold—I would have broken down into sobbing. I'd allowed sympathy before this, but minor, peripheral. More to benefit those who felt grief and needed to express it than for my own comfort.

But Demetrius's kindness and clear simplicity of condolence hit me harder than anything I'd yet endured. Thankfully, my surprise at seeing him after all these months cut short my hormone-ridden reaction—I blamed it on that, naturally, and not my grief lingering, waiting to be addressed—and allowed me to remain calm and lucid myself.

Instead of dissolving into a blubbering mess of sobbing pregnant woman.

Talk about an ugly cry.

"Thank you," I said, proud of myself my voice remained steady. Took his hand, felt his sorcery gently butt up against mine again in greeting as he squeezed my fingers ever-so-softly. "I'm so glad to see you." Really, really. Almost enough to break me down again. "Especially like this."

Whole. Sane. Himself again.

Demetrius's lips pressed to my cheek before he winked, a sparkle in his eyes. "There are many things for which I will apologize to you," he said as his own demons crawled over his face. "But those can wait, I think. For a time we two can sit and discuss matters when you are not so steeped in your joy." His face brightened as I almost tried to deny him. Knew I couldn't. It would disrespect his need to clear himself of his guilt. I would enjoy the talk, I suspected.

Demetrius continued holding my hand as his smile returned. "For now, I will only say I'm sorry it took me so long to return home again," he said. That surprised me, the fact he thought of this house as home. Also brightened my day a little more. "I've been busy making a certain sorcerer's life miserable."

A happy zing of spite zipped through me. Belaisle. Before leaving me on the stronghold plane, Demetrius told me to leave the Brotherhood leader and my old friend-turned-traitor, Rupe, to him. That the former Goth known as Blood and Liander Belaisle were his to deal with. And I had. Mostly because my pregnancy forced me to think of the peanut before myself.

And my revenge.

But seeing Demetrius brought it all back. Sure did.

With a fierceness that surprised me, I snarled and pulled on Demetrius's hand. "Is he dead yet? Tell me he's not dead yet."

The sorcerer laughed, clear and bell-like. "Don't worry," he said. "I promise we'll kill him together."

Awesomesauce.

Even the nugget seemed happy, mental voice giggling.

Made me pause and wonder if I was accidentally growing a smiling, cheerful psycho.

Had to get my act together.

"I've had the pleasure of talking with Eva Southway." Demetrius didn't release my hand, total comfort embracing us as Sassafras sat at my feet, listening in silence, amber gaze blinking slowly. "I've been welcomed back into the Steam Union." His voice turned suddenly thick, large blue eyes blinking a few times. "It's good to be home, Syd."

There was that word again. I understood the use now, though. Not necessarily here. But home, to himself. After decades under Belaisle's influence. Being someone else, an existence he had no choice but to live.

Home was his sanity. And the real Demetrius Strong.

Who was he, exactly? I'd seen glimmers when I'd first rescued him from the Chosen, still draped in the skin of a demon mine had forced him into. Restored him from. Had flashes of him as his gratitude shone through his insanity, his invaluable help despite the courage necessary and the hardship he endured telling me more clearly than words the kind of man he had been.

And the one who saved us all during the battle at the stronghold. The smiling man standing before me now.

I had no doubt I was going to be very happy to have him in my life again.

"I'm thrilled for you," I said, not sure what else to say as my heart churned with a wealth of emotions.

Demetrius bobbed a quick nod, as though knowing, understanding what I felt through those simple words. "Thank you. For everything." He swung my hand a little, an almost child-like motion, two friends in a playground sharing secrets, forming bonds. "For trusting me, back there. When I needed you to." At the stronghold. The hardest thing I'd ever done, releasing my power, my egos, allowing myself to be drained to empty when a man I knew to be broken begged me to let go.

Yup. All on the word of his crazy self.

My hitchhikers reached out to him and surrounded him with soft touches of their multi-colored flames in answer as I answered. "Always," I said.

His answering smile lit the whole basement.

"Such being said," he grinned at me, "I wanted permission to start a North American branch of the Steam Union." Demetrius finally released my hand, bending to stroke Sassafras's head as the silver Persian began to purr again.

"I thought there already was one?" Hadn't Piers told me there were Steam Union here on our continent already? That he was hoping to reconnect with them? Then again, he never did fill me in on why the two factions lost track of each other, either.

So many questions I'd let fall to the wayside in the last nine months. I loved the nugget with all my heart, but it really was time for both of us to be free after all.

I had a lot of work to catch up on.

Demetrius gently took my elbow, guiding me toward the stairs as Sassafras sashayed his way ahead of us. "There are," he said. "But this branch is a splinter group not interested in connecting. We're working on it."

We. Demetrius and Piers? Had to be.

I was very grateful for his steadying hand as we ascended to the kitchen together despite my irritation at being left out of the fun. Knowing the swelling boy inside me was the reason for me being left in the dark. Still.

The steps groaned under my weight, as if in agreement with my conflicting emotions. Yes, my head understood. But the rest of me was pissed.

Oh, and thanks for the reminder of my massiveness, stupid stairs.

"Maybe you should be asking Mom about forming a sect here." She was Council Leader, after all. I didn't really have any choice in the matter. Neither did she, come to think of it. But it would be courtesy, right?

Demetrius laughed as Sassafras opened the door with a push of energy, swinging ahead of us a few steps. His demon shape appeared for a flash, turning to smile down at me from the dear, young man's face I'd only known a short time before the fat cat waddled out of sight. "I honestly don't care what Miriam and the witches think," Demetrius said, helping me into the sunlight.

Fair enough. "I think it's a great idea," I said as Gram rose from the kitchen table, hands trembling, faded blue eyes locked on Demetrius. I followed her gaze to his, saw the eagerness in his expression and let him go. "But make sure you talk to Mom eventually, okay?"

He didn't answer. He wasn't with me anymore. Amazing to stand there, hand pressed to my lower back, and watch as my grandmother anxiously smoothed her flowered dress, touched her white hair with a nervous gesture, smiled with coy adorableness at the sorcerer.

Holy. Freaking. No. Way.

Gram?

And Demetrius?

What the hell?

"You," he said, as he came to a halt before her, their height a perfect match, "are the most beautiful thing I've seen in so long. I'm breathless."

She giggled. Freaking giggled.

"Ethpeal Hayle," he said, opening his arms, "I've missed you so, my dear."

And Gram... stepped into his arms and kissed him. Passionately.

33

On. The. Mouth.

Before bursting into tears and clinging to him like she'd just found her long lost best friend.

No, not best friend.

Soul mate.

So much I didn't know. So many questions.

They could wait.

Demetrius led my grandmother out of the kitchen and down the hall toward her room without a backward glance, the sound of her door closing telling me I might have to wait longer than I thought.

Shenka's dark eyes shone with laughter and a sheen of tears. "Oh my," she said.

Tell me about it.

Sassafras leaped up on the table, eyes locked on the hallway. "I never knew," he said. "I thought there was only Ivan."

Clearly not the case. And since my grandfather was a lying, cheating, asshole traitor who I hoped would burn in hell for the remainder of eternity for what he did to Gram... Demetrius was a nice trade off.

Maybe Gram could finally find her happy after all.

I just needed to go after Ameline, strip her power and return it where it belonged.

As if in agreement with my assessment of the situation, nugget stirred. Kicked me as hard as he could in the spine, bless him.

And grumbled. Mumbled. Complained.

Out.

Um. What? Was that a word?

Out.

I staggered as a band of pain grabbed me in an iron fist and tried to remove all awareness of the world from my conscious mind. A gasp so loud I'm sure it broke the sound barrier escaped my collapsing lungs as I reached out to Shenka with my lips flapping like a suffocating fish.

Owfreakingowdamnitholycrapwhatthehell?

The pain went away while my second gaped back, dark eyes wide and a little wild.

"Syd?" She took a hesitant step toward me, power reaching for me.

Just as the nugget kicked again.

Out!

Oh. My. Swearword.

"Call Lula," I choked around a new wave of agony as I sank to the floor, unable to stand any longer. "I think—"

Out, Momma.

With a surge of panic, Shenka's magic screaming for Mom and the Kennecott healer, I wasn't sure either of them would make it.

The peanut was coming.

And he wasn't taking "slow down" for an answer.

chApTER fIVE

"Syd, look at me."

Nope, no looking, just breathing. I couldn't breathe, though, that was the problem, wasn't it? Air refused to go in and out of my lungs in a normal manner, my diaphragm contracting and squeezing so hard I could barely pull in air.

Which left me gasping, writhing.

"Syd." Power, usually so kind and soft, sharpened into a jab. My eyes flew open, sweat stinging instantly as I stared up at Lula. She smiled at me, gently, but her magic held me in a grip almost as tight as the pain. "You're doing fine." No panic in her voice. Good, okay then. That was good, wasn't it? So why did I feel panicked and freaked out and like I was going to explode all at the same time? "You have to relax or the baby will fight you."

Eep. Ack. Groan.

No, nugget. No fighting, please, no fighting. Just come out, okay?

Out. His little mind knew that one concept, clearly. *Out. Out. Out. Out.*

Hell, yeah. Prior concerns about the consequences long gone, I was with him there.

"Out," I panted. "You got it. But you have to actually do something, kiddo."

Fell back onto my pillow with a choking sob as the pain eased and he rumbled his unhappiness.

Holy. Freaking. Forget it. How long had it been? Sixteen days? A month? Forever?

I must have asked out loud because Mom's face appeared, her fingers cool on my cheek. "It's only been a half hour," she said. "So you're doing fine."

Bull. No. Way.

The baby howled once. *OUT.*

Yeah, no freaking kidding. But this time when the pain subsided, I felt him pouting, sighing, frustrated as I was frustrated. Too soon to quit. Was it really such a short period of time?

Convinced Mom lied to me, I snarled at Lula.

"Just take him out already."

She continued with her evil little smile that was supposed to be all sweet and kind and crap. But I knew better when she said, "Soon, now."

Liar. Such a liar.

My egos crooned to me even as I snapped at them to shut the hell up. This sucked and I wanted it done. Hell, I was done already. No way could I go through this.

"I'm finished, okay?" I rolled on my side, trying to get up. "We can try again tomorrow."

Hands press me down again.

"Syd." Mom's face wavered before me, her familiar magic holding me still as Sassafras's purr hummed its irritating song in my ear. "It's almost over. You have to let go of the baby. That's all. Just let go."

Wait, this was my fault? "Not my fault." The nugget protested, agreed with me.

Loved me, no matter his discomfort, felt bad for hurting me. Wanted me to be happy despite his own need.

Crap, Syd. Think for once.

"No, sweetheart." Mom stroked my forehead, belying what I now understood, her fingers icicles against the flaming heat of my skin. Funny how I could feel heat, cold. My maji power didn't allow me to, did it? What had this kid done to me? "You're fine. Just let him go, now."

Sassafras continued to purr in my ear as I processed my son's need to protect me, to keep me safe, holding him back. "It's okay," he said. "To let him go. Syd, he'll be fine. I promised, remember? I'll take care of him for you, when he's here. But you have to let him be born."

Was it my fault? I gasped as the pain returned, felt my alter egos support me, the ripples of agony passing through me and into them, down to the core of my sorcery. So. Much. Pain.

I wanted him out, didn't I?

Didn't I?

And then, I felt it, what they knew already. There, in the darkest corner of myself. The tie holding him to me, the face I missed so very much, the love I'd lost. And still mourned.

I clung to the peanut as I clung to Liam.

Shaylee wailed, my demon roaring her sadness. The family magic pooled in grief, weeping itself into despair. Even my sorcery closed, the blossom retreating, my vampire shuddering in loss.

How could I let this lovely boy go? How could I let him leave me, knowing what happened to his father, what could happen to him out here in the real world?

How?

Syd, Gram's voice echoed in my head, faint but there. *It's time to let go of Liam, girl. The baby is not his father. And your son has his own destiny.*

We twisted away from her, all of us, even as the nugget rebelled with a surge of frustration, his worry for me gone in a burst of his own need.

OUT, MOMMA.

For one last moment, I clung to Liam. To his smile,

the way he smelled of fresh earth and fabric softener. His deep, steady roots. My oak tree. My sweet, sweet husband.

And then, sobbing for my loss as I hadn't mourned before, I let him go.

Peanut stilled. Sighed. And pushed against me.

This time, I was ready. Helped.

Felt him leave me, my physical body, as Mom cried and Lula smiled and Sass purred. While Gram's thin, remaining magic embraced me.

His first cry was so loud I jerked in response, the sound of Galleytrot howling in the back yard a joyful counterpoint to the boy's lusty cry.

Everything inside me reacted, desperate to know he was okay. Lula's magic severed the cord keeping us together, the last of our physical connection gone.

Even as the magic so much a part of him latched onto me and forged a bond I knew would never part.

Liam was gone. But my baby boy was here. A surge of power from the Kennecott healer and he was sparkling clean, wrapped quickly in a blanket. Lula laid him, now quiet and content, on my chest, and I kissed his soft forehead. He felt soft and warm and smelled of fresh-turned earth, bringing tears to my eyes.

Of joy. Knowing then, through our baby, Liam was always with me.

I whispered my love for our son, wrapping him in my

energy.

"Gabriel Liam Hayle," I said over his fuzzy blonde hair tinted with a hint of red. "Welcome to the family."

chapter six

Amazing how such little fingers and toes could hold endless fascination. Perfectly formed. Tiny replicas of my own, miniature flawlessness in a sweet bundle I wanted to hold forever.

His tiny button nose wrinkled in sleep, bow lips working as he sucked his tongue. Gabriel's scent evolved past his father's into summer and freshness with a hint of the most delicious vanilla, his little body warm in my arms. I feared I'd lose the ability to physically feel that part of him, my temperature sensation curtailed by my power. But though my maji magic kicked in after his birth, returning me to my normal lack of sensation to heat and cold, something about Gabriel made things different. I could sense a change from moment to moment as his body adjusted. Warming in sleep, cooling a little as he woke, rising again when he fed.

But it was the warmth of his power and his darling little soul that made me want to hug him and never let him go.

I was forced to release him, set him down from time to time those first few days, much to my irritation. So what if I needed a shower? Gabriel didn't care if I stank. Or needed to eat? I had enough padding on me to last several years, thanks. The worst? They convinced me to give him up, didn't they? Mom and Shenka and Gram. Charlotte. Meira, who arrived with more gifts and a huge grin. All of them. Talked me into letting my son go.

So they could hold him.

Heartless. Selfish.

Jerks.

I don't think he slept in his bassinet once the first two weeks of his life. There was always someone there to cuddle him. Night time brought Sunny and Uncle Frank, even, to take away my precious moments with my son as the vampire queen and her consort mauled him just like the rest of the damned family.

I didn't mean to be grouchy. But seriously.

Mine.

The best thing about Gabriel was his shining personality. My downfall. Maybe if he'd been the kind of baby who cried for no reason. Or at least fussed a little. I found myself wishing he'd upchuck on someone so they'd give him back to me. But no, not my Gabriel. I don't think I knew what his cry sounded like, the only one he uttered gone with his birth.

Gabriel giggled. Gabriel cooed. Gabriel smiled and wriggled.

Gabriel, in a word, was perfect.

Lula admitted she found it astonishing how mature he seemed. "Most babies aren't self-aware this young," she said as I greedily took my child back from my sad-faced mother. "The fact he was able to articulate to you in the womb... he's a remarkable boy."

I looked up, sharp and concerned at the wondering tone in her voice.

"He's fine, though." I rested my cheek against his fuzzy hair, combing his little person with my power as my egos echoed my act, looking for any flaw, any problem.

Lula laughed, patted my shoulder. "Gabriel is more than fine," she said, echoing what I already knew. "He's perfect."

He was, wasn't he?

"I think it's our fault," Sassafras said from his perch next to me. He refused to leave my side. That was, until someone else took the boy from me. Then he refused to leave *their* side.

Traitor cat.

Lula shrugged. "The power you gave him during the pregnancy could be the issue," she said. "This is my first experience with the birth of a Sidhe soul, though. I daresay it's Cian's influence at work."

Right. The full-grown Sidhe soul inside my son, a part of the Gate creator, had to have an effect.

Sassafras seemed to relax. "I hadn't thought of that."

I felt a momentary pang of empathy for the demon cat. "You didn't hurt him," I said, stroking Sass's fur with one hand, cuddling Gabriel against me with the other. "In fact, you, Mom, Gram. My hitchhikers. The family." Okay, I wasn't grumpy anymore. "You all gave him a massive gift. I agree with Lula." My fingers left Sass and touched my son's soft cheek. "Gabriel *is* perfect."

Despite my need to just lie there and cuddle, nurse, sing to and generally absorb my son back into me through osmosis, Lula had me up and moving right away. I was a little surprised how fast the bloated body recovered, how quickly my hands returned to mostly normal, ankles and knees no longer aching. My lower back rejoiced and thanked me, though my tummy remained a soft, squishy mess for a while. Not that I had washboard abs or anything, but I despaired at the flab until it, too, began to recede and my waist came back.

So happy to see my waist.

Life settled into a kind of joyful rhythm, surrounding Gabriel's every need and whim. Breast feeding took some getting used to, though his power hummed around us at every meal and encouraged my body to give him what he needed without any help from me. Lula told me I was lucky how easily the two of us fit together and I was again grateful for my son's amazing development.

Especially when some of the family came to visit. Shared horror stories about colic and illness that sent me running, stomach churning, Gabriel protectively tucked against me until Mom or Shenka came to softly soothe us both.

Sassafras's constant companionship at least eased the worst of my fears. I woke one morning, about three weeks after he was born, to find my son talking baby talk to the cat who answered with his own version of Gabrielspeak.

The. Cutest. Thing. Ever.

Ever.

I had no idea a three-week-old shouldn't be talking yet. Lula's alarm was well hidden, but I caught it and tensed immediately when she arrived for his weekly checkup.

"He's growing much faster than most children," she said, smile wavering only slightly.

"He's fine," Galleytrot growled. "Leave the boy be."

Was she right? Gabriel did seem quite sizable for an infant. Fitting into six month baby clothes. And how had his face matured so quickly?

"Sidhe babies grow up very fast," Galleytrot informed us from where he lay beside me, earth power a protective presence. "Trust me, Gabriel is completely fine."

Lula accepted his word and I had to. Didn't I? Again, I could have asked Sonja, I supposed. But Liam's mother had been left out of the pregnancy. At this point, I didn't even know if she knew Gabriel existed. She already wasn't exactly my biggest fan, blamed me for her son's death... Since that made two of us, I could hardly hold her animosity against her. And now that my son was here, surely she'd blame me for not knowing about Gabriel—or being kept from him, not putting that past Mom for a second—and chalk it up as yet another reason to hate me.

About two weeks after his early June birth, I finally allowed a large group of guests to come and celebrate. My protectiveness came from my fear and the loss of his father. I knew that as clearly as my own name. But I couldn't release it, not yet. I had to protect him. And exposing him like this was just an open door welcoming in trouble.

Wasn't it?

Shenka almost went into raptures when I finally agreed. "He is going to have the best shower ever." She bounced off, mind churning so loudly I heard it.

Made me smile.

And my stomach clench in fear. I hadn't allowed a before birth shower, as much as Shenka begged. Thinking I might be able to convince her to drop the whole idea once Gabriel was born. Now putting her off seemed like a terrible idea.

When I was pregnant, he was still safe in my belly. Now...

Anyone who came near my son with evil intent better look the hell out.

The day of Gabriel's party dawned clear and warm, passed without issue. By the time the sun started to set, I dressed him in a sweet little blue outfit Charlotte had made for him in the Ukraine, plush corduroy and soft fleece. Meira's booties fit his feet perfectly, and had since he was born. It wasn't until I sat back with a frown I realized she'd magicked them.

To always fit.

So funny.

I descended to the back yard at the touch of Sunny and Uncle Frank's arrival. Felt my heart quiver at the sight of the lights strung in the trees, paused at the door. Grief washed over me, the memory so vivid. The last time we had a party here.

My wedding.

Liam.

Sorrow grabbed me so tightly I had to force a breath. Felt familiar power, caught the scent of summer. Looked down into hazel eyes.

Sparking with green.

And my son smiled at me.

"Momma," he said.

My sadness shattered as I kissed my son.

"Gabriel," I said.

Looked up to the sound of applause. Found the family waiting for me. My friends of many magic races. Clapping like I'd sung an aria or completed some performance to be proud of.

Funny how it felt like I had.

I was forced to relinquish Gabriel, kept my heart tied to his as my happy son made the rounds from witch to werewolf to demon princess. On and on as I tried to smile and nod and small talk even as my gaze was drawn, over and over, to the sweet baby boy giggling and chattering his nonsense to those who held him.

"Syd." Was that Trill? I hugged her on impulse, surprised to see the young Zornov maji. She and her brothers had left shortly after I found out I was pregnant, gone their gypsy way in their rusting caravan. Her smile was kind and full of hope, without a hint of worry. So she was here for Gabriel and not with bad tidings.

"That's a first," I whispered.

Trill must have known where my mind went, because she laughed. "No news is good news," she said. "I'm here to hold the baby and see my friend."

Tears. Hugs. And the feeling that everything was all right in my world.

"Such a lovely boy," Penelope Anders said, patting my hand as she blinked at me through watery eyes behind her round glasses. Her wrinkled face fell a little while her bestie and constant companion, Rodrigua Pernicus, looked on, sipping nosily at a cup of punch. "Too bad he wasn't a girl."

Mom's fury almost buried the woman, only my power holding back her rage. I'd been expecting this, after all. Found a way to smile, to nod.

Hardly a shocker, Mom, I sent as Penelope and Rodrigua trundled off at Shenka's urging while my mother glared hate at the back of the blue-haired witch and her round companion. *I've been thinking about it a lot lately.*

There's no hurry, Mom sent. *You did as they asked. You were wed. There is no law to force you to marry again.*

But I have to, I sent, softly. With resigned acceptance. *And I will. Because the Hayle coven needs daughters.*

Mom's arms hugged me almost as tightly as her energy. And made everything all right again.

Until a slamming car door turned me around, the sound of shouting, a woman's voice. I knew without seeing her, dreaded this confrontation as I understood from the rage in Sonja's approaching mind she'd only just found out.

About Gabriel.

I knew this party would mean trouble.

I tensed, felt my happiness die, guilt taking its place as Liam's mother pushed past the Lawrence twins, her slippery Sidhe magic allowing her to slide through the blockage the scowling twin witches erected.

So hard to hold my expression calm, to keep breathing. I barely saw Sonja approach me as everything inside me went to Gabriel, felt him held carefully in Charlotte's protective arms. Mom's touch as she came to my side, Trill on the other, Shenka stepping between me and Liam's mother.

"No," I whispered. Touched my second's shoulder. "Please, let her speak."

How had we kept Gabriel from her? How had I dared? I knew I was feeling her outrage, but I agreed with it, all of a sudden. Was so selfish, heartless. She'd lost her husband, and her son. And now I was trying to keep her from her grandson.

Of all the guilt I'd ever felt, this was the most powerful. I never should have listened to Mom.

Shenka must have felt what I was feeling, seen my remorse, understood it. Because she nodded once, abrupt and angry, before turning herself sideways. Still protecting me even as Gram took up her position, Sassafras in her arms, beside Mom.

Their united front almost made me smile.

Almost.

"You can't hide my grandson from me!" Sonja's voice shook, her whole body, too, tears in her eyes, fury behind the moisture. "Yes, I know about him, no matter what you all did to keep him from me." Spittle flew from her lips, her makeup black tracks down her cheeks. "He's my Liam's, too. Not just yours." She waved violently around her. "Your little magical clique."

Were we? Paranormal bullies preventing her from knowing her grandchild?

"I'm sorry," I said, dull and drained. "Of course you can see him."

Mom muttered something, her power trying to intervene, but I shook my head, frowned at her.

"Mom," I said. "If it was you?"

Her stern, angry expression faded, shoulders slumping.

Charlotte came to me, her wolf appearing in her eyes as she reluctantly handed Gabriel over. I smiled down at him, a bit of my guilt fading, absorbing his sweetness. But even he was tense, not himself. As though the push of power coming from Sonja troubled him.

Or maybe it was my remorse. Way to lay blame, Syd.

Especially when I felt Sonja's entire energy change as she drew a loud breath, both hands over her mouth.

"He looks just like Liam." She sobbed once, reached out. "Like he did when he was little, he grew so fast." A pile of questions woke in my mind as our eyes met, smiling at each other, mother and grandmother sharing a moment over this very special boy.

It snapped when she froze, her frown returning. She wiggled her fingers at me as she shook her arms, insistent, demanding. "Give him to me."

I held her eyes, felt again, in my memory, the sting of the slap she delivered, the night we sent Liam to his funeral pyre, all connection to her fading as her desperation turned from joy at seeing her grandchild turned back to hate for me.

Wanted to turn and run, to keep my son from the woman who almost killed her own, who supported the Unseelie lordling who destroyed her family. Murdered her husband. Sent Liam's grandfather, Fergus, to the Sidhe realm.

Mom was right. How could I trust her? And yet, how could I keep Gabriel from her?

My arms unbent slowly, my body leaning toward Sonja. For an instant, we held him together, and then, he was in her embrace and I leaned back. Held my breath.

Gabriel looked up into his grandmother's eyes.

And began to cry.

The entire gathering froze, shocked by the sound. I was certain my heart stopped completely, would never beat again. Sonja bounced Gabriel in her arms, trying to soothe him, her agitation growing as my son wailed his unhappiness into the night air.

I didn't snatch him back. Not quite. But his removal from her presence was decidedly fast. He instantly calmed, all smiles and giggles again, as though he'd never been upset. But the look on Sonja's face told me the last shards of her heart were shattered.

And I honestly couldn't bring myself to feel bad for her. Not now.

Gabriel's judgment I trusted absolutely.

"I think it's time you left." Mom gestured, two Enforcers appearing in the air overhead in double flares of blue fire. Sonja coughed a further sob before jabbing a finger in my direction.

"You've ruined everything." She almost sounded like Gabriel, words garbled, voice a scream. "Everything."

I turned my back on her. Felt her spin and stagger away, Sidhe magic flaring as she pushed through the watching, protective circle of magical family and friends. I held still, my smiling baby waving his hands at me, until the sound of her car screeching away faded in the distance.

Mom's hand settled on my shoulder as I turned back. Nodded once to her, as understanding dawned. Sonja had gone back to the Unseelie. The touch of it was all over my son. No wonder, as sweet and innocent as he was, Gabriel rejected her. Because the Unseelie on this plane were nothing like the ones I knew in the realm.

Sonja embraced the darkest part of her race. And Gabriel knew it. Realized my time off was over.

"We need to set up a babysitting schedule," I said, knowing I'd have a million volunteers. "I guess it's time I went back to work."

CHAPTER SEVEN

I suppose I shouldn't have been surprised the Gate chose to knock that very same night. I'd barely settled Gabriel into his crib when I felt the resounding hammer of the knock echo through him and into me.

At first, I had no idea what it was. Freaked me the hell out, to be honest. But when Galleytrot's big head came up, cocked to one side, ears perked, I made the connection.

Feared Gabriel would cry again, the pressure was so immense. But my son instead came wide awake, eyes glistening, a burbling laugh erupting from him.

"Momma," he said.

Okay then.

"Syd," Galleytrot said. "I've never heard of one so young being Gatekeeper before."

Way to add to my worries, big dog. "Well," I said

through gritted teeth as Sassafras purred and rubbed his head against my son, "we're just going to have to wing it and hope it works out."

I bundled him into a carrier, anxiety coming in little waves, strapping him to my chest. What I really wanted to do was put him back to bed and ignore the knock even happened. Just for tonight. We had two more, didn't we?

Instead, my son beaming his delight at being pressed to me with his arms and legs free, face first to the world, I slowly descended to the first floor, his joyful wriggling forcing me to grab the bannister for balance.

Trying to decide if I could take my son into the veil or if we should walk. Drive over in the family van?

How utterly normal that sounded to me.

And, for the first time, normal felt all kinds of wrong.

The big dog and Sassafras trailed along behind me, silent and watchful. Mom took one look at me as I entered the kitchen, Gabriel strapped to my chest, and panic rose in her face. Shenka was already half out of her chair even as Charlotte, a deep scowl pulling at her mouth and brows, came to stand in my way.

Made my decision, knowing magic was as much a part of my son's life as it was mine. And attempting to convince myself my demon grandmother would never let anything happen to either one of us. "We'll be back," I said, hoping I sounded confident. Took Charlotte's outstretched hand. Like she'd let me go anywhere without her.

Drew a breath.

And opened the veil.

Ahbi welcomed me and, with an eagerness I felt suddenly guilty about, my son. I'd failed to even try to connect with her, lost in my own little Gabrielville. Yes, Meira had crossed more than once, but she'd done so without me present. Meaning Ahbi lost the chance to meet her great-grandson.

I really sucked at this putting others first stuff.

Even as I knew without a shadow of a doubt, despite my lingering concern, we would be absolutely safe in the veil.

Stepped inside with my werefriend and the big hound before exiting, a breath later, in the Sidhe cavern under Wilding Springs.

The Gate glowed in anticipation, the power hungry, reaching for Gabriel. He reached back, Cian's soul answering the knock with a heavy boom of his own.

A shivering green line of fire ran around the edge of the Gate as, with a deep and contented sigh of settling earth, it fell still.

"I guess that's that." Phew. Honestly? So much for the no guarantee my son would be able to answer it at his tender age. It appeared, yet again, when it came to Gabriel, I had nothing to worry about.

Kind of anti-climactic, truth be told. All of my

adrenaline skipped through my bloodstream, looking for a target even as I thanked Liam for this gift, this part of himself I could still hold and love.

Galleytrot sat at my feet, tail thumping the ground. "I miss it here."

I looked around, nodding. Felt traces of Liam still lingering. "Me, too," I said. I hadn't been back in months. Stopped spending alternate nights once my size became an issue and Mom's worry about me traveling in the veil made it more inconvenient. Besides, Liam's scent, his presence, really was long gone. The remaining bits and pieces were mostly memory and sad pockets of loss.

Still.

I took the opportunity to show Gabriel around, keeping my eyes from the cleanly scrubbed spot in front of the Gate someone took the time to bleach. Removing all physical, visible traces of Liam's blood.

Didn't matter. My mind could still see him lying there, Ameline standing over him. With a gun. And the blood, so much of it. On her. On the floor.

Then on me as I held him and tried to keep him with me—

No. Not tonight. Tonight would be about happy memories. For my son.

And his.

I crossed to the hall, turned left into the bedroom. Laid Gabriel beside me on the bed as Galleytrot and

Charlotte waited outside, backs turned, giving us privacy.

Whispered stories to him of his father and my love. Let him feel as much of Liam as I could muster as we curled up together on the bed I'd only slept in a few months, though it still felt like home after all this time. The cavern's magic kept the dust away, the air scented with the earth but nothing musty, only fresh and spring-like.

Gabriel's normal giggling was silent, his hazel eyes wide, crackling with green fire, his entire attention locked on me. How much did he understand? If Galleytrot was to be believed, everything. Cian's grown soul would process and pass on all of it.

Freaky. And yet, so very amazing I was able to do this before Liam's memory faded with too much time.

When lying there became too sad, tears pooling on the quilt beneath my cheek as I fought to catch my breath, I stood, hugging Gabriel close, carrying him out and into the hall again. Galleytrot groaned as he stood, shook himself, followed to the archive and Liam's desk.

Neat and tidy, as he left it, a single book open beside his dark laptop, one of my hair elastics used as a bookmark. A few notes scrawled in his terrible handwriting on a notepad beside the keyboard. My usual chair was a heavy, carved thing with a deep purple seat, upholstered in velvet. I'd never sat in Liam's before.

Sank into it, sighed as the chair seemed to hug me,

leather padded cushion firm but comfortable.

Weird, the view from here. How a small change in perspective could alter everything. I suddenly felt like Liam was here with me, in the chair. Working still, lifting his head to smile at me as I came through the door.

Made me smile, too. Through more tears.

Gabriel leaned suddenly forward and I lunged to support him. His little fingers raced over the page of the book, the words I couldn't read, before he sat back and burbled.

Whatever he said, I couldn't make out. But he seemed content.

I stood, carried him into the stacks of the archive. Showed him the endless books. Ran one hand over the spines as Gabriel continued to stare in silence.

The Sidhe cavern sighed and embraced my son as we left the archive. It felt almost greedy to hold him. There had been so much grief here of late, it was nice to feel the shift. By the time I finished the tour, the living wards eased up their attention, satisfied he was whole. And belonged to the cavern.

Through it all, Gabriel remained saucer eyed, silent, mouth open. When I left the archive, stepping back into the entry at the front of the cavern, he suddenly giggled, both hands pressed to his mouth.

And the Gate sang.

Glowed in a flare of green fire.

Swung open.

I spun and stared into the Sidhe realm, hands shaking. Thank goodness Gabriel was back in his papoose. The whole cavern rang like a bell, the music growing louder as I approached the open Gate, Charlotte tense beside me, Galleytrot relaxed in counterpoint.

Gabriel reached out, one chubby hand waving, while Thalion and Fergus appeared on the other side.

I hadn't talked to Liam's grandfather since the night I discovered I was pregnant. Seeing him had almost crushed me. Liam's face, Liam's voice. Not Liam. This time, it hurt—hell, yeah—but Gabriel's steady, sweet power cut the edge and made looking in Fergus's hazel eyes not as painful as I thought it would be.

"He's able to answer, I see." Thalion's smooth voice was light, almost kind. Sidhe were notorious for their lack of empathy. But he'd softened since we'd met and, when he smiled at Gabriel, I knew there was real affection behind his stunning face.

"He is." I stepped close to the veil between our planes. Fergus made baby talk while Thalion smiled at me.

"He's... different." I had to bring it up. Despite Galleytrot's assurances. Despite the brief moment Sonja told me he looked like Liam. I needed confirmation. "Older than he should be. Maturing quickly."

Both Fergus and Thalion nodded, but it was my son's

great-grandfather who spoke.

"We all did," he said. "Trust me, everything is fine." Laughed. "Let me guess: he doesn't cry. Can speak already. And he's what, a month old?"

I nodded, feeling the last of my tension ease.

"Excellent development," Thalion said. Was that pride in his voice? "But I expect nothing less from you. And Her Highness."

Shaylee preened. Bratski.

"You will find he develops rapidly in his first few weeks," Fergus said. "Up to three times faster than a normal baby. It will slow, in time."

That almost made me sad. So much sweet infantness I'd be missing.

Sigh.

And yet. Phew.

"Thank you." I kissed Gabriel's head. "Good to know." Realized this wasn't just about me. "How are things across the realm?"

Thalion's shoulders shrugged elegantly, long, silver hair falling in a perfect spill of silk. "Quiet," he said. "There are still moments of unhappiness between Queen Aoilainn and the Unseelie monarchs, but we manage."

I could tell from the soft sarcasm in his voice just who was causing the trouble.

Shaylee snorted in my head. *Mother.*

No kidding.

"We shall pass along the good news to Their Majesties," Fergus said, stepping back from the Gate. "Both about your healthy son and the Gate's safety." His smile was Liam's smile. "It's good to see you, Syd."

You too, my love.

I waved goodbye as the portal swung shut, feeling Gabriel's power connecting to it, tied up with it until it finally sighed closed, the song silent to the ear but still vibrating inside my son.

But speaking to the Sidhe prince just reinforced my need to finally get on with it. Things might have been settled in the Fey realm—and I was happy about that— but I had my own threads to tie together into neat little bows of revenge and hate. And though the thought of putting my son at risk by leaving him for any length of time made me want to throw up, I had to move on.

Ameline.

I'm coming for you, bitch.

chapter eight

So much for diving into action. I arrived home from the Sidhe cavern to an anxious Mom and Shenka. Ever eager, Gram took Gabriel from me, fighting Charlotte for the chance to snuggle him. Sassafras's clear irritation at my departure lulled me back into keeping my family happy. I allowed myself to settle into that same pattern of care and love for my son.

I did have a moment of intense fear jolt me from sleep only a few nights later, a nightmare reminding me of Fate's words to me:

"You have so much more to do, Syd. I wish I could lay the burden on another, but you were made for this."

Which meant, among other things, I wasn't done, was I? Fate had so much more in store for me.

And, one day, I would outlive my son.

Couldn't go there. Think that way. Lurched from bed

and snuggled Gabriel close while he woke and cooed to me as though in comfort.

Met Sassafras's glowing eyes in the dark where he slept in my son's crib.

Sobbed.

The demon cat sighed, rose, came to me. Set both front paws on the railing of the crib.

"I know," he said. "But you can't think about it yet, Syd. You have so many years yet."

Of course he knew, didn't he? I slipped back into bed, Gabriel beside me, Sassafras purring us both into sleep. How many witches who he'd loved did my dear demon cat raise, only to watch them age and die?

I couldn't bear to think of it.

July rolled around before I knew it, the beginning of Gabriel's second month seeing his accelerated growth finally slow, just as Fergus said it would. Now a dear with the body of a six-month-old, a babbling brook for a mouth, Gabriel's need to communicate led him to words—real and made up as required—as well as a constant magical connection.

Mom hovered close, still living with us, traveling back and forth to Harvard to fulfill her duties as Council Leader. The old Mom would have dropped everything and run at a moment's notice when the Council called. But I would often catch her, holding Gabriel and rocking him gently, eyes far away as she conducted business with her grandson firmly in her arms.

Every day that passed I woke with the conviction I was going after Ameline today.

And every night I kissed my son and told myself he was too little, yet.

Wasn't he?

Besides, it was so easy to forget with him in my life. The light of his spirit filled me with more joy than I'd ever known. Almost made the losses I'd endured worth it. Until I caught sight of Gram making paddy cakes with him. Felt the absence of the bulk of her power. Remembered just how much Ameline stole from me.

From Gram. From all of us.

I was still riding my merry-go-round of indecision when Meira came through the veil one morning with an expectant and upset look on her face.

And I finally remembered what today was.

Dad's formal request for my attendance at his betrothal arrived only a week ago, in the hands of Theridialis who hummed and blushed as he handed it over.

"Forgive him," Sassy's dad said, round face sad, before the veil snapped shut.

And I stared down at the piece of black rock, a shaving from the Seat itself, engraved with fiery amber letters.

"I can't." Panic gripped me now as it had then while

my sister strode up the basement stairs and into the kitchen, pale skin and blue eyes a shock after seeing her in demon form so many times. I had just finished feeding Gabriel, his dirty spoon in my hand, knuckles covered in mashed potato. "Meems." I dropped the spoon, reached for my son, safely in Gram's arms rather than his high chair, watched carefully by a purring Sassafras.

Meira nodded immediately. "It's okay, Syd," she said.

But it wasn't. Her face was composed, but her whole being ached.

Dad's betrothal day.

I couldn't leave Gabriel. But how could I let Meira go through this alone?

My feet rebelled, my knees. I stood up anyway. My heart begged me, my soul pleaded and fought. What if something happened? What if Ameline—

No. I shook off my fear, kissed Gram's cheek. Stroked Sassafas's fur.

"I'll be back in an hour or so," I said, trying to keep my voice light despite my previous outburst.

Hugged my sister who shook in my arms, her human form feeling frail all of a sudden.

And descended the stairs to the still-open tear in the veil.

Ahbi embraced me as we slipped inside. I didn't allow myself to stop moving. Knew if I did, I'd spin and race back upstairs and leave my sister to handle this disaster alone.

Crossed over to Demonicon with my heart hurting in so many ways. For my son. My mother. My sister and me. And, for my father, who had no choice at all.

Meira's demon form shifted back immediately when we stepped out into her bedroom. But, as was normal for me now, I remained human.

Pagomaris stood waiting, her hands clasped in front of her chest. Ahbi's aide, now my sister's, shrieked when I appeared, lunged for me. Stopped, face crumpling, looking me up and down before turning to my sister with a hopeful look on her face.

"Perhaps her demon form...?" Like I wasn't there, or some inanimate object to be repaired. As if Meira could make me do anything—or would ever try.

I rolled my eyes, sank into my irritation with pleasure, welcoming it as a mask for my sadness and nerves. Prepped for the coming fight. From the polished, gem-studded perfection of Pagomaris's horns to the sparkling spikes attached to her face and nails, down to the leatherette body stocking covered in a sheath of frothy gauze the aide wore, she was the epitome of Demoniconian style. Meira took after her, though in a subtler way.

I, on the other hand, refused. I'd allowed it in the past, the dressing, the pretending I was a demon.

No more.

Before Pagomaris could say another word, my egos rose, power flaring, a rainbow of maji magic appearing in flickering flames around me.

"We are maji," I said, allowing their voices out with mine.

She backed off with a meep, bowing almost to the floor. "Of course, maji," she whispered in a quavering voice. "Forgive me, maji."

Oh, damn it.

"It's okay." Reined the girls in, sighing. "But I'm not up for theater today."

Meira grinned at me. "But Syd," she said, "it's so fun."

Um-hum.

Looked down at myself when my sister giggled.

"Maybe a change of clothes, at least," she said, amber eyes sparkling. "Unless you'd like to set a fashion trend where a ripped t-shirt, baggy jeans liberally sprinkled with food bits is *de rigueur.*"

Crap. I barely thought about my appearance these days. As if it was front and center previously. I looked up, sighed.

Nodded.

A compromise later and I was plucking at the thick leather armor Pagomaris altered for me with her own magic. A flowing cape of shining black, strewn with more crystals than I could shake a stick at, cast a rainbow glow around me. I even let her put up my hair, winced I didn't know when I'd showered last, hoping it wasn't too greasy.

Grateful two months post pregnancy and nursing helped me shed the majority of my baby weight, my body feeling mostly normal. The hard shell of black did a great job holding in the rest of my flab.

I'd take it.

But I remained human, normal height, even. Turned down the ridiculous platform boots my sister seemed to adore. Pagomaris was lucky I went this far.

For Dad, had to admit it. Besides, when I checked myself in the mirror, I looked pretty damned badass. Like some modern-day knightess ready to kick some butt.

Yup, this would do, thanks.

With my maji power flowing freely around me—so much for cutting out the theatrics—I accompanied my sister into the throne room, joining her beside Dad, as the family gaped and trembled.

Let there be no mistake. I wasn't interested in Demoniconian politics. And anyone who came near me had better have friendly intentions or they'd be finding out what it was like up there on one of the plane's moons.

The fact my little show was a game in itself?

Touché.

Meira's mind locked on mine, mental giggles almost hysterical.

I. Freaking. Love. You. Her power hugged me in a

fierce embrace.

The feeling was totally mutual.

I spotted Ram standing with Bakari. Weird to see him after all these months. My former kidnapper turned friend smiled, nodded to me. But his attention was all over my sister.

As for Bakari, I grinned at him. I hadn't run into my grandfather's quiet and dangerous bodyguard since the whole fiasco after Ahbi's murder. I wasn't his biggest fan, but Henemordonin trusted him, clearly. And so, it seemed, did Ram.

Speaking of Ram…

Well now, I sent to my sister. *Someone seems a bit taken.*

She gasped in my mind, embarrassment coming through loud and clear. *I'm sorry*, she sent in a rush. *I know you like him. That you two…*

Meems. I let her feel my heart. *Ram and I are friends. Always were. That's all.*

I think she was surprised by my openness and embraced me for my generosity.

Thank you, she whispered in my head. *I think… I think I'm falling in love with him.*

Young love.

So like me to be cynical.

I shoved it aside, wished I could hug her for real. Almost did. Fixed Ram with a glare so sharp he tilted his head at me in curiosity.

You hurt her Rameranselot, I sent, *and I'm going to kick your ass so hard you won't feel it until weeks later. Get me?*

His demon fire mingled with mine. *I think you have more to worry about her hurting me,* he sent, voice gentle.

Hard not to grin.

Okay then.

No time for more chit-chat, not when Dad strode down the center aisle, all official Ruler and crap, draped in so much robe, jewelry and a giant crown I was surprised he could carry the lot. His amber eyes avoided mine as he stomped up the steps, my grandfather behind him, and spun on the spot. Henemordonin took his place at Second Seat while Dad thudded a giant staff topped with a blazing golden jewel three times against the polished stone.

When Dad sat, I shuffled closer to his throne, standing on the left to Meira's right, down a step, feeling my father behind me, wishing I could turn and shake him.

Stop this somehow.

"The betrothed may enter." Someone at the back of the room had an irritatingly official voice. Which carried. I spotted the demon in a uniform standing by the lift entrance. Even as the elevator appeared and a demon woman appeared.

I wanted to hate her. Struggled with the need to crush her like a cockroach the moment she showed her face. Rolled my eyes when she paused—posed—on the lift before sweeping forward.

Her amber gown unfolded behind her in a flaring, endless train, almost half the length of the throne room by the time it unfurled. The cuffs hung to the floor, making soft tinkling sounds from tiny bells sewn into the hems. She was beautiful, small in stature for a demon, almost as small as Sassafras's sister, Avenesequoia. And this demon woman looked at my father like he was the center of her Universe. From her shining black horns to her heaving bosom, Dad's future bride seemed as vapid as Meira said.

Seemed.

Time to find out if she was what she said she was.

I hoped to uncover some plot, some deception. To be able to turn to Dad with a knowing "ah-ha!" and a reason he shouldn't marry her. But as she swept into the most graceful curtsy I'd ever seen, my mind probing hers, I realized my sister was right.

She wasn't stupid. Or as weak as maybe she made herself out to be. But her entire existence was dresses and status and being Ruler's wife. No ambition.

Nothing.

Sucked. So. Much.

"Zinniaperimote, Lady of the Eighth Plane." The same official voice introduced her at last.

"My Ruler." She curtsied again, hands clasping to her impressive chest, amber eyes wide and full of innocence.

"My love.

Choke.

I dug deeper. There had to be something.

Even as Dad rose with a stiffness telling me he wasn't any happier about this than I was.

"Lady," he said in his deep voice. "Welcome." And sank down into his throne again.

The ceremony was short, thankfully. I missed the whole damned thing digging around in Zinnia's head.

Finally came to the conclusion we were screwed. Yes, she had the personality of a carrot stick. But of any of Dad's choices, she was the best.

She wanted to give him kids. Make him happy. Wear pretty dresses and throw parties and be special.

Gross.

She finally spun and strode away after one last curtsy, three demon aides who gathered her train for the return trip carefully guiding it as Zinnia retreated.

I turned half way around. Met Dad's eyes, feeling defeated, seeing the horrible unhappiness in his eyes.

Thank you for being here for your sister, he sent as the court broke and began their usual chatter. *She's so strong, Syd, but this has been hard on her.*

And you. I wanted to be angry with him, but what good would it do? I felt far too much empathy, as it turned out. Being forced to marry sucked.

I should know about that.

I'm sorry I haven't come to see Gabriel. I realized then, with a startled understanding so profound I almost lost it to tears, he was right. How had I failed to realize my own father hadn't met my son?

Self-centered much?

Now that this is over, I'll stop by. Dad rose, bowed his head to me. "Maji," he said.

Screw that crap. I reached up and grabbed his shoulders, pulling him down to kiss his cheek.

"I love you, Dad," I whispered. "I'm so sorry." Had to stop speaking.

Couldn't go on.

Sadly stood there and watched Dad retreat while my sister's rigid face hid the crying echoing inside her mind.

chapter nine

I didn't linger. Went immediately to Meira's quarters, shed the ridiculous outfit, slipped back into my jeans and food-coated t-shirt while my sister waited for me in her bedroom. Emerged to hug her.

"You call me anytime," I said. Leaned away. "Any. Time."

Meira sniffled, shrugged. "I'm okay," she said. "But that was harder than I thought it would be."

"Want to come home for the night?" I reached for the veil, felt Ahbi welcome me. Her sadness joined with mine. Odd to find her upset, considering it was her idea to make Dad Ruler in the first place. But my demon grandmother changed a great deal since her soul bonded to the Node keeping Demonicon's planes in alignment. Softened and became more human, if that was possible. Lost the deep, compelling drive of political maneuvering, which had existed most of her life.

Amazing I loved her way more dead than alive.

Meira shook her head, backed away with a firm smile. "I have to sit through the banquet," she said. A little too brightly.

"Do you want me to stay?" The need to rush home, to hold my son, almost kept me from speaking.

Leave it to my sister to let me off the hook. "Naw," she said. "The rest is just politics and formalities. I can handle it." Her face softened. "Go home," she said. "Hug that adorable boy. Tell him his Auntie Meems will be by tomorrow to visit and bring him treats."

"Done." I blew her a kiss. "Love you."

"Love you, too." Meira softened from her rigidity. "Thank you for being here."

I left her then, returning home, arms aching with need. Ahbi's parting squeeze barely registered as I bounded through the kitchen and upstairs to my room.

Charlotte grumbled about me being home so soon, but handed off my sleeping son before leaving me to sink into the rocking chair and snuggle him close.

Just grateful it was over.

I don't know if Mom sensed the shift or if Sass actually told her about Dad after all, but the next morning she hugged me. Kissed me gently.

"I guess I should go back to work," she said, eyes bright with tears.

And left.

I could tell she was so upset to have to move back to Harvard it was killing her.

And immediately contacted her, promised I'd bring Gabriel to visit so she didn't have to do all the traveling.

A lot, she sent.

I laughed. *As often as you want.*

Now that we knew he could travel safely in the veil, I had no problem making such a promise.

I think Dad was waiting for something like this to happen. Within hours of Mom leaving, the veil parted and he stepped through into the diamond effigy still in our basement. I finally got to hug him, felt the tension ease out of him as he relaxed, human face as handsome as I remembered.

"Syd," he said. Kissed my cheek. "Hi, cupcake."

"Hi, Dad." I led him by the hand up the stairs and into the kitchen where Shenka bounced Gabriel on her knee. Smiled at my father, rose with the giggling boy, and handed him off to his grandfather.

Seeing Dad look down on Gabriel with so much love made my heart crack. I had to turn and run out of the kitchen, standing in the back hall, sobbing silently. Yes, he was still my father. But he should have been with Mom.

Should have.

Dad didn't say anything about my breakdown, instead spending the afternoon outside in the yard with Gabriel and me, playing in the grass and being a fabulous grandfather. By the time night fell and Dad rose, he looked the happiest I'd seen him in a long time.

Didn't last. The moment we descended to the basement, Dad turning in place where his statue stood only a few hours before, his face crumpled as he bent to kiss Gabriel's nose.

"Syd," Dad choked, "next time, only marry for love. Promise me."

And left in a rush of power. Leaving his cold and grief-stricken statue behind.

Heartbreaking. I stood there, staring at him a long time before turning to grab a wrinkled sheet from a box long left unpacked.

Covered him with it in a smooth toss guided by magic as Gabriel watched.

I just couldn't stand to see my dad like that.

As I carried my son up the stairs, heart hurting for my father and mother, I caught the sound of whispering. Followed it through the kitchen, into the hall. Spotted Gram and Demetrius outside her door. Realized I hadn't seen much of the pair of them lately. Almost spoke up.

Until Demetrius leaned in and kissed Gram.

Zing.

I stared like an idiot as they slipped into her room, firmly closing the door behind them. Almost choked. Would have if Gabriel didn't reach up and touch my lips with his fingertips. Shenka appeared beside me, giggling.

"What," she said. "You're just noticing now?"

I turned on my second. "I knew they were… it's just… seriously?" Yes, Gram was a woman. Of course. And from the moment Demetrius returned, it was clear they loved each other.

But… she was my *grandmother*.

"You just mind your own business," Shenka said with a wink.

My grin took me by surprise. "Wouldn't dream of interfering."

Nice to know someone in my family had a happy ending.

chapter ten

I missed Charlotte's steady presence when she returned home at Oleksander's insistence. It was selfish of me to want her around all the time, to want everyone around. I wasn't, it turned out, the Center Of The Universe.

When did that happen?

I never expected to settle into a quiet life as a mom and love it. But Gabriel made everything so much better, simpler. Distracted me from the old angers and sorrows enough I fell into a kind of Mommy haze.

So when I felt spirit power enter the back yard followed by the familiar touch of Sunny's magic, I shook myself free of my stupor and greeted her at the door with a big smile and a giggling baby in my arms.

She swooped forward, a joyful cry on her lips, and lifted him from my grasp, swinging Gabriel around as he laughed, the sound so fresh and sweet I had to swallow the lump rising in my throat.

I made him. Imagine.

Sunny came to a halt, tucking my son against her, kissing his forehead while he ran his little fingers through her blonde hair, hazel eyes sparking green as he gazed up at her with absolute adoration.

The vampire queen lifted her eyes to mine, sparkling with unshed tears. "Syd," she whispered, her own voice thick. "I envy you."

Okay, thanks for crushing my heart. She couldn't have children, she and Uncle Frank. The longing I saw in her whole body as she gently bounced Gabriel brought more tears. My nugget's adorable giggles just made things worse, somehow.

She finally closed the distance between us again, handing him back to me before kissing my cheek with her warm lips. She and Uncle Frank were always careful to feed before coming to see the baby, so their bodies wouldn't be ice cold. Just a little detail, but one that made me love them both more than ever.

Speaking of my tall, handsome uncle, he was conspicuously absent.

"What's up?" Why did I always expect trouble? Probably because trouble and I had a close, personal relationship and no matter how much my son was able to keep me from it, I knew disaster would eventually rear its ugly head once again.

But Sunny just shook her head, smiled. "I was hoping you could come back with me," she said. "We have something we want to talk to you about."

We. As in...

"You could have just messaged me." I turned to go inside, spotting Shenka coming down the stairs. She smiled and waved at Sunny who bowed her head in return.

"And miss a chance to kiss that sweet face?" Sunny bent over Gabriel, nuzzling his cheek while he grasped her long hair in both hands and burrowed his nose into her neck. Sunny sighed when he released her, lifting his little hand to kiss it gently.

I handed Gabriel off to my second who bounced him just like Sunny had. His favorite. Galleytrot hovered, as usual, the giant black dog a silent, watchful shadow. I'd grown so used to him, I almost forgot he was there sometimes.

I reached down, scratched behind one ear and heard his soft groan of contentment. "I'll be back in a bit," I said. "I'm sure you two can keep Gabriel occupied?" Why did my heart clench despite my light words? And would it always be this hard to leave my son behind?

Probably. Sassafras sashayed down the stairs, silver tail quivering at full mast. "Where are you off to?"

Sunny reached out and stroked his fur. "You're

welcome to join us, sweet boy."

Sass's purr rumbled so loud I grinned.

"I have been feeling a little cooped up," he said. Stood on his back legs so she could lift him into her arms. Sunny laughed and obliged, resting her cheek on the top of his head, blue eyes sparkling with good humor. "Let's ride."

What, no hovering over Gabriel? I reached for Sunny's hand as I sent my question to Sass. *That's a first.*

He has more than enough eyes on him tonight, Sass sent. *And I'm restless.*

The veil opened easily, Ahbi's power welcoming me as I stepped through, waving goodbye to Shenka and Galleytrot after a kiss for Gabriel. My son's eyes widened as he watched me go.

So hard to leave with him staring like that.

Besides, Sass sent as we crossed the rubbery membrane and stepped out into the throne room of Castle Wilhelm, *I smell trouble. And I want in on it.*

I laughed at him in my head. *Bored, cat?*

Sass sniffed at me, amber eyes flaring with fire. *More like wanting to make sure you avoid yet another disaster.*

Yeah. That was it. Sure.

Smartass.

I would have responded with a suitably snarky shot. Had one prepared, on the tip of my mental tongue. Didn't get to share it.

Not when a deliciously dark-haired, blue eyed vampire with a huge smile on his yummylicious face closed the distance between us before sweeping me into his arms.

And kissing me.

Oh. My. Swearword.

The last time I'd seen Sebastian was at the vampire mansion, shortly after I'd saved him from almost certain death. My power not only freed him from his close encounter with mortality, but removed his blood need and altered him somehow. No longer tied to his queen, Pannera Sthol, and without the connection to his Blood Clan, Sebastian wasn't angry. At least, the joy on his face the night he'd left me gave me the impression he didn't hold a grudge because I seemed to have changed everything about him.

He'd kissed me that night, too. Not knowing I'd married. And I'd fallen into a serious swoon, heart pounding, fireworks, lightning strikes, sparkles and zingadingdong.

Yeah.

Repeat performance in progress.

This time, I kissed him back, not because I didn't love Liam anymore. And not because I wanted anything to come from this moment. But because I needed it, the flare of passion as his hands cupped my back, one pressed firmly in the middle of my spine, the other dangerously close to the swell under my right back pocket. His full-body embrace included the firm and welcoming presence hiding inside his pants.

I wound my arms around his neck, fingers locked in his dark hair, tongue discovering he no longer had fangs even as he breathed his hot, spicy breath into my lungs.

Um.

What?

I pulled away, stared up at him in shock.

"You..." Gulped. Tried again. "You're breathing."

Sebastian laughed even as he lifted me into the air and spun me around, cheek pressed to mine, arms tight around me. I locked my legs around his waist, feeling his pure happiness embrace me while my alter egos bubbled with excitement.

Yum, my demon sent.

Tasty. Shaylee's chuckle was wicked.

Mine, my vampire sent.

Down, girls.

Sebastian finally stopped twirling, blue eyes brimming with so much emotion I could barely decipher what he was feeling. He leaned forward, pressed his forehead to mine. Whispered, "Syd. I'm alive again. Because of you."

Gasp.

And yet, it was true, I felt it now I allowed myself to focus on him and not, well. Him. My vampire eagerly explored, the other girls following suit. Even the family magic purred around him, my sorcery swelling open, the black petals not looking for sustenance but welcoming him.

And the maji power he now possessed, flooding every cell, replacing the spirit magic keeping his vampire form animated.

I wriggled and he set me down. The moment he did, I pressed my ear to his chest.

Heard the most beautiful sound.

Da-dum.

And sobbed suddenly into my hands.

Sebastian's arms engulfed me, the heat of his body, the scent of him so new, so real, and no longer an illusion created by his need for blood I cried harder.

What had I done?

I backed off, feeling conflicted despite his happiness. One of his hands lifted, caressed the tears from my cheeks as I opened and closed my mouth in an effort to speak before my brain could reassemble itself into some kind of order.

Someone touched my back, the familiar feel of Sunny's magic turning me from Sebastian to look into her eyes.

Her eager, hopeful eyes.

Now I knew why I was here. "You want me to make you like him."

Mind. Blown.

Sunny hugged me, fierce and tight. I caught sight of Uncle Frank beaming at me, now holding a watchful Sassafras.

"Syd," Sunny said. "Just listen to what Sebastian has to say."

My vampire—was he anymore?—friend nodded, stepped away a pace. "You have no idea the gift you've given me," he said. "I've been experimenting with it, to see what I can do. And not do." He laughed. "Stupid, really. Things I shouldn't have risked." My brain went on terror overdrive, unable to picture any scenarios, but certain he'd put his life in danger a number of times in the name of his experiment. "But Syd, I can tell you, I'm still me." He shrugged. "I don't need blood. Or spirit power to sustain me. But I'm also not mortal, and far from ordinary."

He could say that again.

What is he? I sent the desperate question to my vampire who immediately soothed me.

I don't know what you're afraid of, she sent, her normally cool and calm tone rippling with happiness. *He's evolved. Just like the werewolves, you've changed him. But more so. You've helped him develop to his full potential.*

This is what vampires were meant to be? No, that couldn't be right. She didn't feel like him, the vampire essence inside me.

I'm not part of you, she sent in answer. *I reside within you.*

It makes a difference. Besides, you are already maji.

I couldn't stop my hands from shaking as I reached out and touched his hand. "I don't know what I did," I said, a detached part of me wondering why there was a soft wail in my voice. "How I made this happen." Swallowed. "To do it again."

Was I really going to do it again?

Considering Sunny and Uncle Frank could live again... how could I not?

Sebastian shook his head, still smiling, blue eyes deep and full of contentment. "We'll figure it out," he said. Looked at Sunny who remained beside me. "For all vampire kind."

I felt the gathered clan sigh, absorbed their hope. Knew this wasn't a mistake, then, some mutation I'd created to make them vulnerable. Helped me to relax, stop shaking.

Mostly.

Only one mind seemed in opposition, a clear and angry presence. I didn't have to guess, knowing it had to be Piotr Wilhelm who shot his hate at me. Fine, he could stay a vampire.

I was totally okay with leaving him behind.

Wait a second. Did that really mean I was seriously considering—

Breathe, Syd. Vital for survival, remember?

How comfortable was I with this kind of tampering?

"I had no choice when I saved you," I said to Sebastian. "You were dying. It was give you everything I had to heal you or let you go." I was never, ever letting anyone go again.

Ever.

Sebastian nodded slowly. "Very true," he said. "Your point?"

I turned to meet Sunny's eyes, felt her calm as she pushed down her hope. Damn it, I loved her and Uncle Frank and if I could help them live again...

"Ethics." I bit my lower lip, thinking of Iepa and the maji. Of the werewolves and the sorcerers who created them. "My vampire says this is your evolution. But what right do I have to speed that up?"

Sunny's hand fell from my back, but she wasn't angry. She, instead, took my fingers in hers, stilling the last of my trembling.

"We would never ask you to go against your nature," she said. "But, Syd, from what we now know of the creation of our people, how the maji made us flawed, we wish the darkness that has plagued us our entire existence to be lifted. To be the people we were intended all along."

Why was I hesitating?

"What if I can't do it again?" Yeah, there it was. The deep fear. Not just of failing to succeed, but failing in a way that put them at risk. "What if I try and it kills you?" I glanced at Uncle Frank, at Sebastian, Sunny again. "I would never, ever forgive myself."

My vampire sighed softly. *I suppose your fear is grounded*, she sent. *After all, Sebastian was near death. These vampires are fully awake and alive. I'm no more comfortable reducing them to his state to try again than you are.*

"We need someone to test it on." Uncle Frank stepped forward, Sassafras still in his arms. "I volunteer."

Oh, *hell* no.

My demon cat hissed softly. "Don't be an idiot, Frank," he said, tail thrashing as his amber eyes locked on mine. "What are you thinking?"

I had a seed of an idea. But it meant risking an entire blood clan from the queen down. Still, from what Sunny had told me previously of the Sthol queen's condition, she wasn't likely to survive much longer. When Ameline stripped the taint from her, she'd left the vampire so badly damaged her body—and the spirit power sustaining her—was unable to regenerate.

Maybe she was the exact guinea pig I needed.

"We have to go to Castle Sthol," I said. "And test this out on Pannera."

CHAPTER ELEVEN

I half expected to run into resistance at Castle Sthol. Old habits die hard, after all. But instead of the typical animosity of the past, I was instead greeted with awe and more than a little fear by the vampires who stood guard at the front gate.

Yes, I could have landed myself and my vampire friends in the middle of Pannera's throne room. But I was learning diplomacy and figured sugar might get me farther than arrogance and bullying.

Sunny and Uncle Frank took the lead, Sassafras perched in my uncle's arms. Sebastian remained back, with me, his hand brushing mine twice as we entered the large gates at the front of the castle and were ushered inside.

On impulse, I flexed my fingers and felt his slip into mine. Guilt tried to rise, Liam's face. But I pushed it down, tightened my grip on Sebastian's hand.

Liam was gone. Had been for almost a year.

Time to move on, Syd.

I looked up, caught Sebastian's little smile, how his dark blue eyes watched me without pressure, but filled with speculation.

Well, he was alive now, wasn't he? Which opened our little situation to a whole new world of possibilities.

It was the first time I actually allowed myself to think about someone else, at least with a face instead of some vague understanding I had to choose a replacement. To see my life past the loss of Liam. Yes, I knew I had to find someone. A daughter was a requirement if our family was to maintain leadership of my coven. I might be immortal and pretty much invincible, but I had no desire to lead the family forever. Just didn't seem right, somehow.

All of my musings about Sebastian and just how alive he really was—and how willing he would be to show me what his new state could mean for us—came to an abrupt halt as we strode up the central aisle of the throne room and I caught my first glimpse of Pannera.

She looked terrible when I'd left her at the vampire mansion in Sunny's care. I knew she'd been brutalized by the loss of the Brotherhood's taint. Weak and aged, shrunken no matter how much blood she fed, Pannera seemed to be dissolving that night, cracking and powdering around the edges.

No comparison to the present. I barely recognized her, save for her blazing gray eyes that caught and held mine.

"Sydlynn Hayle," her voice snapped, harsh-edged, as she spoke.

I stopped in my tracks, did my best not to stare like a kid at a freak show. Swallowed my rising gorge and pulled my crap together.

"Queen Pannera," I said in my best Mom voice, not a trace of my sympathy and horror showing. I hoped.

I prayed.

The withered, pale gray creature perched on the throne coughed, a racking sound echoing through the throne room. Where the clan of Castle Wilhelm radiated hope, the Sthol blood clan gathered around their queen shivered in despair and terror. They had every right to be afraid. The only part of Pannera holding life were her gray eyes. The rest of her resembled a piece of paper burned too fast, still intact, but fragile, ready to break apart at the briefest breath of air.

Sebastian had been shrunken, but more mummy-like, his skin leathery and hard. As had mine, from what I was told, when Batsheva drained me into nothing. And that very ex-witch, ex-vampire queen, was currently ensconced in my basement to grow mold on her leathery hide while her spirit lived on in torment.

But Pannera had none of that solidity and, as she moved one hand, claws yellowed and cracked, a soft fall of what looked like spent ash fell from her skin to dust across the lap of her gown.

Still dressed in satin and lace, her once glorious hair thinned to stray strands of sickly brown, Pannera Sthol was clearly on her way out.

The perfect candidate for our little test.

"I welcome you, maji," Pannera said, the blunt grinding of her tone making me wince internally. A wet rattle followed as she drew a breath. Not a real one, no lungs to inflate, nothing to hold it as Sebastian's body now did. Not necessary for vampires, of course, but something they carried with them from their days as humans. She was obviously falling apart on the inside as well as the outside.

"Thank you, Great Queen," I said, bowing to her, willingly. My sympathy made me feel more kindly to the old bat, I guess. Considering how far she'd fallen, and that most of our encounters were flavored by the control of the Brotherhood, I figured a little kindness and respect wouldn't hurt.

She gestured again, losing another layer of herself, the pattering of the bits loud in the quiet throne room.

"I would see you clearly," she said. "Please, approach."

Not a moment's hesitation. I walked directly to her,

kneeling beside her throne as the vampires surrounding her stepped back. A quick glance up at the touch of a hand on my shoulder and I reflexively squeezed in return. Anastasia, Sebastian's former lieutenant and the new leader of his old blood clan, bobbed her head to me, sorrow on her beautiful face.

I returned my attention to Pannera as the dying queen offered me her hand.

I expected it to fall apart in mine, took her fingers carefully between my own. She was cold, so cold, and powdery, but the core of her was still solid despite the dusting like baby powder of her deterioration on my skin.

"You have come to say goodbye." Her gray eyes flared once with power before it faded. "I am grateful."

"I'm sorry for what's been done to you." I really was. No one deserved to die this way.

Except Liander Belaisle. Maybe I could arrange that.

Oh, and Ameline.

If this transformation worked for Pannera, I'd think about it.

For now, I could only do my best and try to make things right.

"Your Majesty," I said, "I have another reason for being here. And I hope goodbye has nothing to do with it."

chapter twelve

I hated to give her hope, but felt it rise like a flare of flame, her fingers trembling in my grasp. "You have a cure?"

I couldn't help but turn and look at Sebastian who nodded to me before bowing to his former queen.

Pannera coughed again, softer this time. "My darling Sebastian," she said. "How I've missed you."

He came to her side at once, kneeling next to me, face so sad I wanted to hug him. "Sweet Pannera," he whispered. "Let Sydlynn help you."

Her gray eyes went from his face to mine. "Tell me what you have in mind."

Sebastian's power flared, engulfed her and Pannera gasped. "You know I've changed," he said. "But I'm certain you have no idea just how much."

The Sthol vampires sighed as one as they felt his life,

heard his heartbeat. I held my breath as the sound of it, amplified by his magic, thudded against the stone walls before he let it fall silent.

Pannera's eyes flared with spirit power. "You can do this thing?"

"I can try," I said, suddenly afraid. What if I failed? She was so far gone...

"If you cannot," Pannera said in a voice softened by gratitude, "I will not judge you or call your intentions false. But if you succeed..." The dying queen sighed, the wet rattle shaking her chest under the parody of her satin gown, the bodice barely held in place by her crumbling body. "If you succeed, you can have anything of me."

"I don't want anything," I said. Glanced at Sebastian who smiled, touched my hair with his free hand. "I'll do my best."

I don't know about this, my vampire sent as I retreated, opened my mind to speak to her and the others.

Great, just what I needed.

You mean we can't make it work? Well, that sucked. She could have told me before I planted the seed of possibility.

She's very far gone, my demon sent, her amber magic flaring.

Sunny was under the full influence of the taint for only a short time, Shaylee sent. *She has some residual damage. But this...*

Centuries, my vampire sent. *As queen, Pannera held the*

core of the taint for centuries. Possibly for as long as she's been *queen.*

So much the Brotherhood had to answer for.

Just one more layer on top of a heaping pile of whoop ass.

We can only try, my demon sent.

Yes, of course. Shaylee's earth magic hummed in the floor under my feet.

Indeed, my vampire sent. *But we have one person to ask for help, first.*

I didn't want to call on her. Still held so much fury in my heart toward the maji Iepa. She sat on the same shelf as the drach leader, Max, and the Light Fate. All responsible for Liam's loss. They could have acted, could have allowed me to save him. Didn't. Chose to be all destiny and stuff.

Yeah.

Still.

It had been Iepa who guided me with the werewolves, though she refused to take part herself. And while I'd acted on impulse to save Sebastian, Pannera was going to be an entirely different situation.

A little help would be nice.

I ground my teeth together, prepared for either a) her ignoring me or b) the company line of non-interference and reached out to Iepa.

Was shocked down to the ground when she answered

me immediately and with great regret in her mind.

Sydlynn. Her power embraced me, her sympathy and self-loathing so clear I shrank from her. Didn't want to feel badly, still wanted to hate her. Hard to do when I felt Iepa's own heart aching with Liam's loss.

Damn her.

I need help. Sharp tone in place? Check. Short sentences? Check. Hard heart?

Traitor.

Iepa's magic settled. *I will assist if I can.*

Yeah, here we go, "If I can" all over again. Still battling my anger, I showed her Sebastian. Heard her sigh of happiness.

You've done so well, she sent. *Sydlynn, I am proud of you.*

One of my molars chipped as my teeth ground together. *How nice for you*, I shot back. Then showed her Pannera.

She sighed, her presence nodding. *I'm aware of her deterioration*, she sent. *What do you propose?*

Can I do to her what I did to him? I forced myself to release my tension as a soft, silver body settled next to me, Sassafras's purr easing me a little.

Iepa's hesitation made me worry. Worse when she spoke.

It's possible, she sent, tone heavy with doubt. *But the repair required might be too extensive to succeed.*

I was afraid of that.

I don't know how I did it last time. Hated admitting it to her.

Sydlynn, she sent, tone gentle and loving, *you don't have to know how. How is unimportant. Your power will know what to do.*

Okay then.

I take it you can't help me. Not like I was expecting her to break her track record of leaving me to handle things.

I can't. There was her grief again. *They will not allow it.*

The other maji. *Zeon still being a jerktard?*

While she remained sad, her laugh broke the edge of her sorrow. *My leader, though kind of countenance, can be quite stubborn and short sighted.* He'd shown me his happy Santa side, all right. Even as he sent me away to figure stuff out on my own. So I understood completely. *I've stepped over the line as far as I'm permitted. And I would go farther if I thought it would be necessary. But Sydlynn, please believe, you can accomplish just as much as I.* She hesitated. *More. You are stronger than I am now, stronger than my people here in Center. And I worry their fear of you and how your power continues to grow will only escalate.*

There was a warning if ever I heard one. And a bit of shocking news.

Didn't know which to bring up first.

Naturally, didn't get the chance to bring up either.

I wish you only the best, Iepa sent. *If anyone can heal Pannera, all the vampires, to evolve the magic races to their full potential, it is you, my friend.*

And then, she was gone.

Leaving me to chew my bottom lip and wonder if I was going to have the maji to worry about in the near future.

Shook it off. Drew a breath.

"Okay," I said. "Let's do it."

Didn't give Pannera a chance to argue.

Dove inside her mind. And met a wall. I don't think she even realized it was up. Her magic seemed eager enough to welcome me, but centuries of protecting herself, of wards and shields and being alone in her leadership formed a barrier.

Yes, I could have forced my way through. But in her fragile state, I didn't want to risk it.

Looked down as Sassafras's mind touched mine.

I'm here, Sassafras sent. *For what that's worth. If I can help...*

I don't think he understood what was in my way, only spoke out of his need to assist. But the moment he did, I had an epiphany.

On impulse, I released Pannera's hand, lifting the silver Persian into her lap. His body lit with amber fire, his purr louder than before. Pannera's eyes dimmed, softened, her tension easing under the influence of his magic.

And when I returned to her mind, I felt him there,

the beloved presence of his power softening her edges, taking down the wall, allowing me in.

Thank you, Sass, I sent and moved on.

So much damage. Yes, it was visible on her surface, and I'd felt it when I'd cleared her of the taint originally. But her degradation progressed to the point of near collapse. I didn't know if Pannera was aware just how short her time was. Wouldn't put it past her she was totally in tune with her pending final death.

So, I sent to my egos, *Iepa seems to think we already know what to do. Do we?*

Trust her, my vampire sent. *Though she's proven unfaithful in the past thanks to the burdens of Fate, she's had her own forced path to walk and, I believe, has always had our best interest at heart.*

Agreed, my demon sent. *As much as I hate to admit it.*

When we saved Sebastian, Shaylee sent, *we had to follow him to the edge of death. So that saves a step?*

Yes, my vampire sent as Pannera's life force clung to the tattered remains of her physical form. *He was empty. And we filled him up.*

My sorcery swelled, the blossom parting, widening as the family magic swirled around me.

Right. Pannera was a vampire. But her cells couldn't absorb blood anymore. I could feel it floating inside her, the crimson waste rotting even as it turned to its own dust. She simply couldn't take it in. No wonder she was falling to pieces.

I think I knew even before I tried we were throwing power after a lost cause, but it didn't stop me from giving everything I had to save her. Maji magic flowed out of me in a steady stream, encasing her in a glowing iridescent bubble of energy as I tried to tie her back together, to reassemble what had been destroyed. But even as I rebuilt one part of her, another crumbled and fell to nothing. There just wasn't any part of her intact enough for me to use to stabilize her.

Sydlynn. My vampire spoke softly in my mind as I drew a breath and kept trying. *Enough.*

Damn it.

Just damn it.

I let the bubble collapse, felt Pannera sag with it even as her people cried out as one in grief.

Her gray eyes never left mine as I sank back from her, shaking my head, real sorrow for her twisting inside me.

"I'm so sorry," I said, wishing there was something else I could say. Pannera's slow nod, tiny smile on her dusty face, held no animosity.

"As am I," she said.

And softly wept without tears for her body to shed.

chapter thirteen

I said goodbye to Sunny and Uncle Frank, refusing to even talk to them about their own transformations, at least for now. Not after I'd failed with Pannera, had to tread the walk of shame—at least, in my own head—down the throne room aisle, past the watching, grieving vampires until I couldn't stand it anymore.

Lifted Sassafras into my arms, cuddling him close, as I tore open the veil and returned us to Castle Wilhelm.

"I won't pressure you," Sunny said as we touched down in her throne room, "but I want you to consider it."

I nodded, miserable still, Sass's purr only taking the edge from my failure. No, I didn't care I'd failed. I cared Pannera was going to die and there was nothing I could do about it.

Yeah, she'd been my enemy once. But damn.

Hell of a way to go.

Sebastian took my elbow in one hand as I tore the veil again for home.

"I'd very much like to speak to your mother," he said.

Whatever. He could have traveled on his own, couldn't he? Still, it was nice to feel the warmth of his hand on my bare skin and, with a shrug, I brought him through the veil with me to Wilding Springs.

Not Harvard. Not yet. My heart hurt and I needed a dose of love from a certain little boy.

Found him sleeping in Shenka's arms in the living room while she watched TV. My second rose the moment I approached, eyes a little wide as she nodded to Sebastian.

I set Sassafras down, took Gabriel from her, kissed his soft cheek. He stirred in his sleep, but didn't wake. That was okay. Just holding him in my arms made me feel so much better.

I turned, cheek pressed to his soft, blonde hair and gave Sebastian a wry smile. "You haven't met," I said, keeping my voice low.

The handsome former vampire shook his head, but he smiled, too. Came closer, fingers soft on Gabriel's cheek. Sassafras hopped up on the arm of the chair Shenka vacated, putting himself in the middle ground between me and Sebastian and fixed me with his amber gaze.

"Don't you have work to do?" His thick, silver tail lashed once. Galleytrot's soft groan almost made me jump as his big head lifted from the other side of the chair, black eyes flickering with red fire.

I looked down at my sleeping son and made a decision.

"I do," I said, turning and heading for the stairs. "And I'm taking Gabriel with me."

Mom would love that.

No kidding. As I walked into my bedroom, Sassafras trailing behind me, the heavy, unhappy tread of the black hound's big feet thudding on the carpet, I reached for Mom.

It was early yet, just past 9:30 in the evening. She latched onto me the moment I touched her mind, as though I was a lifeline she desperately sought.

Syd. Was that panic in her mental touch?

Mom. Okay, now my heart was pounding. *What's wrong?* Oh. My. Swear—

Her touch softened immediately. *Nothing, sweetheart,* she sent. *It's just, you never... oh, dear.* She giggled mentally.

Way to work me up, Mom.

We're fine, I sent. *But I have someone who wants to see you.*

And I can't wait to see him. I could feel her reaching for Gabriel like a greedy sponge seeking water and blocked her.

Not him, I laughed. *And he's sleeping.*

Her disappointment came through crystal clear.

Mom, Sebastian is here. I grabbed the papoose, remembering it was Charlotte who gave it to me as a shower gift—among the dozens of presents she'd loaded Gabriel down with since he was conceived—and slipped his warm, sleeping body inside. It was nice to carry him against me like that, all snuggly...

Is he all right? I caught a glimpse of Mom moving from her office toward the kitchen in her quarters at Harvard.

Of course Gabriel was—oh. Right. She was talking about Sebastian.

We're coming for a visit, I sent. *I'm going to let him fill you in.*

Mom's hope was so badly hidden it bordered on pathetic.

Yes, Mom, I sent. *I'm bringing Gabriel, too.*

Can't wait. She cut me off with so much eagerness I knew I wouldn't have much time to cuddle my son after all.

"I'm joining you," Sassafras said. Eavesdropper.

"And me." Galleytrot's deep voice rumbled like a thunderstorm.

I turned on the pair of them and shook my head. "Not this time," I said. "I'm going to see Mom, for goodness sakes. You two stay put for once."

Sassafras grumbled while the big dog's eyes glowed with red fire.

"But—"

"But—"

I giggled.

And left them there to sulk.

Maybe it was mean of me to leave them behind, but honestly, Mom was going to be bad enough. And if she let Erica know I was coming... Mom's former second and my representative on Council would be disgusting in her need to hold my son.

Sass and Galleytrot had him almost 24/7. A little distance wouldn't hurt them any.

And I'd been away from my son forever.

Okay, an hour.

Still.

Sebastian waited for me at the bottom of the stairs. Shenka raised one eyebrow at me, a tiny smirk on her lips as she kissed my cheek, then Gabriel's head.

"Have fun," she said. *Try to find some free time with hottie here*, she finished.

Blush. Ing.

I opened the veil, now totally self-conscious about Sebastian's hand in mine as I took it and strode into the veil.

Didn't help I was having unclean thoughts myself.

Growl.

Ahbi hugged me, cooed at Gabriel. I hadn't considered my demon grandmother might not be as willing to let my baby sleep. As we stepped out the other side into Mom's kitchen, Gabriel woke with a soft sigh and a surge of love for Ahbi. She embraced him with her energy before reluctantly sealing the veil shut again.

Mom's soft cry of happiness immediately preceded her stampede to my side and, as I expected, Gabriel was removed from my person and mauled heartlessly by my over-eager mother.

Okay, fine. She cuddled him and kissed him and he giggled.

Sheesh.

I turned to drop the papoose on the table and caught sight of Mom's secretary, Maurice, hovering, peeking through the crack in the door, watching my son with his beady eyes.

Was his gaze narrowed as he chewed his bottom lip? Glared as if Gabriel was to blame for some personal fault.

Creepasaurus. Anger flared inside me as I stormed to the door and slammed it in his face. Overreaction? Maybe. But I hated the way he always hovered when I was at Harvard, sneaking around, listening in on my conversations with Mom. Her secretary and I had never gotten along. Partly because he was a slimezilla with a serious case of the asshats.

Mom didn't seem to notice, still murmuring nonsense to Gabriel, though Sebastian's eyebrows lifted in question. I shrugged at him, temper draining away now Maurice's prying was cut short.

Mom looked up, cheeks pink, eyes laughing, met mine. "Thank you for bringing him," she said.

I shrugged, gestured at Sebastian. "Did you even say hello, Mom?"

She flushed brighter, bobbed a nod at the handsome former vampire. I really needed a new handle for him. Thinking of him as a former vampire was going to get old, fast.

How about yummynomnom? My demon growled her suggestion.

I like tauthawtness, Shaylee giggled.

Ahem, my vampire sent. *I prefer Captain Delicious.*

Oh. My.

Seriously?

Sebastian approached Mom, bent to look in Gabriel's eyes. Now awake and aware, my son said something in his very garbled language, as though expecting an answer from my friend. The earnestness on his baby face made me press both hands to my heart as it swelled beyond the ability of my chest to contain it.

"It is my great pleasure to meet you," Sebastian said.

That seemed to satisfy Gabriel who laughed his beautiful laugh and reached out both arms to Sebastian, almost flinging himself from Mom's grip. Sebastian took him without hesitation, repeating the happy little bounce most people started up as soon as they had my son in their arms.

Gabriel seemed to examine Sebastian closely before snuggling his head against my friend's shoulder and sighing with a smile, eyes falling closed.

So. Freaking. Cute.

No more so than the look of shock, and then amazed contentment, on Sebastian's face.

Hmmm.

Maybe he was daddy material for real.

All of a sudden, Shenka's suggestion I spend a little alone time with the delicious former vampire—I refused to call him Captain anything—seemed like a really, really good idea.

Following him and Mom to the kitchen, "for a snack," she said, made my mouth water.

And not for food.

How could anyone's ass look that good in jeans?

Growl.

chapter fourteen

We sat at the table, my carnal thoughts making me blush as Sebastian turned and sank into a chair, still holding my son. Those thoughts turned to "awww" as he softly rubbed Gabriel's back with one big hand, while Mom served us wine and some fruit and cheese. I bit into a strong piece of cheddar just for something to focus on as my demon rumbled her continuing interest, hand fisted around my glass of milk.

Sebastian waved Mom off when she made the offer of some cabernet.

"I no longer enjoy the taste of alcohol," he said. Winked at me. "The only disappointment in all this."

Mom's eyes locked on Gabriel as she sat and, without prompting, Sebastian handed him over while a little seed of resentment woke up, cutting through my consideration of his strong hands, the way his muscular chest rippled through the open collar of his white shirt.

I'd tried to save his former queen, hadn't I? And he gives Gabriel to my mother.

Typical.

Sebastian told Mom everything while she rocked my son in an almost reflexive motion, as though unaware she was doing it. At least she seemed focused on what Sebastian was saying, despite my son's proximity.

I was just finishing my part of the story when Gabriel woke again. Turned to me and opened his arms, feelings of hunger rumbling through his magic.

"Ah," I said, a little embarrassed. "He wants dinner." Refused to look at Sebastian. Would not think about him and my son and my very full chest all at the same time.

Would. Not.

Weaning time was coming, you betcha. And then, well. We'd see.

Thank goodness for Lula's magic, I didn't have to endure the ache in my breasts, at least. And, with some encouragement from me, I was able to keep myself from blowing up like a pair of twin balloons until Gabriel wanted to eat. But I could feel myself pushing against my bra in a way I knew had to look freakish. Scrambled to retrieve Gabriel from Mom.

Breastfeeding in front of Sebastian was NOT an option.

Mom saved my life. "I had a crib and rocking chair

installed in my room," she said. Blushed. "Just in case you ever decided to let him stay over."

Sneaky.

"Thanks, Mom." Dipped her a nod and ran from the room.

Fifteen minutes and a happily full baby later and I settled him into the crib. I wanted to hold him, but I knew it was probably better to just leave him and let him sleep. Took me another five minutes to pull myself away from the crib and close the door behind me, but not until I wrapped the cute, wooden bed with a bubble of maji power.

Perfect baby monitor.

Mom looked disappointed when I returned without the baby, but stayed focused.

"How much longer does Pannera have?" They must have been talking when I was gone.

Sebastian looked at me. Right. "I don't know," I said, crossing my arms over my chest, the last traces of my self-consciousness driving me to hide the shrunken evidence. "Not long. I'm surprised she's lasted until now." Glum, I let my arms drop and leaned forward, elbows on the table. "I wanted to offer her release, but I didn't know if she'd accept it."

Sebastian shifted in his chair, eyes distant. "She would not," he said. "Her pride keeps her from such mercy." One hand reached out, squeezed mine as he focused on me. "But your kindness is staggering, Syd. Considering everything she's done."

"Everything the Brotherhood has done." I squeezed back. "This isn't Pannera's fault."

I stood, needing to move, feeling suddenly restless. Walked to the window and looked out over the Yard. Harvard was lovely in the summer, all the looming trees in full leaf. I found I missed it, my time here at school, the measure of normal it allowed me while I studied, if punctuated by the occasional disaster.

"Who stands in line to succeed her?" Mom's voice was soft, aimed away from me, at Sebastian, clearly.

His own sank low as he answered. "I don't know," he said. "The politics of such a succession are complicated. She might name an heir, but unless the entire clan supports her decision, there could be a fight for control."

"That's not good." Mom's frown came through. I pressed my forehead to the cool glass, catching her reflection in the window as she leaded back, the creak of her chair loud in the quiet. "We need to alert Femke of a possible succession war."

I saw the door open, just a fraction. Knew Maurice was back. Almost spun and tossed him physically from the room. But as I turned, fury full-on, he ignored me and entered, bowing to Mom.

"Council Leader," he said in his whiny, nasal voice, round glasses shining in the light, hiding his beady eyes.

"Yes, Maurice?" Mom sounded slightly irritated by the intrusion.

"You are scheduled to confer with Council Leader Braylen." His eyes flickered to me. Just for a second.

He seemed nervous. Was I finally freaking him out? Honestly, I hadn't seen him since the whole Brotherhood last battle thing went down. Could be I'd earned a little respect. Or fear.

I'd take either.

Mom stood, nodded. Turned to me with a hopeful smile. "I won't be long?"

I shook my head and grinned. "We're not leaving yet," I said.

She flashed me a happy smile before taking Sebastian's hand as he rose. "Thank you for coming to tell me in person," she said. "Would you like me to speak to Femke?"

I'd have to pay the European Council Leader a visit myself. Maybe with Sebastian.

And leave Gabriel home…

Bad, Syd. Bad, bad.

Yum.

"Not at all," Sebastian said. "I'm on my way back now, anyway. I'll take care of it."

Crap.

Sigh.

Mom left, hustling after Maurice, who shot me one

more look before running off.

Definitely scared of me.

Wicked.

Sebastian held out his hand to me and, without thinking, I crossed to him and took it. His blue eyes looked down into mine, square jaw jumping a little as though he struggled with speaking.

Made me all kinds of nervous. Especially when my body had such a powerful reaction to his, always had. The moment my hand fell in his this time, heat traveled between us. Woke up some places I'd thought dead and withered. And while I'd never been self-conscious about myself, not really—at least, not physically—the sudden thought of Sebastian seeing me naked...

I'd started working out again, had my body back, mostly. My marital arts teacher, Sage, saw to that. Pushed me hard enough, bouncing Gabriel while chatting with Charlotte, I fit into my old jeans, at least.

Still.

More blushing.

Yikes.

Sebastian finally bent, pressed his lips to my forehead, hand gently cupping the back of my head as his other settled against the middle of my back. I leaned into him, all my worries fading, allowing his power to flow over mine.

To ignite those certain parts of me all over again.

When he pulled away, his smile was sad.

"My darling witch girl," he said. "I owe you my life, so many times over. And there was a brief, happy moment I thought perhaps I could give you what you needed." He sighed even as my heart shriveled a little in understanding, my demon growling as the other girls sighed. "But until I know who I am, of what I'm capable, I know now it would be wrong for me to ask you to commit your heart to mine."

No it wouldn't. Shaylee was quick on the draw.

We just want his body, anyway, my demon sent.

Yes, tell him that, my vampire sent.

Made me laugh, despite my sadness. Sebastian cocked his head to the side, dark curls falling over his collar as I shrugged.

"The girls disagree," I said. "But I get it, I really do." I knew how he felt, didn't I? How long did it take me to accept who I was?

Sucked anyway.

"I will always be here for you," he said, intensity so powerful I almost allowed tears to fall. Almost. "As you have been for me. You only have to ask."

Sebastian kissed me then, gentle and with a soft flare of heat before stepping away.

Flashing into light as he raised his hand in farewell. And vanished.

chapter fifteen

Mom was already back and watching me as I turned away from where Sebastian had stood. Her eyes twinkled, a naughty look on her face as she closed the kitchen door behind her.

Damn flushing reflex. He'd just told me we couldn't be together, hadn't he? And I was still all fangirl gooey over him.

Mom had the decency not to say anything, just crossed the room and hugged me.

"I thought you had a meeting?" I didn't mean to be grumpy. She let me go, retrieved her wine.

"I rescheduled," she said. Shocking. "Not often my daughter and grandson come to visit."

I felt Gabriel twitch in his sleep, disturbed a little. Probably gas. Then, he sighed and settled again.

"He's still passed out," I say by way of a hint.

Mom's pout flashed across her face so fast I giggled.

We sat again, she at the end of the table with her wine, me picking at the cheese tray as we talked. Funny, I wasn't ready to go home yet, just enjoying my mother's company.

Until I had to open my big mouth and ask about the one person I told myself I wouldn't. Because now I'd stirred those feelings again, the memory of being held, being loved, flared into new life.

"How's Quaid?" Oh, Syd.

Syd, Syd, Syd.

Mom acted like I hadn't just torn the lid from Pandora's box. "He's doing very well," she said as the image of his face swam in my mind, the scent of his chocolatey goodness perked by the small tray of cupcakes next to the cheese. "In fact, he's excelling." She sighed, set down her wine. "He's being given more and more responsibility these days."

"You sound like that's a bad thing?" I liberated a cupcake and sniffed the icing, anticipating the burst of sugar while I stuffed down my feelings for Quaid with food.

Perfect coping mechanism.

Mom shrugged, helped herself to her own cupcake. "It's not," she said. "But I can see Pender trying to transition out, Syd. Makes me sad, that's all."

Pender Tremere, the present Enforcer leader, had

been through a great deal, especially when Liander Belaisle had his people killed and their bodies burned, bones crushed so their magic could never join the rest of the order when he took over the stronghold. I didn't blame Pender for wanting out, but Mom hadn't let him resign.

Maybe she'd be better off finding another to take his job if he wanted out that badly.

Which led me to a small ah-ha moment.

"He's grooming Quaid to replace him." Of course he was. Made total sense.

Mom nodded, picking at the paper wrap on the bottom of her treat. "He's the finest young Enforcer we've seen in decades." Like she'd been at this that long. Sounded more like she was just repeating what Pender told her. Still, I believed it.

"I'm happy for him." I really was. Sad for me, though. Yup, yup.

"You two don't talk anymore?" Mom seemed sorrowful herself, blue eyes concerned.

I leaned away from the cupcake, no longer hungry around the churning in my stomach that rose every time I thought of Quaid. I knew it was the magic trying to force us together, but knowing didn't make things any easier.

"I haven't seen him since Mia's trial." And subsequent burning. At least she was in a better place. Her poor, tortured soul gone on.

I hadn't meant for our conversation to turn maudlin. And Mom wasn't helping.

"I want you to know, I haven't stopped looking for Ameline." Mom's gaze dropped, cupcake slipping to the table uneaten, hand clenching around the stem of her glass as my breath caught.

I forced it out again, made my shoulders relax, drew a deep breath. "Thanks." Another long inhale. "No luck, I take it?"

Mom shook her head, curling black hair tumbling in bouncing coils around her. "It's possible she's left this plane, which means she's out of reach." And sight. And mind?

I had to do something about that sooner or later. Thanks to the drach, Max—though I had very little else to thank him for—I now knew how to track her through the vast expanse of the veil. My maji power allowed me to see her trail, though I doubted she'd be foolish enough to leave tracks behind if she could help it.

And with Gabriel now two months old in the body of a boy much older, maybe it was time I stopped playing Mommy and went after her at last.

I wanted to be able to tell my son, when he was old enough to understand, I'd killed the bitch who took his father away from him.

"The Steam Union has been very helpful." Mom must have decided herself to change the mood because her tone grew lighter. "They've rounded up most of the Brotherhood at this point and are keeping track of those who joined their ranks just in case."

I still thought accepting former Brotherhood sorcerers under their wing was a bad idea, but the Steam Union leader, Eva Southway, didn't seem to give a crap what I thought. Considering her son pursued me at one point and her concern about our possible marriage didn't make her my biggest fan, I was sure with Liam's loss she'd be worried all over again.

Let her. I was taking Dad's advice. Yes, I loved Liam, but my hand had still been forced. This time, I was only going to marry who I loved. Who I chose to spend the rest of his life with.

And that wasn't Piers Southway.

"What about the witches?" I welcomed the distraction as Mom rolled her eyes and laughed a little.

"As stubborn as ever," she said. "But working together, for once."

Would wonders never cease?

I knew as soon as Mom's face fell the forced lightness was a façade hiding something deeper than I'd suspected at first. And winced when she spoke.

"How was your father's betrothal?" Oh, Mom.

She just had to ask.

I stood, went to her. Hugged her as she clung to me, but didn't cry.

"Sassafras told me," she said. Right. He said he would and was good to his word. Is that why she left after all? To give Dad space to see me and Gabriel? If so, she was a bigger woman than I was. "Is Harry happy?"

I could have lied to her. Would it have made her feel better? Or worse? Didn't matter.

Couldn't do it.

"He's miserable," I said, choking up. "Like you."

That did it. Mom sobbed once, hands clutching at me. I pulled her to her feet and hugged her, doing my very best not to cry, to just embrace her with my power and my heart and let her release her sorrow.

She finally pulled free, sniffling, half-smiling.

"I'm sorry, sweetheart," she said. "You don't need to see me break down like this."

"Mom." I gripped her upper arms, shaking her a little. "I love you. And I'm not a kid anymore. I know exactly how you feel." First Quaid. Then Liam.

Yeah. Did I.

Mom nodded. "I know," she whispered. "That's why I didn't want you to see me cry."

I hugged her again and she hugged me back, not the desperate hold of a moment ago. Just a loving embrace between mother and daughter as we supported each other.

I leaned back, met her eyes. "I know you want me to move on," I said, amazed my voice was steady. "And I

125

will, I promise. But someone needs to take her own advice."

Mom's face paled, two bright points of red on her high cheekbones as her eyes widened, then softened as she nodded.

"I know," she said. Drew a shaking breath. "It's time." She stroked my hair. "For both of us."

I couldn't bear it, this hovering weight of grief, the bubble of pain we stood in.

Couldn't.

"Maybe we could try a double date." Mom winked, shattering it just before it could smother me, suck all the air from my chest. "I'm sure we could find a father/son pair who would be very happy to find themselves having dinner with us."

Choke.

I loved my mother so much.

"Don't ever suggest that again," I said with a grin, wiping at the single tear that escaped. "Ever."

Mom laughed, wicked gleam back in her eyes before she fluttered her hands in front of her like a nervous bird. "I just… Syd, it's been so long. I don't even know how to date anymore."

Surely there was someone much better than me to give her advice on guys.

Shudder.

Saved by the boy child. Gabriel stirred, suddenly

upset, agitated. He never cried. Well, only around Sonja O'Dane. His distress drew my immediate attention. "Nugget's fussing," I said, frown pinching my forehead.

Mom's mirrored mine. She followed me as I hurried to her room, his anxiety rising as I reached for the door handle.

Turned the knob.

Whispered his name in the dark as he fell quiet—

chapter sixteen

Why is everything all black and fuzzy? Numbness pulls at me, hums to me to return to the dark and be still. I almost do, want to, for some reason. There is great comfort in it, in the embrace of the black and the haziness of the nothing.

Have I fallen into my sorcery? Into a gaping hole made for travel from the hungry black of my power, only to be lost?

No, that can't be right. I can hear voices, can't I? Familiar voices, ones I know very well. They make me want to focus, to listen and understand why I am here, floating in the dark.

Even as I do, my soul flinches. Cries out. Tries to retreat. Something isn't right. A fundamental something, tied to the center of who I am.

But what? And do I really want to know?

Light assaults me, bright and terrible, and only then do I realize I'm blinking. Looking up into Lula's face while she talks from very far away. Not to me.

To Mom. Who hovers over me, face lined in strain, hands clenched tight to her chest.

Why are they upset?

And should I be?

Lula looks at me. Her face crumples a moment before she opens her mouth and says my name in slow.

Motion.

Syyyyyyydddddddd...

And then, I'm falling again, away from her, my soul running from the light. My stomach heaves, I feel a terrible grief try to take hold of me, only to be embraced in the numbness.

I know this numbness, have felt it before, this lack of emotion hazed in a cloud of confusion. Lived it for a little while. But when? And why? Lazy, indistinct, a face appears. Beloved face, with hazel eyes and pinpoints of green sparks, the scent of the earth and fabric softener sharpening the memory.

(My dead husband,) Liam.

Yes.

But he's gone already. So from where comes this numb and empty feeling I find myself in?

Another flash of light as I surface once more, Mom sitting beside me, weeping. Meira next to her, hand holding mine. So odd, she's human. Yes, I feel her touch, if only for a moment. Meira comforts Mom. She must be so sad Dad is getting married again. Lovely of my sister to come and help when I'm not feeling well.

Yes, that's it. I'm sick, aren't I? Just ill, some odd malaise holding me captive in the black and the numb. I should act on it, heal myself. Rise again. Mom needs me, it's so clear to see, can barely hold herself together against the pain of Dad's marriage. Something wet escapes the corner of my eye, touches my cheek. Sweet, this tear for my mother's sadness.

But I when I try, when I reach for my magic, it takes so long for me to find them, to feel them, my hitchhikers, my alter egos. Hiding, deep inside me. Torn up with sorrow. Turning slowly toward me, the truth of what's happened in their magic.

And, in a gasp of need I

Run

From

Them.

Back into the darkness. The quiet.

Without hearing or knowing or understanding. Because I don't want to.

I know that now.

All I want is to stay here.

Where it's perfect.

Lula's voice again, breaking through. "She's fighting me. I can't keep her still."

The family finds me, the coven's power, grief and love and support but I can't can't can't—

Can't.

I jerk awake, into night this time. Lying in a bed. Blank. Empty. What?

What happened?

Meira's room. At Harvard. I recognize it immediately. What am I doing here? I need to go home, the family needs me—

Lula appears, sits beside me. Sassafras's silver body presses against me as Lula eases me back down onto the bed. I don't resist her. Maybe I should stay here a bit longer. I've been sick.

Haven't I?

Sass's misery is almost too much for me to bear, because I don't know (I do, I know, I just don't want to, never want to, never never) why he's so upset.

"It's okay, Sass." My lips are thick, I can only mumble. "It'll be okay."

He sobs, unable to purr.

Mom is there, too, replacing Lula. Her magic wraps around me, her hands holding my hands. "Syd," she says, voice steady though I can hear the tremor behind it, feel the subtle touch of her sorrow masked in her power. "Syd, sweetheart."

Something happened to me. "What happened?"

She shudders, looks at Lula.

"Her mind is still protecting her," the Kennecott twin says. "But it's time we try to bring her back to us again, Miriam. We must keep trying."

Mom's face crumples, her hands shaking before she nods and meets my eyes. Sassafras is still weeping on my shoulder.

I feel them, then, my egos, shivering and crying within. The thrum of the family magic. The deep and mournful touch of the earth through Sidhe magic.

Galleytrot. Did someone hurt him?

Did someone hurt—

Flinch.

"Syd," Mom said. "What is the last thing you remember?"

The memory coaxes forward. Mom's kitchen. Sebastian.
"Cupcake," I said.

Mom sobs once, stills. "Yes, sweetheart," she says. "Then
what?"

I hugged her, she cried over Dad. And then someone—

"Crying," I say. "Someone was upset." Who was it? I struggle
to retrieve the recollection, my mind skipping around it while my
soul screams at me to stop.

Asking.

Questions.

Stop.

But I can't stop, not now. I have to know. Who was upset—

And then.

My mind.

Exploded outward.

Images, memories. His sweet face, his tiny hands, his
dear scent. The way he giggled and loved everyone. And
never, ever fussed.

Never.

Gabriel.

My body bucked in answer to the truth, seizing,
power tossing me as the girls howled their loss.

My loss.

Gabriel.

Lula's power barely skimmed over me, unable to hold me. I knew that, they couldn't keep me here, I was done, so done—

"She's breaking again." Lula's desperation was clear in her voice, but I didn't care.

The family tried to hold me, Mom, Sunny and Uncle Frank, Sassafras. Charlotte, weeping. Meira and Ahbi.

Only Galleytrot shared my grief. And wanted to leave with me.

But this departure had to be solitary.

Lonely was a single digit.

"We can't lose her this time." Sassafras's power slapped me, hard. Jabbed me over and over. The shock of each impact jerked me back, but he wouldn't win.

He couldn't keep me here.

Don't you leave me, girl. She had to come, didn't she? She had to force me to listen, to sit in my mind and harp at me. *You stay with me. Because if you go, you take me with you.*

Gram.

Syd, they whispered, all of them. *Syd, stay with us. You have to stay.*

No. Please. Just let me go.

Don't make me.

I can't.

I won't survive without—

My mind takes me out of Mom's kitchen. Down the hall. To

the door. The knob. Gabriel fussing in my mind, against the shielding I left around him.

Mom's room in the dark. The crib. His name on my lips as he falls silent—

Deathly silent.

NONONONONONONONONO—

They cling to me while I howl and fight them and try so hard to leave. How many times have they forced me to come back, to face what's happened? The numb and the dark wait, pulling me close, embracing me. And I go to it, hide in its cool embrace, their presence falling away as I run.

Run from my shattered heart. My broken soul.

My life.

I want to die. Please, just let me die. Go with him. Be with them both.

My husband is dead.

And so is my son.

chapter seventeen

They pulled me back at last, finally jerking me from the black to face it. To face my loss, a loss so deep it smothered the sadness I felt for Liam. Devoured any caring for my own personal safety. Destroyed any hope I had to ever, ever be happy again.

Never again.

My son was dead.

Crib death, Lula called it. Which only rarely happened to witch babies, for obvious reasons. Because their mothers took care of them, didn't they? Used power to protect them, guard over them, keep them breathing and alive and beautiful.

What the hell kind of mother was I?

Trill lay down next to me, resting her head on my pillow, hand under her cheek on my shoulder. "Please don't run again," she whispered. "I almost didn't find you this time."

I wished she hadn't. Stared at the canopy above me and willed myself to die.

Just die already.

A giant face appeared at the foot of my bed, topping broad shoulders, scaled skin, diamond eyes. Max. My hate raged.

"You brought me back." Spit flew from my lips. "You made me."

Another reason to despise him.

But he remained. Sat ponderously in a chair. Watching me.

So he thought he was going to keep me here, did he?

I turned my head away from Trill, away from Max. Stared at the curtained window. Fine, whatever. I was too tired to fight, for now. But they couldn't watch me forever. And then I'd go. I'd run to the veil. And I'd find a way to hide where no one would find me.

Maybe Center? I could go to Iepa, appeal to her. Surely she could erase my memories and I could live there, with her and the maji. Blissfully ignorant of the life I once lived, the people I loved.

Of my dead son and my dead husband.

Quite the track record you have going there, Syd.

And then I couldn't breathe, choked on my grief, so powerful it sat in the middle of my chest and whispered horrible truths. That Gabriel was dead because of me. If

I'd only let Sassafras and Galleytrot come to Harvard, they would have been with him. Watched over him where I failed. Kept him safe, alive.

My fault.

No Ameline to blame this time, no Max or Iepa or Light Fate. No Liander Belaisle to point the finger toward. No evil coming for me, my family.

Not this time.

My. Fault.

My egos coiled inside me, keeping themselves apart, unable to offer each other comfort. To offer me any. That was okay. I didn't want it. Didn't deserve it. I let my son die.

I let my son die.

I let my son—

Why was I here again?

How much could I be asked to bear, how many hurts, heartbreaks, losses, endless pits of agony could I be expected to tolerate? And there was no hope for me, was there, not at all. I had FOREVER to suffer.

Maybe that was a good thing. Maybe I needed to spend forever remembering I'd failed, I'd lost the one person who needed me to protect him the most. My own son.

Liam would have hated me for this.

I hated myself.

I stayed, despite my need to go, the desire to run

cycling over and over, each time easing just a little more until the numb found me and hung out, not needing the dark to sustain it.

I'd fought it off once before, wouldn't let it take me. When Liam died.

Not this time.

This time, the numb was an old friend, more welcome than the seemingly endless parade of faces and powers coming to my bedside. Who tried to talk to me. The cool, white power of the vampires. Sunny's tears did nothing to break through. Uncle Frank's either.

What did they know of grief? How dare they think they deserved tears? I lost my son.

I killed him.

They earned their tears of grief more than I had.

The sympathy of the string of visitors burned like a fire that wouldn't go out, beating me with whips of flame. Hurt more than anything, their sadness for me. Their attempts to try to cajole me into eating, conversing, being present.

They could keep me alive, but they could not make me live.

They came, in pairs, in groups, in singles. Charlotte. Meira and Mom. Dad, weeping openly. Femke Svensson, her fair skin blotchy, blonde hair shining like an angel's. Even Eva Southway. Sebastian whispered in my ear. Sassafras with his calming purr.

Gram.

And always, watching me from his chair, as though he would never leave.

Max.

Quaid wasn't welcome. I wished he'd stayed away. But he tried, sat next to me, took my hand. And the touch of his skin, the warmth of him, the surge of magic between us pierced my empty.

He shouldn't have done that.

I let him go, fought to retrieve my place of nothing after he was gone, to sink back into the numb.

Found anger in its place. Fury. Hate. And the burning fire.

Trill slipped into my room. Met my eyes.

And I embraced the rage, gathered it to me like a weapon.

Threw it in her face.

"This is your fault," I screamed. "Why didn't you just let me die?"

Trill ran from me, weeping.

Let her.

I was done.

More than done. Alone at last, they'd left me finally. Only Max watched as I fell out of bed, legs weak, body shaking from hunger and thirst and overwhelming fury. A robe lay on the end of the bed. I jerked it on, felt him rise, come to hover over me.

Didn't touch me. Speak. Nothing.

Good.

The veil opened, Ahbi there, reaching for me. I jerked the tear closed.

No. I couldn't go that route. How could I? She'd tell.

There was another way. Escape into a black so deep I knew I'd never get out. But I wasn't interested in escaping, not anymore. Just this room. This building. The constant pressure of the magic around me.

Air.

Outside.

And then, I would decide. What next.

A black circle opened before me as I called on my sorcery, the petals blossoming wide. I drew on the supporting magic of my family, my friends. Screw them. They were so worried about me, they could feed my need. I touched on Mom's fear, Lula's attempt to grapple with me.

But Max held them back.

Nodded. Pointed to the gap.

And together, the drach, who I'd thought my friend once, and I walked into it.

I didn't make it far. Gasped for oxygen as the portal opened again, my desperate need to escape it more powerful than my grief. Horrible, terrible the place of total nothingness. I'd thought I was in empty, but I had no idea.

Was reminded just how bleak and soul-sucking empty really was.

A building I recognized, a bench beside it. I sank into the seat, the Memorial Chapel behind me, Harvard Yard dark but for a few lights lining the trees in the center. This place had so many memories. Of Alison attacking me, trying to steal the vampire essence. Crossing with Gram into the stronghold through a secret path right here, in this spot. My life, spinning out from those memories as my egos continued to hide.

To grieve and blame.

To hate.

I reached for Iepa. No answer.

Freaking typical.

Max stood off to the left, watching me with his damned diamond eyes.

"What?" I snarled the word, flung it in a dagger of spite.

He didn't reply. Just nodded to me.

Only then did I feel I wasn't alone.

Turned my head.

And met Alison's blue eyes.

chapter eighteen

Maybe I should have feared her. What she might have become. The last time I saw Alison, she'd attacked me, tried to steal my crystal from Demetrius.

Was blown apart by the power.

Instead, the boiling hate woke in full force as I grasped her by the front of her shirt—part of me remembering she was corporeal at the last minute—and shook her.

And shook her.

And shook her.

Until my arms ached. Until I was sobbing for air, pouring all of my rage and bile over her, dumping the shreds of my guilt and fury and shattered remains of my heart.

Alison simply sat there.

And took it.

Which made it worse. I jerked her toward me, pressed my nose into hers as I screamed at her my final shred of need in this world.

"Show me my baby!"

Alison finally reacted, twitched.

"You gather echoes. Where is he?" I pushed away from her, stood, spun to face her, power crackling as the girls woke. Finally, something to do, to focus on. Someone to punish.

Someone else.

Her tears, her sadness, cracked me down the middle. Broke me open like no one else had been able to. A monster didn't look back at me.

Alison Morgan did. My old bestie. The girl who just wanted to be loved.

"I sent my echoes across," she said, voice soft, edged with tragedy. "They are where they were meant to be."

Hope, cold and sharp, but hope nonetheless, drove a gasp of air into my lungs.

"You have him?" I almost fell at her feet, hands outstretched. "Did you help him cross?"

My Gabriel.

Alison shook her head. "The power shift changed me," she said, as though I wasn't desperate to know. As if she didn't hear me at all. "When Demetrius touched me with the crystal's power, it devoured me. And the taint. And healed me." She looked up, met my eyes. Smiled despite the tears still trickling down her cheeks. Alison wiped at them, magic sparking.

Maji magic.

It was only then I understood. She felt like Sebastian.

And I cared, why?

Didn't. And yet.

"I finally remembered who I was, Syd." Alison stayed seated, hands tucked between her knees, blonde hair in a ponytail. Just like always. My anger receded, hope fading as I sank down next to her on the bench and sagged into my grief all over again.

Too hard to sustain the temper, it seemed.

"I went looking for my parents, did you know?" Alison seemed thoughtful despite her sadness. "I hated how they seemed happier without me, like I was the reason they didn't live together." She shrugged, shook her head. "Until I was healed. And realized they came together because of me." Alison turned to look at me, managed a little smile. "Mom stopped drinking. Dad's not a workaholic anymore." She took my hand and I didn't fight her, though I also didn't offer any comfort as she squeezed. "So much has happened to me since I died," she said. "I've hurt you, Syd. Please, forgive me."

A weak shrug. Why did this matter? And yet, it did, as she went on. I found myself listening, my egos, too.

"You didn't use magic on me to change me," she said. "I'm sorry I lied." Right. She'd told me I'd used my power on her, that someone like her would never be friends with someone like me. "The truth was, if you hadn't been my friend, I think I would have self-destructed long before I did."

"Now what?" She was healed, kind of real, whatever. Good for her.

Alison turned, held my hand between hers. So warm. "I can't cross over," she said. "I've tried. I'm too real now. Alive again." She tapped her chest over her heart before returning her hand to mine. "I'm part a lot of things." Laughter. Foreign, that sound. "But I don't know where to go from here."

Was she really asking for my help? When I could barely help myself? When my son was dead and I killed him?

"I know someone you should talk to." The words were out, my sense of duty roused before I could suppress it. And in that moment, as I looked at Alison, really looked at her, light dawned again inside me.

She'd done what no one else succeeded in doing.

She made me care.

Alison hugged me, her chin over my shoulder. "I'm here for you," she whispered. "Your sadness drew me to you, drove me to complete my healing. I was there, Syd." I flinched and she leaned back. She was there, when… "I've been trying to reach you, but I knew if I showed up your mother would have me taken by the Enforcers."

True that.

"I've been watching, waiting. This was the first chance I had to see you alone." Her eyes lifted to Max. "Mostly alone. But I had to take the chance."

The big drach nodded. "Fate, Sydlynn Hayle," he said in his gravel voice, making me shiver from it as his magic reached for me, surrounded me. I wanted to shrug it off. I still blamed him for Liam's death. But Alison was talking again and I found myself focused on her.

"I so hoped you'd listen." Alison's tears ran again. "I had to do this in person or I knew you'd block me out."

"Do what?" Some giant disaster waiting to be solved? Screw that. Max's comment about Fate could bite my ass.

"Syd," Alison said. "I went looking, when he died. For Gabriel's echo."

At first, I shivered, rejected what she said. Gabriel died. My son. Dead.

And then.

The world.

Stood.

Still.

"I searched for him," she said. "But I couldn't find him."

Gasp.

Choke.

"What?" She was lucky I managed that one word. Especially while my egos all sat up, hyper focused.

Waited.

His echo—

No. Why allow any thread of hope? Gabriel was dead. Mom wouldn't lie to me.

"That just means he moved on already." Sidhe didn't have echoes anyway, did they? I knew that much.

But Alison was shaking her head.

"I know what you're thinking," she said. "And I thought maybe, too, he'd gone on. Or, like other Sidhe, he wouldn't have an echo at all. But he was as much your son as he was Liam's." Don't take me there, I beg you. "And even Sidhe bones have traces left of their power."

"You." Air, Syd. No passing out. "You checked his"—gasp—"bones?"

She nodded, firm, up and down. That was a yes.

A yes.

Hope?

No, I couldn't.

And yet.

Hope.

"I'm sorry for doing it," Alison said, leaning away, wringing her hands. "For intruding on his remains like that. I didn't know what else to do. I felt so terrible for you, and I wanted to be sure he made it across okay, if he did have an echo."

"What does it mean?" What could it possibly mean?

Hope.

Shut up.

Alison stiffened. Paused. Then spoke the words that cemented my heart back together.

"It means," she said, "whoever was on that funeral pyre, it wasn't your son."

Chapter Nineteen

I gaped at her for a long, long time. It felt like forever as the tiny hope I'd fought bloomed like a rose, flared and woke inside me while my soul leaped up and shouted in joy.

Gabriel.

Not his bones.

My egos freaked out, shouting, buzzing with power, so violently I had to hold myself very still for fear I'd fly apart. We reached out for him, found nothing, not a trace, a sniff.

If he was alive, if I could let myself believe… where was he?

Alison continued to watch me, concern on her face, breathing heavily as she, too, must have fought her emotions.

I finally felt my egos still a little, reined them in.

Listen, I snarled.

And they did.

"Whose bones are they?" Teeth clenched, throat tight, barely able to force the words out.

I managed.

Alison shrugged. "I don't know," she said. "Usually bones carry an imprint of the person who lived in them." Shiver. "But these felt blank. Black."

Empty.

Sharp pain wrenched at my insides as truth woke and punched me in the gut.

Alison went on, oblivious. "No echo, no imprint of Sidhe, no Gabriel." She touched my hand one more time. "I don't know if your son is still alive," she said, "but the body they interred wasn't his."

The veil parted before me, Ahbi's eagerness turned to fear as I grasped Alison's hand and jerked her inside, Max following after. My demon grandmother's spirit fought me, buffered at Alison with energy, but I shoved her off and forced the veil open.

In the middle of Mom's bedroom.

She stood there, panic on her face, everyone with her. Charlotte barked in fury at the sight of Alison, lunged forward with her wolf in her eyes, twisting her face even as Mom's power crackled.

And Max stopped them. All of them. Sassafras. Trill and Lula. Shenka and Gram. The vampires I loved, even

Sebastian. And Quaid.

"Listen to her." I shoved Alison forward, harder than I intended, making her stagger. But she didn't seem hurt by my rudeness. Instead, she bowed her head to Mom and spoke, though her voice shook.

No one moved as Alison told them what she told me. Every time she said Gabriel's name, my heart healed a little more. A rising passion washed away my hate and guilt, leaving behind a powerful need, so strong it almost tore me apart.

I had to find my son.

And kill the person who stole him from me.

Lula looked troubled when Alison was done. Troubled and doubtful.

I would not allow doubt, not now.

"Syd," the healer said, "I checked Gabriel myself. There was no mistake."

Screw her. I focused on Mom. Who looked at me with a mix of her own concern and fear, as though I'd lost my mind, somehow fallen under Alison's spell.

"Just take me to him," Alison said. "I'll show all of you."

There. See? I stared at Mom, glared at her. Expectant.

But it was Sassafras who broke the dangerously growing silence.

"Oh, for the love of the elements," he snapped, hopping down from the bed and waddling his fat cat body to my feet. "What can it possibly hurt at this point?"

Mom exhaled.

"Miriam," Quaid's deep voice shook. "I'll take her if you won't."

I smiled at him. Beamed, wanted to go to him and hug him for speaking out when everyone else seemed ready to deny even the possibility I was right. Even Sass didn't trust me. I could see it in his face. Or that Alison knew what she was talking about.

I'd kiss Quaid later for his faith.

Mom finally nodded. Turned to Lula who also nodded.

That's right. Just nod your freaking heads. I'd show them.

Gabriel was alive.

All that mattered.

I knew what they were thinking as I spun and left the room, could feel the murmurs in their minds. Whisperings of "closure" and "This will be good for her."

They had no freaking idea.

Alison took my hand, hesitant and I smiled at her. Beamed.

Knew in my heart he was okay.

Dragged her along, Max beside me, Mom hurrying ahead to lead us out. To the elevator.

But not into the Yard, not yet. Down deeper, underground. I knew the bones of fallen North American witches were archived and kept safe at Harvard, could only guess European families had their own storage at Oxford, others around the world in safe caches like this one. But I'd never been down into the catacombs, had no real desire.

Until now.

It was dark, quiet, a little humid. Mom lit the way as the elevator opened, disgorging the near dozen of us into the stone hallway. Her witchlight cast blue over everything, long shadows chasing down the corridor. I drew a sharp breath at the feeling of echoes around me. It had been years since I'd been troubled by them. Aside from Alison, that was. But down here, surrounded by the history of our race on this continent, it was impossible not to sense them.

Gram joined Mom at the front, scooting around me as we passed a corner, not meeting my eyes, her fuzzy socks silent on the stone floor. It wasn't until we rounded the bend I saw someone waited for us up ahead, a flare of blue fire dying as Varity Rhodes joined the party.

Weird how it felt like a party to me. I wanted to dance, sing, shout, laugh. No, I didn't have proof. But I didn't need it. How had I allowed myself to believe he was dead? Now that I understood, I knew he was still alive. I'd fallen into the gray out of reaction to Liam's loss. But Gabriel…

No, I couldn't find him. Feel him. Yet.

Didn't matter.

My son was alive.

Had to be.

We neared Varity who stood outside a heavy steel door. The hall was lined with them, going on into the darkness, more bends, branches. I knew I'd be lost down here in a heartbeat without a map.

Good thing I wasn't alone.

Mom gestured at the door, blue magic flaring around the edges. It groaned and creaked, the hinges grinding as it swung outward. I wanted to be the first inside, but something hit my legs, made me look down.

Sassafras stared up at me, paws rising to my knee.

I bent without thinking, swept him into my arms. Buried my face in his fur.

"Thank you," I whispered.

"Syd," he said. "I hope she's right."

I nodded into his mane. "She is."

"And if she's not?"

No. Stop.

"She's right." I strode forward then, looking up, finding we were the last to enter, though Max and Charlotte remained at the door, flanking it like a pair of bodyguards.

I kissed my werefriend on the way by, caught her as she turned her head, cheeks wet.

Let her cry.

I was about to prove to her—to all of them—my son was fine.

Well, Alison was going to prove it.

Good enough for me.

I wasn't expecting the reception I received. Stopped dead in my tracks—no pun intended—as I started down the narrow room toward the back of the vault.

They lined the way, echoes of witches long passed. A stunning dark-haired woman held a tall, handsome man's hand. They waved at me as I walked by. The gorgeous woman who was next made Sassafras shudder and look away. I glanced down at him. Stopped and met her eyes.

"Who is she?" I peered behind her at the small plate over the stone box holding her bones. "Thaddea Ethpeal." I looked up again as she smiled and Sassafras sighed.

Turned his head to look at the witch who gave me my middle name.

"Hullo, Thad," he said.

She blew him a kiss, laughed silently.

The beautiful red-head beside her did the same.

"Auburdeen," Sass said, voice dull and sad.

So this was the infamous Burdie I'd heard about. I stopped in front of her, too. She pressed both hands over her heart, pointed at the tall man beside her.

"Gabriel," Sass whispered, making me jump.

I smiled at Burdie, at her husband. Nodded. Turned

and went to Mom, passing more witches who waved and beamed and gestured me onward.

Toward the back of the vault. Gram waited with Varity beside a tiny stone box, a little gold plate carved, fresh and bright.

I knew what it said. Gabriel Liam Hayle. His birthdate and the lie of his death.

Alison paused next to me, shivering, hugging herself, but she kept her eyes focused on the box.

"Coven Leader," Varity said softly, though her voice carried. "You're certain?"

"Just open it," I said.

She turned without another word and touched it.

The top gasped, as though a life escaped. But no echo rose. No hint of Gabriel.

More hope. Yes, yes.

Gram stepped back, Varity keeping her position as Alison slipped forward.

The old Enforcer leader reached into the box.

Lifted out the tiniest little human skull I'd ever seen.

So. Tragic. But not my son.

Not.

The moment she exposed the baby's bones, the whispering began. My name. Gabriel's. Over and over, as my ancestors spoke to me, promise in their echo voices. And a hand, steady and strong, settled on my shoulder, warm breath over my cheek, the welcome, familiar support of Quaid's magic holding me up, feeding my belief with the steady presence of his own faith my son was alive.

Varity cradled the skull, pouring power into it as I'd seen Gram do once before. She'd raised the echoes of those she knew could save Mom when she was on trial. A lifetime ago.

If anyone could find Gabriel's echo, it was Varity, I knew that.

All I could do was pray she failed.

chapter twenty

I could see the tension in Varity's face as she performed her necromancy.

And nothing happened.

A frown pulled at her lips, lining her already wrinkled face with surprise and frustration.

"He was young," Lula said softly. "Have you raised a baby before?"

Varity shook her head, deeply troubled as her power swirled around the skull. "I haven't," she said. "But he should have an echo."

"He was Sidhe," Mom said, bringing up the argument I feared the most. "They don't have echoes. It could be he simply doesn't have one to show."

But Alison was already shaking her head, her nerves gone, face determined as she held out her hands to Varity. For the skull. As though it were some special gift.

"Please," she said. "Let me."

Varity met my eyes, but Quaid spoke before I could.

"Just give it to her," he said, voice rough, gruff and graveled. With grief? I didn't know. But his power around me never wavered and I sent silent thanks to him for his continued support.

For his belief in me.

I nodded, sharp, impatient. Pushed forward, Quaid's hand leaving my shoulder, slipping in between Varity and the box, taking the skull myself. It was lifeless, empty. I felt what Alison meant, the black, darkness of nothing. Spun and handed it to her.

And now, hope lived without a shadow of a doubt. Certainty.

Alison was right. These were not Gabriel's bones.

I followed Alison as she went into the bones, searching. It was odd, but no more so than when I'd chase Charlotte into death. Sebastian. The principle was the same. Alison linked magic with me, shy but pleased when I latched onto her and let her lead me.

Here, she sent. *You feel the weakness?*

I did, like a shadow over light. But not a flaw in the bone itself. In the dark hiding the echo from us.

Alison scraped the surface, her power parting it at last.

A dull groan escaped me as a weak and wavering image rose from the skull to hover over it.

Gabriel's image.

But I didn't have time to despair, to fall into the fear Alison was wrong. Because the moment it appeared, the image began to alter, shift. Still wavering, it wasn't long before another face graced the echo, this one far different than my son's, and so fragile when I reached for it, the likeness shattered into a million pieces, dying with the cry of a child.

Silence, utter and complete, enveloped the vault as we all stared.

Until Alison spoke.

"These bones belong to a normal child," she said. "Used to carry Gabriel's impression. To pass immediate inspection." She gently set the skull back in the box. "But it was never meant to stand up to someone like me."

I grabbed her, hugged her, entire body vibrating as I pulled back, choking on air that wanted to fill my lungs, to keep me alive.

"Syd." Lula looked broken, desperate and hurt. "I'm so sorry."

I waved it off, just grateful this was true, all true.

"Why would someone want Gabriel's bones?" I shivered as Sassafras spoke up. I hadn't considered that. Hadn't I searched for him, reached out to him and came up empty?

Didn't mean anything. Except that whoever had him was hiding him from me.

Temporarily.

"No," Alison said to my demon cat. "This was the body on the pyre. I swear it to you." She replaced the lid. "It wasn't Gabriel you burned."

Rage woke again as my fractured mind made multiple connections. Tied up loose ends, bound together the whole into a hate-filled story I finally understood.

Because it makes perfect sense, doesn't it? My vampire hissed her fury.

I'm going to eat her heart, my demon snarled.

Right after we kill her a dozen times and bring her back so we can do it again. Shaylee shivered, the ground shaking under my feet.

They knew, as well as I did. Hadn't Max mentioned Fate? And the very fact he was here at all…

It had to be her.

The black emptiness on the bones. The diabolical scheme to convince me my son was gone. So she could take him.

Just like she took Liam.

"She wanted me to think my son was dead." I faced my family, the ones who loved me, shaking with so much rage I felt like I was about to bring the tomb down on top of us. "She wanted Gabriel and she took him."

Just. Like. Liam.

Mom's shock grew on her face as Lula looked at me in confusion.

Only Quaid seemed to register what I was already thinking, darkness taking his handsome face when Mom spoke up.

"Who, Syd?"

I guess she was the only one not in the know, wasn't she?

"The only person who would conceive of a plan like this," I snarled. "The same person who killed Liam now has our son."

Ameline.

Time to pay the piper, bitch.

chapter twenty one

I had already taken a step toward the door, reaching for the veil.

Power rippling in waves of near-uncontrolled vitriol.

Mom's hand on my arm, her magic touching mine, broke enough of the hold hate had on me to stop me from going after Ameline right then and there.

Barely.

"Syd." She pulled me back, face calm, though I knew it was a mask. That she was trying to keep me from tearing off.

Good luck with that.

"We need to form a plan," Mom said, slowly. Steadily. Like she was talking to my son and not to me, as if I were the child.

"No." I staggered, feeling my physical weakness, reaching for strength to hold me up. Found it as Enforcer power slipped in beside me and supported me as it did only moments before. I looked up at Quaid who lifted one hand, pressed it between my shoulder blades, feeding me energy and healing magic.

"You need to eat," he said, chocolate eyes soft around the edges though his lips pulled tight in concern. "Get some rest. You've been gone from us for so long." He swallowed, throat working. "Please, let us take care of you. Of this."

Mom's power joined his. "So we can bring Gabriel back safe and sound."

Gulp. Her words were a bucket of ice water splashed over me and I was suddenly very grateful Quaid's power held me up.

"She won't hurt him," I said. Panicked. Look up into kind brown eyes full of calm and focus. Dragged my gaze back to Mom. "She won't, Mom. She took him for a reason."

"But how did she take him?" Gram's grim anger simmered in her faded blue eyes, the magic she had left to her sizzling around her edges. "Miriam, how did she get in?"

It hadn't occurred to me to wonder. And part of me didn't care. But Gram was right, I supposed. Understanding how Ameline stole him might help me find her. Yes, I was full maji and she wasn't—at least to my knowledge. With the loss of my demon grandmother's spirit, Ameline was down a soul. Unless she'd found one here on this plane to steal.

The possibility was so real I staggered.

What the hell was I thinking, just letting her roam free?

You were thinking of Gabriel, my vampire sent. *Now, stop with the guilt and listen.*

Roger that.

Mom's hands shook as they ran through her hair. "I don't know," she said. "There shouldn't have been a way in. The wards are tied to my Council magic. I would have known if Ameline breached them." She paused. "Even if she used sorcery, the empty touch would have triggered the wards." Her hands fell to her sides before she wrung them at me. "Syd, sweetheart. I'm so sorry. But there's only one explanation for how this happened."

My brain agreed. "Inside job."

There, you see? My vampire sighed. *There will be more than enough guilt floating around us in the next little while. We don't need yours added to the mess, muddling our thoughts.*

I ignored her, hugged Mom immediately. "This was not your fault." Wasn't. My vampire was right. As I pulled free of my mother, I suddenly felt fresh, the most clear-headed I had in ages. Even before Gabriel was taken.

Since Liam died.

"That makes the most sense." I should have been running off looking for the culprit, not calmly discussing the matter. But my relief made me hyper rational. "Not only are your quarters warded," I said, "but I had Gabriel fully shielded with maji power. So it had to be Ameline with help from a witch with access to your quarters."

"Could she have found a way to break through the wards, Miriam?" Varity's arms crossed over her thin chest, scowl remaining. "Without help? If so, we need to find out how and plug the breach."

"I doubt it very much," Mom said. "I have no illusions as to the power of the shields. If Ameline assaulted them with all the magic she has at her disposal, she could easily break through. But."

But. Mom would have known. Felt it.

Which meant…

"We need a list of all of your staff," Quaid said, hand still firm on my back. "Leader Tremere will want to round them up and question them immediately."

"Is anyone missing?" Sassafras's voice hissed out, ending in a furious whine. "Surely the traitor must have known the possibility existed we would uncover the deception. Turned tail and ran."

Mom shook her head. "No one," she said. "All present and accounted for." She looked so distressed it could have been one of her people, but I couldn't bring myself to care.

Not when puzzle pieces began to shift and fall into place.

Yes.

Of course.

I knew exactly who Ameline's little helper was, didn't I? The fear he showed for me the night Gabriel went missing wasn't a reaction to my battle with the Brotherhood.

Maurice.

This time I didn't allow Mom to stop me. Ahbi roared her answering rage as I jerked open a hole in the veil and dove through, power building around me as I slammed into the rubber membrane, propelled by Ahbi's anger, and out the other side.

He barely had time to see me coming, but turned as I leaped from the veil. His round face formed a shining "O" of terror as I closed the distance between us, pinning him against Mom's desk as he scuttled back. Maurice's head whipped from side to side, seeking escape, no doubt.

No escape for him.

My maji power formed a solid bubble around the two of us. Ameline would likely ignore a plea for help from this little sack of wasted life. She'd used him and discarded him, I had no doubt.

Still.

Wasn't risking him contacting Ameline at this point and alerting her to the fact she was next on the dead meat list.

Maurice's beady eyes blinked behind his round lenses, jiggling belly bouncing as he fought for breath.

"Coven Leader!" He grasped at the collar of his elaborate white shirt, paisley vest straining over his paunch as he cowered before me. "How lovely to see you up and… and…"

My jaws ached. My cheeks. I was smiling, grinding my teeth at the same time. And from the amber glow cast around the edges of my vision, my demon was in full theatrical release.

"Where." I slammed against him with my power. Not too hard. Not yet. Needed to soften him up a little before I ruptured his nasty little mind. The large desk he pressed against squealed in protest, sliding an inch back from the pressure. "Is." I hit him again, controlled, precise, right in the breastbone, knocking the wind from him. Maybe I didn't want an answer to my question, not a verbal one. I'd tear it from his mind soon enough. "My." But he needed the chance to spill it, didn't he? Another hit, cold and calculated. My alter egos joined the fun, impacting him so hard the buttons in his vest popped and flew wide, bouncing around the inside of the power bubble with the sound of heavy hail. I drew a giant breath. Pressed my face almost to his, the moisture from his terrified sweat steaming his glasses. "Son?"

And crushed him with my magic.

Tried to. Someone held me back. Almost gently, but

with firm insistence, the same warm magic touched with chocolate. I spun with a snarl, animal hate rising all over again, to find Mom, Sass, Gram, Varity. Quaid holding me back. All of them. The doorway packed with those who couldn't squeeze into the room. Staring with huge eyes.

And Max.

"Stay out of this." I pushed against Quaid with my power, stepped out of his grip. And right into the drach. He I couldn't fight, knowing it wouldn't matter. Max was so much stronger than me, proved it when he let Liam die.

I should have stayed with Quaid.

"Please, listen." Max nodded his head toward the terrified secretary, now blubbering before me. "Use him to find your son first. Then kill him."

Logic. "But I want him dead now." I really, really did.

Max nodded. "I understand," he said. "But sometimes waiting makes the killing sweeter."

Maurice wailed, collapsed to the floor. The distinct scent of released urine rose from him as the front of his pleated pants darkened with moisture. I backed off in disgust, even as my demon howled and Shaylee shook the entire building in her fury.

"Actually," Alison said, tone clinical and head cocked to the side, her perky cheergirl expression oddly hilarious. "If you kill him now, I can just raise him for you. So, go for it."

I grinned at her, vicious and joyful. But the moment was past. Max was right. And as much as I wanted to squash Maurice, I would take what I needed from him and allow the law to send him to the stake.

Where he belonged.

Enforcers flooded the room, Pender's grim unhappiness etched deeply in his face as Mom gestured at Maurice.

"Take him to be questioned," she said even as I opened my mouth to argue.

Too late. Max's magic broke my hold for the brief moment Pender needed to form his own shield around the quivering secretary. The Enforcer leader then latched onto the mess of a witch and vanished in a flare of blue fire.

I lashed half-heartedly at Max as I spun on Mom, my power surging around me, the need to hurt someone so vivid I had to gasp a breath of air and remember who she was to me. To Gabriel.

"I will question him," I snarled.

"You will not," Mom said. "Until you've calmed down."

Shut. Up.

"Sydlynn, listen to me." Mom came to me, hands settling on my shoulders despite the sparks cascading from my agitated magic. "If you go into his mind and destroy information we need, finding Gabriel will be all the harder."

"I won't," I said, teeth clenched again. I really needed to invest in a bite-plate. Or a mouth guard. Something.

"Syd." Mom's mind touched mine. "Do you really believe that?"

REND TEAR DESTROY, my demon sent.

I'll rupture every organ in his body. Shaylee's enthusiasm for her pet project shifted the building slightly while everyone gasped and held on.

My vampire sighed, her agitation a burning white light in my mind. *I hate it*, she sent. *I hate him. But your mother…*

My mother was right.

Damn. It. All. To. Hell.

I jerked away from her. "Fine." Rubbed my upper arms, gooseflesh rising in a rippling wave as my egos crouched and fumed.

"I know we failed you once," Mom said, grief-laden face now slick with tears. "But Syd, I swear to you, we won't fail you again. Or my grandson."

Breathing became easier. Rage settled into a simmering pot of bubbling expectation.

I nodded. And Mom spun and left.

Maurice better look the hell out.

Quaid looked like he wanted to say something. Took him a long moment to muster his voice. "I'll kill him for you, if that's what you want."

I shook my head. "Please let me," I said.

Quaid bowed his head. Hesitated. "I'll do my best," he said. Looked up, face tight with anger and traveled on his own flare of blue.

Leaving me behind. He'd better save me some torture and guts.

Or he'd be in big freaking trouble.

Charlotte and Shenka, meanwhile, grasped onto me by either arm and dragged me out of the office. Through the sitting room. Into the bedroom I'd only just recently vacated. And forced me into the bathroom.

"Coven Leader," my second said with an attempt at joviality, "you stink. Shower."

I didn't have time, couldn't she understand that?

She slammed the door in my face. Locked it.

Like that would keep me from leaving. But the moment I unlocked it, pushed it open, Charlotte slammed it again. And from the thudding sound on the other side, she was now firmly pressed against it.

Sigh.

With Charlotte standing stern duty outside the door, I finally did as I was told, though it took a constant, muttered string of the worst swearwords I could think of to keep me moving. When I finally stepped into the stream of water, I waffled between giggling into my hands under the steaming stream of hot water at the thought of holding Gabriel again and intense passion wrapped around Ameline and her demise. I scrubbed and cried and laughed and swore at the top of my lungs until I felt clean again.

Inside and out.

The reflection in the mirror gave me pause. I'd looked like crap before. Like the time I'd come back from my mummy state after being drained of blood. But I'd never looked hopeless, truly helpless. The dark circles aged me ten years, a crease formed between my eyebrows reminding me of Mom. Skin so pale I could have rivaled a vampire.

But hey, I could see my ribs. Lost the last of my baby weight, go me.

Didn't recommend the weight loss program to anyone.

Ever.

When I emerged, ready to go, I discovered my two charges still weren't done. Charlotte firmly escorted me into the kitchen. Sat me down and hovered as Shenka and Gram dished up some food. And though I just wanted to go, had to leave, the smell made my stomach cramp so hard I bent over the plate and shoveled in a few bites just to shut it up.

I sent my power out, in an almost constant search for traces of Gabriel as I gulped a glass of milk, Lula's magic hard at work around me as she sat next to me with a worried look on her face.

"You don't want to lose everything you've just eaten," she said.

Antsy, feeling a little sick, truth be told, I jiggled my knees up and down as she soothed my upset stomach before nodding. Taking my hand. Crying suddenly.

"I'm sorry."

My vampire hit it on the money. I was going to be hearing that a lot over the next little while.

"Lula," I said. "Thank you for taking care of me."

She shook her head, but I didn't let her speak, deny it out loud.

"Just promise me," I said, "when we bring Gabriel home, you'll always be his healer."

She choked, face twisting in self-loathing. "You still want me around?"

Guilt sucked.

I hugged her, as I hugged Mom. Then stood. Grabbed Charlotte who shook and cried silently while we embraced. Kissed her cheek before hugging Shenka. My second whispered her love for me in my ear, her support, as always. Alison hovered nearby, had a hug of her own. So nice to have my Al back.

And Gram. Gram most of all. She stood watching me, fuzzy-socked feet tapping the tile as she looked up through her lashes, faded blue eyes teary, white hair floating around her as her thin shoulders hitched up around her ears.

Sister soul, I sent as I squeezed her so hard I heard her back pop. She did the same to me, wiry arms straightening a few vertebrae.

We'll find him, she sent, mental voice strong thanks to our physical connection. *And he'll be fine.*

But Ameline won't be, will she? I leaned back, smiled. A happy smile.

Gram grinned, pinched my arm. *Nope nope*, she sent.

We laughed together. Because killing Ameline was going to be so. Much. Freaking. Fun.

I turned to the amazing women watching me and shared my smile with them, too.

"Thank you," I said. "For loving me. For loving Gabriel. But it's time to put our grief and guilt aside and focus on the real villain."

Shenka nodded, murmured, "Here, here."

"Now," I said, "if you ladies will excuse me, I have a date for an interrogation and I don't want to be late."

Clean, fed, head on mostly straight.

Time to talk to Maurice again.

Personally.

chapter twenty two

I was going to go alone. But there was no way my posse would allow me to leave them behind.

Lula was called away before Gram and her bully pack made themselves very clear.

"You're taking us," she said, linking arms with Shenka even as Charlotte crossed her arms over her chest, scowling at me. Sassafras appeared through the kitchen door, leaping up on the table, tail thrashing in agreement.

Made me happy, despite my one-woman crusade addiction. Filled me with a kind of brilliant joy, as though I'd swallowed the sun. Had to take a second to keep the lump rising in my throat from emerging completely.

Nodded.

Reached for the veil.

We formed a magical daisy chain, my friends and family following behind me as I stepped through and into

Ahbi's welcoming embrace. Sassafras leaped at the last minute, landing in my outstretched arms, first through with me as my demon grandmother released us and allowed me to take over.

My maji power sought Maurice—and my son all over again. Though I knew I wouldn't find him, I looked anyway even as the beacon of Mom's secretary drew me to the only place I knew he'd end up.

Almost wished I could leave the others behind and check the full veil for traces of Gabriel anyway. But I'd have his location soon enough.

Sure would.

The power of the stronghold welcomed us as we exited the veil into the main mirror room. A handful of nervous Enforcers bowed to me as I strode past and headed to the elevator, following the pull of Mom, Maurice, Pender. Up, then. Into the tower, the heart of the stronghold.

Light One, his grinding voice spoke in my head, the shivery depth of the earth itself moving. *I am pleased you've returned.*

I wish the circumstances were better, I sent.

As do I. His sorrow was the sadness of the ages. *I am sorry for your progeny's theft. If I can assist you in any way, please ask.*

Sure, he was a big castle and everything, but me and stronghold, we were tight.

We didn't rise the entire way, the elevator only taking us up two floors. As I stepped out into a mirror of the circular stone hall I was more familiar with, I immediately noticed differences. There were doors in the middle, not the outside. How much of the tower was solid rock? I approached the central core, rising up to the ceiling, touched the stone.

You are always welcome here, stronghold sent.

Thank you. I patted the cool wall, feeling the rough texture under my fingers before turning and heading around the corridor.

Only took a second. Spotted two Enforcers standing guard outside a door. Almost stopped my forward motion when the one on the right looked up. Met my eyes.

Of all the Enforcers Pender could have assigned. What was he thinking?

Payten's face fell, her head dropping as I hardened myself against seeing her. Quaid's little girlfriend. Was it fair to hate her? Of course not. He'd made his choice, hadn't he? But there she was, and I was already full of fury.

So when she looked up again, met my eyes, opened her mouth, my heart chilled to ice.

"I'm so sorry for your loss, Coven Leader," Payten said.

"Go fuck yourself," I threw back at her with all the venom I could muster.

And pushed past her through the door.

Okay, I didn't normally swear at people, mostly in private or in my head, like I had in the shower.

But somehow, just then, that particular word seemed uber appropriate.

Pender emerged from a smaller door, into the round chamber I now found myself as I entered. He came to me, shoulders sagged forward, anger on his face.

"We've let you down so many times," he said. "Forgive us. Forgive me." His hands clenched at his sides, blue sparks falling to the floor, smoking on the hem of his black robe. "I should have realized it wasn't your son. But we were all so heartsick, and you were in such peril." Pender bowed his head to me. "And it was the best illusion I've ever seen."

My anger toward Payten cooled my jets enough I didn't blow at him, but my ability to feel sorry for other people died with her little attempt to make it all better.

I hoped she and Quaid were happy together.

Not.

I stared up into Pender's aged and weary face. "Where is my son?"

He shook his head, stepped aside, and gestured toward the door. "We have been unable to make him talk." Regret and resignation.

We'd just see about that.

The door opened for me, the stronghold's power

ghosting across it. I strode inside the tiny square room, windowless and lit only with a hovering witchlight. To find my mother losing her crap all over the place.

Her power crackled, her face beet red, hair a mass of electrified crazy as she shuddered in front of the small stool where Maurice sat, sobbing.

"YOU WILL TELL ME WHERE HE IS!" Her voice made my bones tremble.

He shook his head. Glanced at me. Paled, his eyes rolling back until only the whites showed.

Teetered from the stool and collapsed, passed out, on the cold stone floor.

Mom spun on me, magic in a frenzied fit. I reached out for her, soothed her, but not with kindness and love, not at all. With the need to take over, to tear him to pieces.

And my mother snarled a smile and backed off.

"He's all yours," she said as Lula appeared, revived Maurice from his faint.

He must have heard her last words because I could feel Lula's magic doing its best to keep him from passing out again.

Mom backed off, my friends and family lining the wall behind me as I slammed the door shut. Sealed it with iridescent fire. And smiled at Maurice.

He squealed like an unhappy piglet, scrambling back away from Lula, hitting the wall hard with his shoulders and the back of his head. The dull echo of his skull bouncing from stone made me smile wider.

I didn't move. Didn't have to. Just watched him as he devolved into utter terror.

Maybe Mom was right. Killing him outright would have been a waste.

This was way better.

"I can't I can't I can't I can't." What I first thought was a panting whine finally evolved into words. "I can't!"

"Can't what, Maurice?" I stepped forward, kicking the stool out of my way. Stood over him. "Because you know I'm going to make you."

He shook his head in a whipping motion, glasses already askew flying free to tinkle on rock.

"She'll kill me." He sobbed into his chubby hands, feet scrabbling on the ground, trying to push himself further from me.

Ameline. Had to be.

I crouched, nodding. "She's not the one you need to worry about."

His whining stilled, whole body frozen. "You have mercy," he whispered. "You won't really kill me. I've seen it, watched you let those who oppose you get away with it." His jowls bounced as he bobbed a crazy nod. "I've seen you."

He thought me weak, did he? Incapable of revenge.

Maybe once. Before my husband died. Before my son

was taken from me.

Oh, how things had changed.

He must have seen the truth in my eyes. I'd often joked about killing people, my demon eating their hearts, making fun party decor from their entrails. But I'd seen death, been shocked and horrified by it. Never really thought I could be capable of killing.

I was capable. And absolutely willing.

And he knew it.

Even as my power wrapped around his frantically beating heart and squeezed.

Maurice screamed, body convulsing, falling into panting sobs as I released the pressure.

"You don't know anything about me," I said. "Now, tell me where that bitch has my son or you'll find out just what it is I'm prepared to do to save Gabriel."

Maurice's brain seemed to flare, spark. Settle. I felt the broken pieces of him rupture and float off, but held them together as his mind snapped.

I didn't need him to be coherent. Or all there, not really.

I'd dig around in his head until I had what I wanted. No matter how long it took.

Lula bent beside me, touched his wrist, her healing magic reaching out to him. But she'd shed her own kindness, no matter her natural inclinations to helping others. She met my eyes, sweat standing out on her upper lip.

"I'll keep him together as long as I can," she said. "Ask quickly."

Bless her.

"Where is Ameline?" Because she would be where Gabriel was.

Maurice's lips lifted into an angelic smile. "Don't know," he said in a sing-song voice.

I knew he was telling the truth, didn't need Lula to nod her affirmation.

Damn it.

"Who is she working with?" Mom came to stand behind me, hand on my shoulder.

"The dark," he said. "Rainbows and darkness, all together now."

And my stomach fell to my feet.

"I need to talk to Trill." The dark maji. My friend mentioned them in the past and I'd let it go, allowed her to deal with them. But Ameline was dark maji, followed Dark Fate. And I now understood leaving things to others had been a huge mistake.

Time to rectify the situation.

Mom nodded at my order, spun and left as I unsealed the door and allowed her to go.

Maurice's smile remained, but tears gushed down his cheeks. Gram took Mom's place, sitting cross-legged beside me.

"They have names and faces and places," Gram said.

I glanced sharply at her, at the crazy tone in her voice I thought she'd shed ages ago.

She met my eyes a moment.

I've been down this road, she sent. *Trust me.*

I did. And held my tongue.

Maurice bobbed a nod. "So many faces," he said, picking at the empty button hole on his vest. "So many places. Close and far, like a star."

Gram's thin, remaining power wove around him. "Star," she said.

"All the time I serve them." Maurice leaned forward, took her hand, whispering in a voice loud enough we all heard. "All the time I watch the witches and tell the dark ones what I see."

A traitor all along. He'd better hope he didn't regain his sanity.

I couldn't imagine being fully aware was a benefit when one burned at the stake.

Then again, I hoped with a fever heat Lula could revive his mind after all.

So he would know when they set him on fire.

"Find the rose." He tugged on Gram. "At the Star. All will be revealed."

What the hell did that mean?

I was done with Lula's control, with Gram's coaxing. I reached past them both and into his shattered mind.

THE ROSE, I sent.

He showed me, reflexive and instantaneous.

And I gasped at the face he showed me.

THE STAR. But this time there was nothing. Only darkness.

At least I had one clue to chase down.

I turned with my heart pounding in desperate hope and met Alison's eyes.

"Well," I said with a snarl in my voice. "Looks like your old maid, Rosetta, has a lot to answer for."

chapcer cwency chree

No more waiting. Not when I had a target to track down. And I knew the perfect person to help me do it. A small jolt of worry followed as I thought of Galleytrot. Realized I hadn't seen him since my wakening.

Sought him out as I left Maurice to his broken mind. And I wasn't alone in my departure as the group crowding the room thundered after me, out into the open room then past the second door and into the hallway.

Touched the veil with my maji power, through the kindness of the stronghold. Chased back home, to my plane. Floated above it, power seeking Galleytrot.

Touched down in Wilding Springs as his trail led to town hall. Through the wards underground.

Felt the black hound at last, in the first place I should have looked, his power, weak and distant, in the Sidhe cavern.

Of course.

Did another search. For Ameline. Came up empty.

Gabriel. Same.

And Rosetta… damn it.

Galleytrot it was.

I released my search, shaking myself a little as I returned to my body. Reached for the veil with a huge thanks to the stronghold for allowing me to use his heart as a hub.

Froze at the sight of two Enforcers, heads bent together. One in tears, the other rigid and full of anger.

Chocolate eyes lifted, met mine.

Poor thing can't handle her job, I sent at Quaid. Not to him. He'd been with me in the catacombs, but the connection I felt to him was shattered by her presence, my gratitude poisoned as he comforted her. Now I knew where he went. Not to question Maurice, but to hold his little girlfriend. *Might want to tuck her in a read her a bed time story before she hurts herself.*

Quaid didn't answer, still simmering with fury.

But.

Not at me.

Interesting.

What had she done to piss him off that much?

Not my problem, not when Gabriel waited for me. I could hear his giggle, feel the weight and warmth of him in my arms even as I tore open the veil.

Spun and faced my posse as I realized a plan of some kind might actually be a good idea.

"I'm going to get Galleytrot," I said. "We need to find Rosetta." Alison's old housekeeper, a witch, traitor to her own race, working for the Brotherhood. Twisted and fanatical about destroying those with magic though she was one herself. He'd sniffed her out once before, tracked her when nothing else could lead me to her. And I knew he would do so again, in a heartbeat.

To save Gabriel.

Why wasn't Galleytrot here?

Didn't matter. Not now. "I'll be right back. Wait for me here."

And stepped through the veil.

One breath.

Out again. My feet touched down on more stone, this full of Sidhe power as I strode, heart pounding, into the Gate room.

A large, silent mass of black fur lay before the portal, ribs barely rising. I felt how weak he'd become, his own sorrow devouring him, as mine tried to devour me. But I had help, didn't I? And left him to deal with this on his own.

Galleytrot. The others thought they failed me. But I failed him.

I sank to my knees next to the big hound, touched his shoulder. His fur had matted in places, ribs sticking out of his coat, tongue trailing across the rough floor as his eyes blinked once, not a glimmer of fire inside.

How long? It was the first time I wondered at the amount of time passed, though I registered my own weight loss, knew a considerable amount had passed. Now, seeing him, how emaciated he'd become, magic the only thing sustaining him, did I realize I'd lost a larger chunk of my life than I thought.

Three weeks, my vampire said, voice soft.

Three—

Wow.

I shook off the knowledge. Didn't matter now. All that mattered was my son, now almost three months old.

In Ameline's clutches.

For three. Freaking. Weeks.

New urgency spurred me to act as I sent Galleytrot power, Shaylee embracing him, filling out his wasted form, polishing his black fur from the dullness of despair to health and vitality. But he didn't move, even when his body stretched and expanded into his former glory.

"I'm sorry," I whispered in his ear. "I shouldn't have allowed you to go through this alone."

He groaned. Fell still.

"Galleytrot," I pressed my cheek to his. "I need you now. And so does Gabriel."

No response.

Until I showed him. Let him feel and see and

experience what I did. The tomb. The bones.

His head shot up, whole body tense and shaking. Blazing red fire lit the dog's eyes as his met mine, tail thumping once in pathetic hope, tongue sweeping over his snout.

"Syd," he whispered.

"If you ever want to see Gabriel again," I said, "you'd better get your ass up and hustle."

Galleytrot surged to his feet, shaking his huge body, green Sidhe fire flaming around him as the coals of red in his eyes blazed in answer.

His howl rocked the chamber, shook the foundations of the Gate, and Shaylee screamed along with him.

When his head fell, his jaw gaping as he panted, I did my best not to crumble. Hard to do when he approached, nudged my hand with his big nose, leaned into me with a soft groan.

"You'll have to fight me for her," he said.

"How about we kill her together?" Sounded like a plan.

Galleytrot chuffed his agreement as I tore open the veil and, on impulse, carried him home with me.

The kitchen felt cold despite the summer sun and my imperviousness to temperature. Because it was empty. I'd grown so used to the sound of laughter, lots of voices, the feeling of layered powers and the excitement of my growing family.

The giggling, bright green joy of my son.

I'd have it back. Shivered and hugged myself as I felt around the house. And encountered the empty place I'd been hoping to find.

Demetrius bounded up the basement stairs, blue eyes huge and full of hope.

"He's alive," he said.

He had to say it, with all that happiness and excitement in his voice? I crumpled for the first time, unable to stop myself, Galleytrot supporting me as Demetrius rushed forward, held me up and guided me to a chair as my knees buckled and the world swayed around me in a film of moisture.

"He's alive," I whispered. Smiled through my tears. Bounced in my chair.

Demetrius laughed. "Syd," he said. And that was all.

It was all he had to say.

I found my voice again, told him about Rosetta. Demetrius was nodding immediately, anxiety and anger mixing together as his sorcery butted up against mine.

"They were owned by the Brotherhood," he said. "The Chosen. But I can see how easily they could be shifted to a new belief system since theirs fell apart." He sat back, fingers tapping on the table. "And the dark maji—especially led by Ameline—would make excellent candidates." He'd know. He was one of them, set up as their leader by Liander Belaisle after the Brotherhood leader broke him and drove him mad. "I've been keeping an eye on them, peripherally. The Chosen are more a danger to themselves, now, or so I thought." He shook his head. Opened his mouth. And I know he was going to say it.

I'm sorry.

I shut him down. "Doesn't matter now," I said. "Galleytrot can find Rosetta."

The big dog nodded. "I recall her scent perfectly," he said.

I scratched his head, turning back to Demetrius. "But I was hoping you might take the fight out of her for me. If Rosetta sees you, will she crumble?" Not that I wasn't interested in a fight, hell yeah. But an all-out battle would put Gabriel at risk and that, I wasn't willing to contemplate.

Demetrius stood, took my hand, helped me to my feet. My knees were working again, at least, nice and solid.

"I will speak to her," he said, voice shaking. "And she will tell me what she knows."

chapter twenty four

They were waiting for me at the stronghold, my faithful ones. Gram took Demetrius's hand as he joined the others, facing me. I dug my fingers into Galleytrot's fur, the big dog sinking to his haunches beside me while I addressed them.

"I know I won't be able to convince any of you to stay behind," I said. Silence and grim expressions. Answered that question. My heart swelled with love and eagerness as I went on. "Okay then. Listen up. Charlotte, you're with Galleytrot." She'd been with me the night we tracked Rosetta and her Chosen and with her keen nose tied to his, I knew we'd find our target that much faster. "Sass, you stay with me." Amber fire flared in his eyes. "Demetrius, if you could handle any stray sorcery and intimidate your old followers, that would rock."

He gave me a thumbs up, so odd to see him make

such a normal gesture.

"Shenka, you and Gram clean up the mess I make, *capiche*?"

Because once I found the Chosen and the dark maji, I was going to make a mess.

Oh boy, was I.

Mom hurried toward us down the corridor, Trill trailing with her head down. I almost forgot my request for my mother to find the Zornov maji and grabbed Trill's arm, shook her a little. Caught the tiny rebellion in her eyes as she met mine.

Grinned at her.

I'm sorry, I sent. *Thank you.*

She stilled, shivered inside with sorrow, nodded.

"The dark maji," I said.

Trill cracked her knuckles. "Don't worry," she said. "I don't even need the boys anymore."

Her brothers. Where were her brothers? Didn't matter.

"Stay close," I said. "And shield. If they fight back, there will be a lot of flying debris."

"And people," Shenka said. Like flying people were a given.

Loved. Her. So. Much.

Alison hovered on the edge of the group, hugging herself, looking lost. I held my hand out to her and she came to my side, took my fingers in hers.

"Rosetta is yours," I said. "At least, until I need her."

Alison bobbed a nod. "I won't let you down," she said.

Only then did I realize Max disappeared. I'd lost track of him when I'd taken a shower. He hadn't come with us to the stronghold.

His part was done, I could only guess. And actually sent thanks to him for his help, no matter what happened between us before.

Emotion almost overwhelmed me as I spun and faced the tear in the veil, felt Ahbi's need to hug me.

"Let's go get my son," I said.

Galleytrot chuffed deeply as the stronghold reached for me.

I wish you only the best of luck, Light One, he sent.

Thank you. And tore the veil. Stepped through.

To Harvard. Mom's room.

The empty cradle.

It was the first time I saw it since—

Breathe, Syd. Gabriel is alive.

Galleytrot snuffled it. Shook his big head with a sneeze. "I have the traitor's scent," he said.

Maurice. "Ameline?"

"She has no scent," Charlotte growled. "Remember? But I don't think she was here." She snuffled as Galleytrot followed her to the back of the room. Pressed against the wall with one hand.

And the wall parted.

Stupid secret passages pissed me off.

"The horrible little man who works for your mother went through here." Thunder rolled in Galleytrot's voice as he refused to say Maurice's name.

With Gabriel?

I followed, we all did, down the narrow passage, to a service elevator off the kitchen.

Outside into the trees behind Massachusetts Hall.

Around the building and into the Yard. Harvard was quiet, new students preparing for their first day just beginning to arrive. We stopped in the grassy center of the university while Galleytrot scented the air and Charlotte growled.

"Close," the dog said. My werefriend nodded. Pointed.

Off campus. Even as Maurice's babbling suddenly made total sense.

I kept my peace as we walked, an odd bunch, across Massachusetts Avenue and to Holyoke. Stood in the dark of a broken street lamp and stared at the narrow steps leading to a dark door and the climbing rise of a brick building.

One I knew very well. Had been forced to invade during my first year at Harvard.

Sassafras snarled as he slunk to my side, staring at the quiet building on the other side of the street. We'd stood here before, he and I. With Sunny and Uncle Frank. He swatted the air in the general direction. "Why am I not surprised?"

Yeah, me either. "The Star Club." Maurice wasn't babbling. Find the rose, he said. And the star. "Close and already tainted," I said. By Ameline, the very bitch, the basement bleeding that night so long ago. The night she turned my old friend Simon, when she did her best to kill me with her creation power. Killed the young witch, Darin Mavore, used his blood to feed her power. So long ago, and yet, the memory was sharp edged and painful. I lost Rupe that night, too. And Alison had begun her long journey into evil only the battle at the stronghold freed her from.

Idiot.

Why didn't I think to check?

No beatings, my vampire sent.

Right.

Focus on Gabriel.

I knew it wouldn't do to draw attention to us out in the open, where normals could watch. Still, it was the hardest thing I'd done since forcing myself to stay not to blast the front door off from right here and shake the place to see what kind of creepy crawlers fell out.

Temper, temper.

Instead, I strode across the street, my legs stretching out into a giant power walk, ignoring the tooting of a driver's horn as I stepped out in front of him, eyes, magic and soul locked solely and 100% on the door.

Only the door. What came after… I'd think about it when Gabriel was safe.

By the time I took the flight of six steps to the top, I was running, leaping up them two at a time, a small ball of focused power hovering in front of me. The last time I was here, I did blow the door off. But this time I had more finesse.

The lock slagged under the pressure of my power, swung inward as if possessed as my vampire blasted it with spirit magic. The moment I crossed the threshold into the dark hall I felt him.

Felt.

My.

Son.

And almost lost it.

Charlotte and Galleytrot pushed past me, sniffing and searching, my werefriend's low growl a warning. I wasn't listening, too tied into the deliciously sweet feeling of my baby. He was here.

Was, being the operative word.

I realized his touch, though present, was too faint for him to still be in residence about a heartbeat before the door at the end of the hall—the one leading to the basement—burst open and a flood of people rushed through.

And Rosetta led them. Her face had aged, her small, round body now hunched and twisted, but her power blazed strong. Fed by the blood magic around her.

Not fresh, at least. But these dark maji—for it had to be them—used creation power recently. Did they somehow know we were coming? Didn't matter.

I'd crush them all even if they spilled blood recently.

I took one second to reinforce the shields around my friends before opening up to my maji power and blasting them with the full force of my magic.

They flew back as a unit, lifting from the ground, Rosetta's mouth open in a black hole of shock as an iridescent fireball took her full in the chest. The house protested, groaning when my power hit the wall, crushing the dark maji, pinning Rosetta to their writhing mass.

I stormed down the hall, hand in a claw before me, stopping inches from her face with my fingertips pressed into her chest.

"I want my son," I snarled. "You have exactly five seconds of life left. Use them wisely." I repeated my performance with her as I'd done with Maurice, my power engulfing her heart, squeezing. She coughed for air until I let her go. "Tell me where she took Gabriel."

He was here. Must have been brought here that first night. Maurice delivered him to Rosetta, to the dark maji. And Ameline…

She had to have taken him from there. But where?

"WHERE." I crushed her further, hearing bones crack and snap beneath her, the cries and screams of the others. Pushed harder, wet popping sounds rupturing who knew what.

Still. Didn't. Care.

Rosetta shook her head, dark eyes huge.

Gasped out, "Never."

Dead. She was dead.

Until a hand settled on my shoulder. Drew me back. And Demetrius smiled at me.

At Rosetta.

She quivered in my grasp, tears falling from her eyes as she fought to reach for him. "Master," she croaked with the limited air I allowed her.

"Rosetta," he said, cherub face and huge blue eyes just as I remembered. Making me shiver when I thought of who he used to be. Who the Brotherhood made him. "We need the boy. She's played you false. You must tell me." He touched her cheek. "Where is he?"

She groaned, sagged but didn't respond.

"Mistress," she finally said.

And gasped a scream as her gaze settled on Alison.

Who smiled back at her, waved and tossed her blonde ponytail. Drifted close, her skin fading from solid to ghostly as she passed her fingers through Rosetta's cheek.

The horror on the woman's face should have been filmed for a Hollywood blockbuster. Already a superstitious woman, I could only imagine what she was thinking, seeing Alison's ghost up close and personal. I think she would have broken as Maurice did, right then and there, if Alison hadn't reformed to solid and snapped her fingers under Rosetta's nose.

"The baby," she said in a voice filled with arrogance. "Now."

Rosetta blubbered as I eased up a little, let her breathe. "We need him," she wailed.

Need.

Wait.

What?

"Damn it." I kicked at a stray shoe one of the maji lost in the blast, dropping all of them, into a weeping, suffering heap. A few tried to crawl away, only to be rounded up by Trill as Shenka guarded the door. "She doesn't do anything without a reason."

Sassafras pawed my leg. "Syd, I assumed she took him to hurt you."

Okay, I wasn't the only one. "So did I." Demetrius bent over Rosetta who lay, one hand over her face, gasping and wailing. "But Ameline always has a plan." I kicked the weeping woman firmly in the leg, made her jump. She looked up a moment before trying to cover her eyes again. "What does she want with Gabriel?"

Fear, deep and vibrating, woke inside me all over again. If she took him to use him for something... did that mean she was going to kill him after all?

Of course my mind went there. Where else would it go?

Doom and disaster were my two best buds, yup yup.

Rosetta's evil returned in a slow wave over her face, her hate for me as crisp and sharp as it had always been. "We will rule all through his gift," she said. "The Gateway will lead us to our salvation."

What the hell did that mean?

Rosetta's madness crackled around her as she cackled a laugh.

"It is foretold," she said, jabbing at me with one finger. "It is his fate."

Oh. *Hell.* No.

I jerked open the veil without thought, and dove through, leaving the others to clean up.

Because this was something I had to do myself.

Fate was about to get her damned ass kicked.

chapter twenty five

I landed in Center with my full rage on, not even blowing through on the edge of the city, but tearing a giant gap in the veil right smack-dab in Fate's lap.

Tried to. Instead landing in the middle of the huge building with giant Zeon towering over me.

Right. The little growing trick that seemed to keep the maji so amused. I forced myself into massive size, quickly rising to face him. His normal Santa Claus expression was missing, face pinched and guarded as I slammed him with my power.

"Out of the way," I said. "I'm not here to see you."

Iepa appeared over his shoulder, fear on her face. Let her be afraid.

"You will go no further," Zeon said, power pushing back against me.

Only then did I realize Iepa wasn't kidding. He was

strong, don't get me wrong. But millennia of hiding out here must have weakened him. Either that or the combination of the magicks I carried packed a powerful punch, because, to his very obvious shock, he couldn't even budge me.

This must have been what Max felt when I attacked him and didn't get anywhere. From the expression crossing Zeon's face, he liked it about as much as I had.

Sucked to be him.

Careful, Iepa sent.

Screw that.

"For the last time," I said, forming a solid wall of power between Zeon and before adding pressure as I pushed against him, "get out of my way. Before I hurt you."

He fought. Might as well have blown on a forest fire.

When he backed down, I had a moment of worry. Not about the maji, though Iepa seemed to think I'd gone too far, her hands over her mouth in shock and fear. But by my own ability.

Forget it.

Gabriel first. Worry about the state of my growing magic later.

I hadn't for a moment wondered where Max ran off to after I'd fled the tomb in search of Gabriel. Had the unasked question answered as I strode past Zeon's scowling face and approached Fate's door. Didn't get a chance to pound on it, as much as that would have given me great satisfaction.

Not when the drach calmly opened it for me and gestured for me to enter.

I glared up at him, smacked him on the arm. "You could have cleared the path," I said.

"My mistake," he said. "You're early."

Grunt. So Fate didn't know everything. Should that have made me feel better? Or worse?

Fate waited by her stupid damned pool with her stupid damned hair floating in the stupid damned water. I stomped my way to her side, power in a tight tornado around me. It was the first time I'd seen her since Liam died. Since I swore I'd give her this very ass kicking.

She rose from her place and came to me, hugging me with so much empathy all the rage ran out of me in a rush that hurt down to the core of my soul. I found myself clutching her, fighting more tears, tears I refused to shed until my baby was home safe with me.

When I pulled away, I managed to muster a fraction of my temper. "You let him die," I whispered through a choke hold of grief. "And then you let Ameline steal my son. And make me think he was dead." That was the worst part. The lies and deception. "I thought we were on the same side."

"We are," she said. "Oh, Sydlynn. I know you will never forgive me. But Fate isn't allowed to pick favorites.

I must follow the paths laid out before me. As much as I would have liked to allow you to save Liam, he was not meant to be." She paused. Nodded as if making a decision. "But Gabriel is necessary. And so Liam was until your impregnation."

Okay, felt worse. "So you're telling me he was a sperm donor." I would never think about him that way.

She sighed. "In a way," she said. "Your destiny leads you to another heart, one not his. And had he lived, your path would not have taken you where you needed to go." She wrung her hands, lower lip trembling. "I know you hate me, and I understand. This burden I bear, it grows heavier by the year. But I must fulfill my tasks, just as you must yours."

"You're Fate," I said, not at all sorry for the spite that came out. "You can do whatever you want."

She smiled, soft and sad. "I am the voice of the Light Fate," she said. "All answers go back to the Creator. I am merely a vessel."

"Well, he's a jerk," I said.

"I'm sure she'll be happy to know you disapprove," Fate said with a soft laugh.

Creator was female. Of course she was.

Explained all the damned drama.

"Had Max allowed you to go after Ameline upon the death of Liam," Fate said, hand on my arm, "Gabriel would have died in your womb and you never would have known he existed."

Shudder. "Got it," I said. Not a great trade, not even a little. But I understood. "I suppose you're going to tell me I'm not allowed to go after my son."

Over my dead body.

Fate's brow creased as her young face frowned. "Not at all," she said. "The maji have tried to keep the truth from you, but I am not allowed to pursue you with it. I am forced to wait for you to come to me before I can help."

Assholes. "I'm here now," I said. "Tell me where my son is and we're all good."

Fate's frown turned to a sad expression. "That path is unclear," she said. Held up one hand as I drew a breath to yell at her. "To me."

Right.

Ding, ding, Syd. Stop running around with your temper in control and *think*.

The Dark Fate was Ameline's guide, wasn't he? My Fate's brother.

I was on the wrong plane for the answers I needed.

"Gabriel is the Gateway," Fate said. "He must be protected, nurtured. No matter the outcome of this path, he will survive and thrive. So do not fear for the state of his physical being."

A huge shudder of relief passed through me. She might have been on my crap list for a long time, but Fate had never lied to me.

"So, the Gateway." Why was I not surprised my son was special? "Hey, hang on. He'll be fine physically?"

Fate nodded, her sadness remaining. "If he is allowed to continue in Ameline's care, his heart, once pure, will begin to darken. And when it does, he will no longer be able to become the man he must be. Or fulfill his destiny. The Fate I see for him."

"Which is?" She had to give me something.

"As I said," she went for vague, of course she did, "the path is muddled by Ameline's involvement. But great things are coming for him. And, as the Gateway, he will be pivotal in maintaining the safety of all through the troubled times to come." Paused. "Or be the downfall of us all."

Lovely. She'd already warned me my tasks weren't over. But knowing my son would be wrapped up in them wasn't making me feel any better.

"Tell me what you mean by Gateway." Surely that wasn't a topic she could avoid? Direct question and all.

"Ameline left the battle at the stronghold and went directly to her own Fate." Another feint. This was getting irritating. "That was how she knew to kill Liam, to take Cian from him. And that Gabriel was important, vital."

No brow beating. I didn't need my vampire to remind me this time.

Though I should have realized it.

"Ameline didn't fulfill her fate." The girl standing before me told me Ameline was part of the battle with Liander Belaisle as a power source. She had another task? "But you said killing Liam was her thing." Had told me so when I wanted to go after Ameline, to destroy her for hurting Liam. Only to be held back, to watch him die because his death was Ameline's task to fulfill.

"And taking Gabriel," Fate said. "I'm sorry. I wasn't permitted to share the rest."

"So his kidnapping was necessary." Way to try to cut your guilt, Syd.

"It was," Fate said.

"Well, that's nice," I said. "But I want him back now, thanks."

Fate nodded. "I have no doubt you will succeed, Sydlynn Hayle." She gestured past me. "Take Max with you. You'll need him where you're going."

I immediately balked, spinning on him, no matter he'd helped me uncover the truth. That was well and good. But my son's life was at risk.

Like Liam's had been.

"No way," I said. "Not this time."

But Max hung his head, scales rippling over his bald head, his gray cheeks. When his diamond eyes met mine, they sparkled with silvery moisture. "If I could have changed my own fate," he said, "I would. I have never been so ashamed. But my task was as impossible to avoid as yours."

I wanted to keep hating him.

Kicked myself a couple of times.

"Fine," I said. "But one sniff of betrayal from you," I jabbed a finger in his direction, spun to face Fate, "or you," poked at her too, "and I'm taking this up with Creator."

Fate hugged me, lips cool on my cheek.

"I wouldn't have it any other way," she said. "Now," she pushed me back, "it's time you finished this particular part of your journey. Say hello to my brother for me."

chapter twenty six

I didn't go right to Core. There was something I had to do first.

Max didn't say a word as I returned to the house, expecting to sneak in and do what I had to do then out again before the crap hit the fan.

Before the family could react to me releasing the coven's magic.

I'd already made my decision to leave the leadership even as I turned from Fate and marched back the way I came. Zeon continued to scowl at me, Iepa hanging back. I offered the maji leader a flash of my middle finger—while Max chuckled—before tearing open the veil and returning home.

Good thing Max was on the ball. I'd have forgotten to shrink myself and probably torn the roof from the house. Yes, our neighbors didn't notice much when it came to magic, thanks to centuries of Sidhe influence, but I doubted they'd miss it if the top of the two-story was suddenly in the back yard.

To my surprise, I landed in the kitchen in the middle of an anxious group of people, one cat and a very agitated black dog. The room was so packed I was grateful Max held the reins when he set us down in the far corner, out of the way of the arguing bunch.

They fell silent the moment we appeared, staring, shocked, before they all started shouting at me at once.

I stood there and waited for them to calm down, crossing my arms over my chest, tapping my toes on the floor until the din died down and Mom's voice won.

"Where the hell?" She stormed to my side, grasped me in a bear hug. Looked up at Max.

"I had to talk to Fate," I said. "Max tagged along to help."

I felt their hesitation. I'd blamed the big drach leader enough times in their presence I knew their doubts were fed by my prejudice regardless of his participation in my own saving.

"It's cool," I said. "Fate and I had a talk."

Mom nodded, stepped back while Charlotte glared at me like she used to when we were still bonded and I tried to give her the slip. Galleytrot paced back and forth, Sassafras on his back, crouched and hissing at me. Shenka even looked pissed off, jaw jutting forward.

"You could have said something," she snapped, tears in her voice. "Instead of just leaving."

I sighed, nodded. Suddenly tired. Let my arms fall to my sides as Gram and Demetrius watched, they and the vampires in residence the only ones who didn't look like they wanted to beat me senseless. Uncle Frank and Sunny flickered with spirit power while Sebastian leaned back against the counter, hands in the pockets of his jeans. Piers leaned against the wall, a little smirk on his face, though from the snapping anger in his gray eyes, they'd filled him in on the attack at the Star Club. Alison hovered, pouting, while Trill's crossed leg bobbed up and down with growing agitation.

I loved them all. Sent my power out to them, embraced them. Let them feel my excitement, how sorry I was, and that I had a plan.

They softened as a group. Though I was sure as soon as I told them what I had in mind, they weren't going to stay that way.

"I'm not coming back from this without Gabriel," I said. "But I have places I need to go. One in particular." I glanced at Max. "I have to go to Core to talk to the Dark Fate. And I'm not sure what kind of reception I'm going to have."

Enforcer magic trickled through the wards, the sound of the back door opening and closing breaking the silence. And then, Quaid was there, standing behind

Shenka, chocolate eyes locked on me.

I fumbled for words a moment, brain wondering what the hell he was doing here before I pulled myself together again and focused on my grandmother.

Held out my hands to her. "I can't run the risk the family magic will be lost," I said. "And it's clear now I'm meant for more danger than is wise to risk the coven." So hard, but necessary. "I want you to take it back."

She gaped at me. "Are you cracked?"

I laughed. "Maybe," I said. "But I have more than enough power without it." The coven's power pleaded with me even as I gently began to detach it from my other egos. "I've put the family in jeopardy too many times over the years to risk it again. If this whole mess has taught me anything, it's that now, more than ever, I need to protect the ones I love." The family magic groaned softly. "And that means stepping down as leader of the coven."

Gram shook her head, held up both hands. "Not me," she said. "Find another patsy."

Damn her. "Gram, this will restore your magic."

"No," she said, sharp and abrupt. "It will simply mean a weak leader buoyed by the power of the family."

I hadn't thought of that. Wished she'd stop being stubborn and do it anyway.

Turned to Shenka who laughed with a softly hysterical edge to her voice and shook her head.

"Absolutely not," she said.

Stubborn bratskis.

"You're stuck with us," Shenka said, reaching out to the family as she did. I felt her share what I wanted, cursed her mentally as they rejected my proposal down to the last coven member. Their rejection stuffed the family magic back inside me where it burrowed deep, refusing to leave. "You are our leader, through dark times and happy ones. And no matter how this turns out, what Fate has in store," I shivered when she mentioned Fate, "we will stand beside you. Your coven. Even if that means we fall with you in the end."

They agreed, all of them. The idiots.

Loved them.

Cried a moment as I felt their embrace, their undying support. How far we'd come.

"All right, you fools," I whispered. Let them go. Looked up and smiled at Shenka. "All right." Shook it off. "Rosetta and her crew?"

Mom sank into a chair. "In custody," she said. "And under Lula's care."

She was healing them?

"I want them all alive and well," Mom said, "when I have them burned."

And the family temper was clearly passed down from my witch side.

My demon snorted in amusement.

"I'm coming with you." Quaid said it casually, breaking into the conversation as though he was welcome. Had been invited. Everyone stared, even Demetrius, as I frowned at the Enforcer.

"No," I said. "You're not."

"Yes," he said. "I am." Paused. "Want to try that again?"

Grrr.

Syd, his mind touched mine, despite my resistance, *I can't let you go alone.*

Can't let? I threw the words in his mental face. *Since when do you let me do anything?*

That's not what I meant. His power stirred with anxiety, determination. *I've let you down so many times. I can't allow this be another of them.*

Let me down. *None of this is your responsibility*, I sent. Without adding "anymore". Because I was nice like that.

It is, he sent. *You are. I want you to be.*

Too late for that. I intended to slap him with the truth, but ended up too sad to use the words as a weapon. *You followed your own calling, Quaid. I understand. I really do. And you don't have to feel guilty—*

It's not guilt. He trembled, his power shivering. *Syd. It's not.*

Then what? This conversation was making me tired. I had to rescue my son.

He had to come before whatever was eating at Quaid.

"I'll follow you regardless," Quaid said. Shrugged. Met Max's eyes.

I looked up at the big drach who had a small smile on his face. Bowed his head to Quaid.

"Of course he will," Max said. "It's what you do for the people you love the most in the world."

I guess I should have been all swoony and whatever.

The word "love" just pissed me off.

"Who says you're the best one to go?" Sassafras bristled from his perch on Galleytrot as Charlotte growled under her breath.

"Precisely," Piers said in his crisp British accent. "I would think sorcery would be more helpful against Ameline."

"As if," Quaid growled.

That wound everyone up again.

"No one is going," I said over them as they started to argue. "Me. Max. End of story."

"If you take me with you," Quaid pushed past Shenka, past Mom, stood in front of me, black robe hanging open, his death-metal t-shirt tight over his muscular chest, "and something happens, I can return the family magic home again."

Jerkasaurus.

I glanced at Gram who sighed, rolled her eyes and nodded.

"He's an Enforcer," she drawled, giving him the stink

eye. "Damned fool has that ability."

While no one else in the room did.

Damn it.

"Good for you for knowing which of my buttons to push," I said, punching him in his very hard stomach.

A tiny smile, quite the match for Max's, raised the corners of his mouth, the short stubble on his jaw darkening his features even as his eyes smoldered.

"I'm at your service, maji," he said.

"Well, if he's going, I am, too." Charlotte pushed him aside, her wolf in her eyes.

Piers grinned. "I'm tagging along for the fun," he said.

Demetrius raised one hand with a beaming smile. "It's likely Ameline will have more of the Chosen with her," he said.

"And dark maji." Trill's leg stopped bouncing.

"Some vampire magic might be in order," Sebastian said.

"You're not a vampire anymore," I griped at him.

"Syd." Sassafras's amber magic touched me as he spoke. "You're not going without help. No matter what you're afraid of, if you fall, none of us want to survive. Because if Ameline wins, we might as well pack it in."

Mom nodded, grim. "We won't be able to stand against her," she said—way to be a realist at the wrong moment, Mom—"especially if Ameline has the dark maji under her control. We can no more counter them than we could the sorcerers, especially since we are still geased against using blood magic."

I hated they were right. Still, if I fell, I didn't want to think they were helpless.

Too much pressure.

"So take the help," Sassafras said, "and kick her ugly butt once and for all."

I intended to. If Fate would let me.

chapter twenty seven

In the end, despite my outward grumping, but private joy at just how much they loved me, it was Charlotte, Sebastian, Alison, Trill. Demetrius and Galleytrot. Quaid. Piers.

Me and Max.

Okay then.

I had to bite my tongue when Piers came to my side, hugged me. On freaking purpose. Like I didn't know he was torturing Quaid who glared at the tall, handsome Steam Union sorcerer with fury in his eyes.

Boys.

I would never, ever be free of their ridiculousness.

Sassafras pouted, back to me, tail drooping. I went to him as the others backed off, talking quietly as they made their preparations to leave. Saying goodbyes.

I wished they wouldn't. Though I knew there was a

chance none of us would survive.

Touched Sass's fur only to have him hiss spitefully at me.

I know you're mad at me, I sent. *But I need you here.*

I get it, he snarled in my head. *The cat is useless. Take the damned dog. See if I care.*

I swept him into my arms, endured his wriggling, the claws digging into my arm. Kissed his head. Felt him sag against me.

You, I said, *are my only solid connection to the family.* He shivered. *Shenka is second, yes, but she wasn't born to the coven. She needs your support. And Gram is weak.*

I know. His mental voice was barely audible.

You have always told me duty and the family come first, I sent. *I'm trying to make sure I follow your orders. And I need to know you're taking your own advice.*

He looked up at me, amber eyes filled with misery.

I'm afraid, he said. *When we thought Gabriel died… Syd, you wanted to go, so badly. What happens if he does die?*

I shook my head, kissed his nose. *Fate promised me*, I said. *Gabriel will survive, no matter what.*

Sassafras absorbed that. *You trust her?*

I do, in this. Felt him relax.

Then I'll stay, he said, one paw rising to touch my cheek. *But you'd better come home with him, Sydlynn Thaddea Hayle.*

I set him gently down in Shenka's arms as my second

reached for him.

I'll do my best.

And turned away.

Face to face with Mom. Who just hugged me. Let me go abruptly.

"Hurt her a little for me," she said. Before flashing into blue fire and vanishing.

Gram took her place. Patted my hair back from my cheeks. Pinched one with her thin fingers. Hugged my neck so tight I couldn't breathe.

This feels scarier than when you fought the Brotherhood, she sent. *And I don't know why.*

I agreed with her. At least then I'd really only had myself to worry about. Sure, I was married, had the coven. But I'd always focused on keeping myself alive and unharmed.

Now I had Gabriel ahead of my own safety.

You bring that boy home to his great-grandmother, Gram sent. *And trust Demetrius.*

I will. I squeezed her hand. *And, if things go the way I hope, I'll have a little something for you, too.*

She just shrugged. And smiled, wistful and soft.

I couldn't bear her expression. Turned to find Uncle Frank and Sunny waiting. More hugs. More whispers of love and wishes of ill on Ameline. I returned their affection and promised she'd suffer.

Just some quality family time plotting the death of an

enemy.

I glared at the big group waiting for me. "Does no one find it odd I'm leaving fewer people behind than I'm taking with me?"

Crickets.

Um-hum.

I gestured to Max. "You want to take the lead?"

He bowed his head to me. "My pleasure." And opened the veil.

It felt different when he did it. No Ahbi, for one. And more elemental, almost raw. I joined him, linking hands with Piers who beat Quaid to it, trying not to roll my eyes. Again.

"You two," I snapped. "Behave or I'm leaving you home."

And followed Max into the veil.

The last time I'd been to Core was with Ameline. We'd been ignored, for the most part, their leader rather pleasant. But I had no idea what to expect this time.

A kind and awe-filled greeting wasn't it, I have to say.

Max landed us near the large pillared building that mirrored the one in Center, smack-dab in the middle of a group of maji. Who bowed in the dark, their black skin shining in the soft lights hovering in the sparkling night sky, pattern of stars so brilliant I sighed over them.

Looked down to find the leader smiling at me. "Light One," she said. "Be welcome. We've been expecting you."

Um. This was a good thing...?

"This way, please." I followed her, my friends gaping around. I left them at the bottom of the stairs, growing almost without thinking about it, Max at my side. The door to Fate's chamber stood open and, with a bow so deep her hair brushed the ground, Yosha, the leader of the dark maji, gestured for me to go on without her.

I was half-tempted to thank her, but held my tongue—and my breath—as I faked some serious attitude and confidence and passed through the arching doorway.

He sat under a statue carved of he and his sister, the Dark Fate smiling my way, blind eyes as clear white as hers. But he rose, unerring, coming right toward me, taking my hands and pulling me down beside him while Max stood over us, silent.

"You're right on time," he said. "I love that about you."

Happy to oblige. "Where's Ameline?" I had no desire to play any games, thanks.

"She's not here," he said, tilting his head to one side. "Surely you know that by now."

Okay, so I started looking for her the moment we crossed over.

Grumble, mumble.

"You were meant to come here, surely my sister told you that." Fate waved at Max. "My sister's love, be welcome."

Max bowed his head, but didn't speak. I risked a quick glance, but the terrible sadness he'd worn the last time we talked to the Fates wasn't present. Only calm.

I'd take that as a very good thing.

"There is much I'm not permitted to share," Dark Fate said. "But I can tell you this. Only one of you will survive your last encounter and the winner will only succeed because of the Gateway."

Gabriel. "Why did you call him that?" Maybe this Fate would be more likely to give up extra info.

"That, you will discover for yourself," Fate said. Paused. Smiled. "You're not afraid."

And I realized he was right.

"I'm ready," I said. Felt a weight lift from my shoulders. "I take it this will get easier over time? I'm cool with just being dropped into the disaster and fixing it without all the decorative preamble."

He laughed, a young man's sound of joy. "How I wish you were mine," he said. Sobered, though he still smiled. "I'm sure Creator will take your needs into consideration. If you are the one who survives."

There was that.

"Why are you helping me?" It was a fair question. Didn't matter, but I had to ask.

Fate just smiled. "I'm not," he said, gentle and kind. "I'm Fate." Sighed. "How do you know talking to you isn't helping her?"

Yeah. Thanks anyway.

"Now," he said. "Time for you to go." Took my hand before I could ask him where, and showed me.

Clear as if I stood there on the lawn of the vampire mansion.

Flashed to the stone stairway underground, passing a face I knew.

Celeste.

The maji chamber waiting at the bottom, a black-cloaked figure standing in shadow.

The oh-so-delicious touch of a Sidhe soul bound to the body of a boy.

"She's already there," he said as I jerked to my feet. "You'd better hurry."

I ran.

chapter twenty eight

I was practically flying when I hit the ground at the bottom of the stairs, already shrunk to my normal size. The urge to keep going, pound my way through the veil and to the vampire mansion, smear opposition and cut the bitch's throat was so powerful I had to force myself to breathe. Knew it was my demon's impulsiveness driving me.

Sure it was, Syd.

I fixed my waiting friends with a grin of evil delight. "The mansion," I said.

Sebastian groaned softly, tapped his forehead with his fingertips. "When I left them, Anastasia gathered the blood clan and took them home to Austria, leaving the house in the care of their human servants."

I thought of Stewart and the helpless staff who were now, quite likely, dead. Just another tick on the tally against Ameline.

She was racking up the points, yup yup.

Time to cash in her ticket.

I almost giggled at that. Even in the face of trouble—hell, usually in the face of trouble—there were times I cracked myself up.

"According to this Fate," I jerked my thumb over my shoulder in his general direction, "only one of us is going to come out of this alive." Way to be blunt and everything, Syd. But my friends didn't comment, their grim expressions telling me who they expected to live and who they planned to make sure never saw the light of day again.

Ameline was in so much freaking trouble.

"The only problem is, I know she won't be alone." If the small selection of dark maji and the few Chosen she left behind at the Star Club were only a selection of bodies she left behind, that meant she'd likely gathered an army of opposition against us. Had to be expecting me to show up at some point.

And I refused to disappoint.

"I have access to a lot of magic." Went without saying. "But my focus has to be Ameline and Gabriel. Which means we need a plan."

Why were they laughing suddenly? Quaid snorted, smirked. Charlotte coughed, looked away and then back, eyes sparkling. Piers grinned at me while Sebastian's eyebrows shot up. Trill giggled, hands over her mouth. Even Demetrius chuckled like I'd said something funny.

"What?" I glared around at them as they pulled themselves together.

"Sydlynn Hayle wants to make a plan." Quaid's deep voice was warm with amusement. "Wow, I think I can now die with my life complete."

They all laughed again.

Smartass friends.

And yet, I grinned, hands on hips, feeling a huge swell of joy and love inside me, excitement stirring as they waited for me to go on. Without question, hesitation. Ready to act.

I couldn't have asked for more.

"Trill, you and Piers are to take care of the dark maji." She sobered immediately, nodded while my Steam Union friend bobbed his head in answer, gray eyes intent on Trill for a moment as they met eyes with determined expressions. "Demetrius?"

"The Chosen." He bowed a little to me with his cherub smile making my grin wider. "I shall endeavor to convince them of the error of their ways."

"If I may," Sebastian said, "might I pursue Celeste and any vampires who might remain in her thrall?"

I wanted her for myself. But his grudge seemed much bigger than mine these days, so I nodded.

"Just don't kill her," I said. "If you can help it."

He snarled a smile, handsome face flickering with iridescent magic. "I will do my best to take her alive," he said.

Yeah. Wasn't holding my breath.

So much fun to be had.

"Quaid, I want you to back up Demetrius." He looked like he wanted to argue, but I wasn't going to give him the chance. "When the Chosen are subdued, follow us."

He nodded abruptly and moved sideways, putting himself behind the sorcerer who smiled over his shoulder at the tall Enforcer.

"I promise you'll have lots of time for fun," Demetrius said. "My old order won't last long against me."

Quaid grinned and squeezed the sorcerer's shoulder.

Bloodthirsty much?

Charlotte's flat expression told me I'd better not expect her to leave my side. Made me laugh and hug her before stepping back.

"Princess Sharlotta," I said, "if you would be so kind as to escort me in your old capacity one last time?"

Tears rose in her eyes, lower lip trembling as she caught her breath. I hadn't expected that reaction and impulsively hugged her again.

"My honor," she whispered.

I stepped back, met Galleytrot's eyes, filled with red

fire. "You, my friend, I want scouting ahead."

He chuffed, tail thudding against the ground.

It took me a moment to find Alison, hovering in the background. I held my hand out to her and she came to me, shy and nervous, eyes down.

"Alison," I said, pulling her close to me. "I need you to find Gabriel."

She looked up, blue eyes wide.

"You saved my heart and my life," I said, tears trickling while my old friend's face crumpled in sadness. "Now save my son."

She nodded swiftly, wiping at her own tears. Kissed my cheek.

"I won't let you down," she whispered.

"You can't," I said.

Quaid's eyes lifted over my shoulder before settling on mine again.

I knew what he was asking. Felt the hulking form behind me, sensed the incredible power of the drach. Turned and looked up into Max's eyes.

His sparkled, diamonds full of calm, his face composed. Not a trace of the sadness he'd worn the last time we'd been together, a sadness I thought he carried for another reason, but I now knew foretold his fate. Forcing me to watch Liam die.

There was no such expression this time, only steady willingness.

"I will do as you ask, Light One," he said. "And am happy to serve."

Fear so powerful it made my stomach clench tensed my entire body a heartbeat before I let it go.

"If you betray me again," I said, "I'll pursue you to the ends of the universe, no matter the cost, no matter how much time it takes. And I will kill you."

He nodded. "I would expect nothing less."

Okay then.

I turned back to the others, all of them tense and ready.

And smiled one last time.

Opened the veil.

"Let's get this party started," I said.

And stepped through.

Knock, knock, Ameline. Time to end this one way or another.

CHAPTER TWENTY NINE

I reached for Ahbi the moment we were in the veil.

I need to go right to the maji chamber, I sent, knowing it wouldn't work, but hoping we could figure something out.

Ahbi grunted softly, showed me a wall of power.

And the lawn of the mansion.

At least I knew where we'd be ending up. Sent the image to the others, the exact image Dark Fate had shown me. He hadn't been generalizing, it turned out.

I felt their acceptance and understanding.

Drew a breath.

Gabriel. I'd be holding him again very soon.

Or I'd be dead.

My egos hugged me.

Nothing will keep us from him, my demon snarled.

We will move the very earth to get him back, Shaylee sent.

And that bitch will die. My vampire's spirit magic blazed inside me.

The family power surged in agreement. Even my sorcery blossomed open in the hope of devouring her soul.

So be it.

Grandmother, I sent to Ahbi. *If you would do the honors.*

She hugged me tight with her power before ripping open the veil and letting us out.

I stepped onto the dew-wet grass and didn't miss a beat, striding forward toward the front door, a woman on a mission. Shouts answered our appearance and approach, the guards Ameline placed to watch for us—of course she had—raising the alarm. I felt the power guarding the mansion tighten on reflex in answer to the uproar and grinned.

Ameline.

So happy she knew I was coming for her.

They lined up in front of the entry to the mansion, easily a hundred of them, while I could feel others flanking us, closing us into a circle. Ameline must have told them they stood a chance.

It almost made me laugh.

I caught a glimpse of Demetrius in my peripheral vision only to have him move past me on my right, his short legs carrying him with great speed though he looked like he was out for a stroll.

He threw his arms wide as he went, a smile in his voice as he spoke and I could only imagine he was beaming.

"My children," he said in a booming voice. "My Chosen. Come to me."

The outcry fell off, a few of the figures in the front pushing back their hoods, staring with huge eyes at Demetrius. Someone shouted, "Master!" Triggered a mass of collapse, half the front row falling to their knees while the gathering behind them thinned still further.

The remaining guards—dark maji, had to be—looked around in confusion and growing concern as Demetrius strode, without a moment's hesitation, all the way to the front line. I giggled in barely contained anxiety and adrenaline as not one of the gathered attacked him, stunned and overwhelmed by his approach.

I was right behind him, stopped just shy of his shoulder as his power stretched outward, the edge of it touching my sorcery.

"Oh, my children," he said. "How far you have fallen."

One of the men in the front—I knew him, didn't I? Annick, one of his lieutenants from so long ago—crawled forward on his hands and knees, groveling.

"My master," he wept, tears shining on his cheeks in the lights surrounding the entry. "Forgive us, we thought you lost."

They moved forward as a mass, coming to worship their lost leader.

I knew it would only be another moment before the dark maji were forced to act.

Trill, I sent.

I'm already on it, she sent. *Boys, you out there?*

Reading and waiting, sis. Owen's mental voice shocked me, not at the depth of it—he'd grown so much since we'd met—but at his presence.

Apollo? Trill's irritation came through.

I'm here, her older brother sent with a mental wink. *Just let them try it. The Zornovs are ready for action.*

Trill glanced sideways at me, rolled her eyes. Grinned.

Gave them a call. Since they were bored. They popped over. Her grin deepened. *I thought I might need them after all.*

Brilliant.

Trill moved to the outside of our little pack, focusing on the front line. I caught sight of the tall, angry looking dark maji who turned and opened his mouth, probably at the same instant she did. Someone in authority finally decided to act, did he?

Unlucky for him.

He froze where he was, hands going to his throat as Trill began to glow. I felt the answering thrum from the right and the left, sorcery racing toward us as the Zornov brothers made good on their word and backed up their sister.

Dark maji dude hit the ground with his eyes bugging out of his head while his people stared.

I took a step forward, ignoring the groveling Chosen who wept at Demetrius's feet and grinned at the line of bodies in my way.

Waved.

"Boo," I said.

They shrieked as a unit just before Trill and her brothers attacked.

The sky was suddenly filled with rainbow light, bracketed by black so deep no stars shone through as the Zornovs contained the dark maji and hit them hard.

Syd, Trill sent, mental voice tight, *go. I don't know how long we can hold them.*

She didn't have to tell me twice.

I squeezed Demetrius's arm on the way by as he soothed his people, winking at me with one blue eye.

Good luck to you, Sydlynn, he sent before spreading his arms again, this time to the sky.

"MY CHILDREN!" His voice boomed like thunder. "OUR CREATOR HAS SPOKEN. THE DARK MAJI ARE OUR ENEMIES."

Oh, clever. Very, very clever. I felt them stir as I hurried past them, saw their faces darken, turn toward those they had once stood beside.

"ATTACK!"

I formed a quick shield before me, pointed like the

bow of a ship, and pushed my way through the last of the guards as they turned on each other like animals.

One hurdle down. Who knew how many to go.

The front door of the mansion was warded, sealed around the edges. I scowled at it, drew back to ram it with the shield. Only to have Piers step past me and bow with a smile.

"Light One," he said, voice airy and full of humor. "Allow me."

He spun and gestured, black emptiness engulfing the door.

Wood groaned, metal squealed and sighed.

And the entire front entry collapsed into dust, leaving a gaping hole in the front of the house.

"Nice," I said. "Thanks."

He bowed again. "My pleasure," he said.

I scowled suddenly. "You're supposed to be helping Trill."

Piers shrugged, gestured for me to enter. "It appears she doesn't need me," he said. His gray eyes filled with concern. "But you might."

Way to stick to the plan, Steam Union. Not that I was surprised.

"Just don't make me rescue you," I said. And stepped over the threshold.

Reached out for my son.

And almost fell to my knees much like the Chosen in

front of Demetrius.

"He's here," I whispered even as my heart sang and screamed and rejoiced.

A flicker of shadow to my right told me I had to pay attention. But I needn't have bothered. Celeste appeared, stepping out of the darkness with a dozen vampires at her back. She looked terrified, especially when Sebastian smiled. Saluted me. And rushed at them, his power roaring around him, no longer just the white of spirit, but touched by mine.

"You." I jabbed a finger at Piers. "Help him." And toward the vampires.

To his credit, he didn't hesitate, threw himself toward Sebastian.

Even as I turned and marched through the foyer, to the hall. All the while pushing against the magic trying to keep me from veiling down into the maji chamber.

On foot, then. Fine. I could walk. Just meant my fury and need to smash and maim increased with every step.

Galleytrot loped ahead of me, green fire tracing over his fur, sparks falling to the red carpet in the dark hall. He stuck his nose into the door at the end, the one we aimed for, turned to look at me.

"Clear," he said.

Weird. Would she have thrown all she had at us so soon?

"Wait." I held out one hand as he moved to enter.

"For us."

Charlotte joined him, sniffing around. Tensed even as Galleytrot did. He touched his nose to the air just inside the room.

And fell back with a howl of pain, writhing on the floor with a black shadow fighting to devour him.

Ameline was up to her old tricks. I lashed at Galleytrot, cutting the cord of the shade before it could draw out his power. He panted, furious, howling his rage into the air as I came to his side, hugged him.

"Careful," I said.

"I'm going to play tug of war with her intestines," he snarled.

"Sounds like fun," I said.

Faced the doorway. She'd done this before, used her sorcery as a kind of trap, leaving part of it in the person she attacked. I hadn't seen the actual trap before, though. Could never figure out how she managed it.

Piers panted to my side, jogging to a halt as Max came to stand next to me, head tilted to one side. Quaid supported the panting Galleytrot as Charlotte paced back and forth between me and the rest of the house, a low growl humming in the back of her throat.

"Interesting," Max said. "It's alive."

Piers's magic touched it before he flinched back. "Holy mother of…" He turned and was noisily sick, whole body convulsing around his need to rid himself of the touch of what Ameline had done.

I reached for it myself, needing to know, to understand.

Almost wished I hadn't.

There was a soul tied to the sorcery trap. A normal's soul. Stolen from a woman who never knew our world, though she had a latent ability in her spirit. That latent magic fed the sorcery, kept it alive until the trap was sprung.

When she attacked Gram. Galleytrot in the cavern. Liam.

She used the souls of latent normals to do it.

Sick. So freaking sick.

I wanted to puke like Piers had, barely held it together as he straightened and wiped his mouth with the back of his hand.

"Sorry," he whispered.

"Don't be," I said. "I know exactly how you feel."

Alison ghosted to my side, her face fallen into sadness. She turned to meet my eyes. "I think I can free her."

I reached out and squeezed her hand.

"Yes, please."

Followed her power, the soft-edged touch of it, more echo than mortal, felt her sever the tie to the sorcery and embrace the woman's soul.

The saddest part, it wasn't even her echo trapped, but

her actual spirit. I watched as the form of a woman, short brown hair and staring eyes, formed in the doorway, blackness fading from around her. A very bright light woke behind her and she turned with a smile and dove into it before the glow went out in a flare so bright I had to look away.

When I turned back, Alison was crying into her trembling hands. Looked up to meet my gaze with hate in hers.

"She's going to pay for this," Alison said.

"She's going to pay for a lot of things." I turned toward the now empty doorway. "Eyes open," I said. "Everyone pay attention."

They formed up behind me, Alison taking the lead as Galleytrot came to my side.

Onward.

chapter thirty

Charlotte stalked past me as Alison's form wavered from corporeal to ghostly and back again. I really should have learned the combination of stones to press to open the secret staircase to the underground, and this time actually watched as my werefriend followed the combination with unerring accuracy.

The floor beside her groaned and collapsed, falling down into a set of stone steps leading into the dark. A giant ball of witchlight burst into existence at the top of the staircase as Quaid shouldered past me, face lit with blue light.

"There will probably be others downstairs," he said. "Let me handle them."

Another one who couldn't follow orders. Though Demetrius had the Chosen well in hand the last time I saw him. And from the echoing booms and faint screams

I heard coming from outside, the battle was still going strong.

I nodded, let Quaid lead the way. As much as I would have loved to barrel my way into the underground, he was right. Focus on Gabriel, let the others do what they came to do—keep me moving forward until I could reach the maji chamber.

And my son.

And Ameline.

He and Charlotte, Piers following close behind, clattered down the steps, not even trying to be quiet. Because she knew we were here already, didn't she? The sound of the stairs opening would be alarm enough. A visible wall of power preceded them, Charlotte's golden rainbow mingling with Quaid's glowing blue, edged with Pier's deepest black.

If I were a nicer person, I would have pitied the idiots waiting for them at the bottom.

Didn't.

Alison drifted ahead of me, fading into ghostly as I went after her. Before I'd taken two steps, I caught the sound of a magic fight breaking out and knew my friends were doing what they could to clear the way for me. I continued to try to tear at the veil, but from Ahbi's bits and pieces of growling and snarling as I managed tiny holes, she was as frustrated by Ameline's blocking us as I was.

I should have rushed forward and helped with the fight. But feeling just how much Ameline was able to resist me told me I had to have access to as much of my power as possible. She would want me to wear myself out on her little army. It was probably the point of all this. She knew I could handle the crap she threw at me. But would I be able to stand against her weakened by the effort?

So sad she didn't have anyone in her life to have her back like I did. People who cared about me and fought, not for power or out of fear, but for loyalty, honor and love.

That she would never have. Or understand.

The moment I touched down in the main hall at the bottom of the steps, I was engulfed in energy. Well, my shields were. Smoke filled the corridor with a thick haze, though my wards held off the worst of it. Flashes of fire and bursts of power flared back and forth as my friends fought off the dark maji and, from the surges of blackness trying to take them out, a handful of sorcerers Ameline had obviously held in reserve.

"Light One," Max said softly in my ear, bending over my shoulder. "Allow me to shield you as we go."

He knew what I was thinking, obviously believed as I did that Ameline wanted me to waste power on useless fighting. Walking through that mess would suck up a lot of my energy, just keeping us safe. I looked up at him, nodded.

"Thank you."

The feeling of his magic engulfing me made me shiver as he released it. A giant bubble of humming light pushed back the haze, even as blackness slammed against it when the sorcerers attacked. It was surreal, seeing my friends in flares of light as they fought, wanting to help them, almost silent inside the circle of protection Max made for me. Like watching a 3D movie with the volume turned way down.

I couldn't think about them. Had to believe they would win. Focused on the entry to the circular room above the maji chamber and the wide-open archway.

I felt Max's power test it for a barrier, but it was clear. He stepped through first, nodded to me and gestured for me to enter. I followed his lead, trusting him now, hoping my trust wasn't unfounded. The moment we were inside, Max's magic snapped a tight seal over the stone archway, sealing off the smoke and the rest of the noise from the fight, though the flares of light continued at a regular pace.

"I will allow this to fall when we are below," Max said, diamond eyes lit with rainbow light. "So our friends may join us when they are victorious."

"Someone will have to watch the door." I turned to Galleytrot. Saw his instant rejection of my need. I bent over him, hugging his big head. *Please*, I sent in a whisper.

You are the only one with enough power to keep us safe.

Max could stay. The hound of the Wild Hunt let me feel his unhappiness, the rumble of thunder and the scent of an approaching storm powerful in my senses.

I nodded against Galleytrot's head. *He could*, I sent. *But I need you to do it.* Because if Ameline won, I had a job for the big drach. A Gabriel rescue mission.

He just didn't know it yet.

Galleytrot pulled away, licked my cheek. "I'll stay," he said. Whined softly. "Save him."

I kissed his furry head. "Is there any doubt?"

He shook, fur cascading more sparks. "No," he rumbled, the floor beneath us vibrating with his voice. "There isn't. Don't forget to save me some of her guts."

I grinned. "You got it." Turned to the pedestal. Pressed my hand onto it, hearing the song of the maji as the floor in this chamber sank as well. Galleytrot stepped back out of the way of the collapse, standing close to the exit, eyes locked on the spiral stairs descending into faint light. The walls, etched with the history of all races glowed with maji power for a moment, as though welcoming me home before falling dark again.

As I stepped toward the top stair, I felt the whole house shake above me, the echoing boom of a massive explosion giving me pause. Even the fight outside the chamber fell still for a heartbeat as we all waited for the place to cave in on us.

When it didn't, the fight resumed, though there were far more flashes of light now than surges of black, so I had hope my friends held the upper hand.

Regardless, I had to let them go.

Gabriel waited for me below, and I was done holding back.

My foot touched the top step. And went no further as a shimmering skim of shielding blocked my descent.

The bitch. She'd managed to wrangle some demon power, had she? Not as much as mine. My demon snarled, my other egos joining her as we pounded ourselves against the shield.

Nothing. It stood firm, ignoring me as though I didn't exist.

"How?" I turned to Max, frustration so powerful suddenly, I would have beaten Ameline to death with my bare hands if she'd showed her face.

He touched the power with his own. Nodded once.

"Were we on the other side," he said, "we could break through easily." I'd heard of this phenomena before, hadn't I? The cavern that held the Firbolg magician, Cesard, was weak on the outside. "But because all of the power is focused on this side, it creates an unbreakable seal."

"Can you break it?" He was drach, of the first race.

He shook his head. "I could break the ground around it," he said, "but I have a feeling she's set it for the entire floor. And it would take us far too long."

DAMN HER.

Alison frowned, head tilted. Walked past me as her body faded into ghostly thinness.

And descended through the barrier, down the stairs.

Turned to smile up at me with a bright happiness I hadn't seen for years.

She held out her hand to me. "I think I can get you through," she said.

Anger flashing over into joy, I reached to her, touched her hand, solid and real where it poked up through the shield. Felt her magic slip around me, change me. The world became thin and hazy, grayed around the edges. Galleytrot growled as I looked down at my free hand and realized I could see through it.

Alison tugged gently on me, her hand now as transparent as mine. "Coming?"

I turned and took Max's hand, watching in wonder as the transparency spread up his arm and over his body, his head and sparkling eyes the last to fade.

Together we walked through the barrier, the soft zing of it an odd sensation as my body passed through it, until we were two steps below. Alison released me while we all looked up, just as the shimmering barrier vanished in a flash of light.

And Ameline's voice stabbed into my head.

Come then, she snarled. *Let's end this.*

chapter thirty one

I pushed past Alison, taking the stairs two at a time, not caring I might fall, mind locked on Ameline as my power built around me, before me, flaring outward as I thundered toward her with her death in every fiber of my being.

And Gabriel.

The bottom step almost took me by surprise and I found myself pouring the last of my forward momentum into leaping into the maji chamber. It hummed with power, but not Ameline's. With the magic of the maji who created it, welcoming me, embracing me.

Troubled and angry and happy I was there.

I didn't pay attention to it, too focused on the black-robed figure standing beside the long stone slab in the middle of the room, cloak spread out, back to me. I'd seen this, too, Dark Fate's premonition right on the money.

I just wished everything else was decided.

That was, I guess, my job, right?

"Ameline." My voice vibrated with my hate, the world closing in around me as blackened tunnel vision hyper-focused me on her bowed shoulders, her hood-covered head. "It's over."

Galleytrot barked above even as Max's power sealed the door behind me. Alison drifted to my left, eyes locked on Ameline, though the big drach's looming presence remained still and watchful.

Didn't matter. Not when I felt him. And not just a trace of him this time. Or a hint of his passing. Gabriel was here. With her.

My hands clawed beside me, my magic ready to tear her apart. And Ameline turned slowly toward me, face wreathed in shadow.

"Welcome to your death," she said.

I didn't respond. I was too busy staring, in open shock and disbelief, at the little boy sitting on the stone slab.

No, this couldn't be. This wasn't Gabriel. My baby was only two months old. Yes, he looked more like a year, acted even older. But it had only been three weeks. And this child was at least two.

A trick? But no, it was him, his heart, his soul. His sweet magic, reaching for me as his hazel eyes lit up with sparks of green, sullen scowl a blazing smile as he locked eyes with me and reached out with his little arms, heels pattering against the stone as he tried to come to me.

"Momma," he said. And laughed.

Oh. My.

Heart broke, shattered, knitted itself back together again as I choked on tears and sobs and screams mixed with happiness and grief.

"Gabriel," I whispered.

His strawberry blonde hair hung in waves around his cheeks as he wriggled his joy. "Hi, Momma," he said.

And then there was no doubt, curiosity gone. However it happened, my son was here and I had come for him.

Ameline's fury hit me like a wall of bricks. I'd let my shields fall, felt the sting of the blow just before I snarled and shoved her back, my wards slamming into place. I reached for Gabriel with my magic, felt him shielded as the stairs had been. Knew then I would never reach him unless Ameline was dead.

Alison, I sent. *Get Gabriel. That's your only job.*

She didn't answer. Didn't have to.

Ameline's hand grasped Gabriel's little arm, shook him. He glared up at her, green power flaring in his eyes. "No my Momma," he said. Pointed at me. "Momma."

She. She tried to. Convince him.

"You bitch," I said. "You tried to convince him you

were his mother."

She glared at me. Only then did I see past some of the shadow of her hood, her face lit by his magic. And then, she smiled, pulling at her skin, leaving valleys of darkness on her cheeks. "Surprised to see him this way?" Her voice was no longer the cultured, careful voice of an emotionless ice queen, but gravelly and harsh, as though she was three days into a bad cold. "The accelerated aging process his body naturally began had to be sped up." She didn't release him, but my son didn't fight her, either, just staring at her with fury and a clenched little jaw. I wavered between staring at him in longing and glaring at her with as much anger as he did. "My connection to Cian made it simple enough to push his body to age faster." She shrugged under her robe, hand clenching tighter around his arm. It had to hurt, but Gabriel's scowl just deepened.

Didn't mean I had to like it. "Let him go." I barely recognized my own voice, scared myself a little. The very air vibrated from my words, tore at her shield with pin-points of rage.

Ameline ignored me, shaking Gabriel ever so slightly. "His power won't peak until he's older, you see." She snarled herself, shook him again. "But it's too soon, isn't it, my pet?" She tossed her head, shrugging the hood from her, turning her face toward me, letting me see her at last. "And the price... I had no idea how much this would cost."

My breath caught at the sight of her. Sunken cheeks, paper thin, lips a slash across her once generous mouth. Her eyes were deep pits, though the ice blue of them shone as bright as ever. She reminded me of a vampire mummy, drained of blood, though it was power she lacked. She'd poured everything she had into this, into the shields. And into my son's aging process.

"I just need a few more days." She howled, jerking on Gabriel's arm so hard he finally cried out and my fury added another blow to the slowness of her impending death. "Just a few more."

Alison stirred, smiled. "My pleasure to ruin your plans," she said. "But I thought Syd should know you're a deceitful, thieving bitch who had her son." She grinned at me. "You're welcome."

Ameline snarled at her, spitting hate. Struck at her through the barrier she'd created. But my old bestie simply faded into ghostly form and the magic passed through her, absorbed into the walls of the chamber. Which sighed, sad and hurt at the blow.

"It doesn't matter." Ameline pulled Gabriel closer as he started to fight her, kicking at her with both feet, hitting her with one little fist. I could see the Sidhe magic behind the blows, but when Ameline's blue eyes flared I knew his fighting back only fed her. When he fell still I realized he'd processed that himself.

My brilliant little boy.

Ameline pulled him into her arms, stepping away from the slab, holding his wriggling body against her with one arm while a ball of shimmering power formed in her right hand. "When he dies, it's all over. A new Fate will be made. Maybe one that's easier for me." She cackled a laugh. And raised her hand over my son's head.

My brain exploded.

And so did my power.

Right. At. Ameline.

chapter thirty two

She blocked me. Of course she did. But that didn't keep me from attacking her again.

And again.

And again.

The power I released ricocheted around the room, hitting the walls, the slab, passing through Alison, reverbing back from Max as he protected himself.

Can you help me? I threw my need at him, heard him grunt.

I will feed you what I can, he sent. *But right now I am the only one keeping this house from collapsing.*

Crap. *Never mind,* I sent. *And thank you.*

Let Max go. Focused on Ameline. Panted a little as I pulled back, felt her for weakness. There had to be weakness. Just look at her. But no, nothing. Not a hint of a way through the shields surrounding her.

No matter the power she expended, she had accessed the magic of the chamber. When I tried to tap into it myself, the same shielding blocked me, the reason, I understood now, for its sadness.

Thanks to the magic she hoarded behind her wards, we were equal.

Maybe so, my vampire sent as I fumed over the truth. *But she carries souls who do not wish to be in her company, does she not? Magicks that would rather return to their rightful owners?*

Very true. Instead of looking for a way inside, I reached for the individual powers making up her maji.

And found them. Demon, one I didn't know, his masculine energy still and quiet. Sidhe, Cian, so familiar because he was Liam's, also silent. The hungry power she'd stolen from Belaisle, a black pit always seeking more sustenance. And Gram. The blue magic flickering, barely registering, in a coma.

My own egos roared at them, prodded. We did our best to wake them, even the family magic tried to stir the witch power inside Ameline. But even as I did, as we did, she laughed in my face.

"I've learned from my times taking souls, liberating power." She bounced Gabriel higher as he slipped down her grasp. "I know now how to make them quiet, to be mine at last."

They were more than quiet. Almost blank. Like she'd killed something vital inside them.

No, not dead, my demon growled. *Just sleeping.*

And might give us the edge we need, my vampire sent, soft and speculative.

Explain, I sent.

We work as a team. She laughed a little. *For the most part.*

Even my demon chuckled through her anger.

But Ameline is at a disadvantage, Shaylee sent. *Yes, brilliant.*

Thank you, my vampire sent. *Perhaps our individual strengths can be of advantage when she only has herself to lean on.*

As always. Ameline was alone and I had everything. No wonder she wanted me to love her in her sick and twisted way. I could see it on her face even now, feel a thrum of it run through her magic. And while I knew I could play that card, try to convince her we could work together, I just couldn't go there.

Was too bad a liar. And my son…

Let's try it, I sent. And let my egos loose.

Again we attacked, this time in concert, but also as individuals, my maji power not suffering for it as I privately feared. Instead, we seemed even more powerful, working as a team. We'd fought together so many times I think it was natural for us now to work as one while using our own strengths against Ameline, in perfect accord with each other. Sidhe, demon, witch, vampire and sorcery came together and flowed apart in perfect harmony.

As we did, for a moment, I felt Ameline wither and

weaken, but not from the force of our attack. But under the realization I wasn't alone.

And she had no one.

She flinched as she felt me winning, her alter egos unable to keep up as she tried to divide herself against us and failed over and over again. I grinned, took a step closer.

Until Ameline released the shield around her and drove her power into Gabriel.

Wrapped it around his little heart.

His eyes flew wide, struggles ceasing. Locked gazes with me. Shuddered.

And my own heart stopped beating. My power dropped off, hitchhikers falling still as we locked into place, terror forcing us to stop.

Stare.

Hold our breath.

Hadn't we used this same threat twice already?

Were ready to make good on it, too. And despite Fate's assurances Gabriel would survive, Ameline's mention of a new path of fate made me doubt.

The sounds of battle came closer, finally penetrating Max's shield as it weakened. I felt it falling, the pressure of the house above in his magic as he fought to keep tons of mansion from collapsing in on the maji chamber. But the fight, our imminent deaths by crushing, none of it mattered.

Only Gabriel. And Ameline's power around his heart.

And then, Alison's ghostly form flew at Ameline, lashed at her. With a startled snarl, Ameline's power withdrew a little from my son's chest, even as she struck Alison with a black film of magic.

The taint, the vampire filth left behind by the Brotherhood, the very power fueling Ameline's inner undead, flowed over Alison while my stomach clenched. She'd been under its control before, only won free when Demetrius attacked her with my crystal.

Alison cried out, fell back, writhing under the devouring shadow, screaming once as it ate through her echo.

And began to change her. I could see the altering of her face, the return to the evil she'd once endured, my focus suddenly split between saving my son and saving my friend.

I threw energy at Alison even as I fought to free Gabriel, knowing I wouldn't have enough magic to do both.

Wouldn't be enough.

Gave it everything I had anyway.

Ameline's triumph rippled over her as she fought back. "I knew your ridiculous caring for others would be your downfall," she laughed. And hit me so hard I crumpled.

Pulled away from Alison, knowing it was too late,

barely enough magic left to shield against Ameline. She continued to pound on me, driving me to my knees as my power faded and groaned and gave way under the constant onslaught I was unable to get ahead of.

My vampire screamed, demon roaring her pain, Shaylee sobbing as she fought. The family magic spun in endless circles, my sorcery's blossom closing over as the spark I held was beaten down, siphoned off.

Gabriel sobbed, began to glow with Sidhe fire. But no, not pure green, more like me. Iridescent, though he seemed to cycle through the colors of the powers until he returned to green again. His fighting began again in earnest as the air behind Ameline shimmered and sparkled.

She turned to look, a maniacal smile on her face as she laughed over the sound of his screaming. I could barely hear either of them, my ears dull as I fought to keep consciousness, keep fighting.

Refusing to let my son see me fail.

"It's working!" Ameline spun back to me, eyes full of madness as her skin began to fill out again, her body swelling with my stolen power. But I could see her siphoning it into Gabriel, the thin trail of sparkles leading from her to him, a straight shot into his heart. "He's not old enough for the full affect yet, but this will do."

Gabriel suddenly fell silent, eyes glowing green as she turned back toward the large portal. She stopped pulling power from me, left me there, weak and useless, barely able to lift my head from where I'd collapsed on the stones, to watch as my son's hand lifted, face blank, and the portal opened.

Into blackness as dark and empty as my sorcery.

The Gateway. Gabriel was a Gate, not just a Gatekeeper. But a maker of ways.

But, to where?

A deep and threatening boom emerged from the black as Ameline threw her head back and laughed.

"Come to me," she screamed. "Come and remake this Universe!"

And from deep in the darkness, something approached.

"What?" I barely whispered it, but she heard me. Turned to smile at me with insane scorn.

"The maker of worlds," she hissed. "The dark one of legend. The Creator's foul brother. He will give me everything, for I am his handmaiden."

She was freaking nuts. But regardless her state of mind, whatever was coming toward the Gate that was my son—no matter its real identity—would not be allowed to emerge.

Not if I had to die to stop it.

With the final scrap of power I had at my disposal, the power keeping my heart beating, I reached for the veil.

And exhaled my last breath.

Into failure.

And darkness.

Flicker.

Flash.

Sydlynhamitra.

Inhaled.

My heart hurt as it thudded back to life, Ahbi's power filling me, stirring my demon.

Grandmother. I showed her what I needed.

And she threw open the veil to home.

To Mom and to Sassafras. To Shenka and Gram and the family.

As I gathered what remained of the family magic, the final trace of it, and pulled back to throw it through the veil.

Only to have Gram seize me with the last of her own magic while Mom's panic almost shattered our connection, and pressed it into my heart.

Save him, she whispered.

And the veil snapped shut.

Felt Gram sizzle inside me, reconnecting pathways long sealed, felt myself wake, pulling magic from the chamber now that Ameline's shields were down as she poked and prodded me. Looked up to find Ameline snarling, shaking Gabriel.

Who fought her with his power even as the Gate hc

made began to shimmer and fail.

While the gaping red mouth and burning eyes of the creature on the other side roared so loud my bones shook.

I love you, Gram's magic said. *Now, finish this.*

I gathered the precious power she'd given me.

And threw it at Ameline.

chapter thirty three

Gram's power burst over my enemy in a wash of blue fire. Ameline spun on me, snarled, Gabriel turning to look at me with his glowing eyes.

Even as my grandmother's power slapped the magic Ameline stole from her and woke it up.

Joined with it as it jerked awake.

And hit Ameline so hard from the inside blood burst from her nose to spray over Gabriel's cheek.

She bent in half, my son falling to the floor. He landed hard on his sturdy little feet, straightened and turned. Gestured at the shimmering portal.

The roaring face of evil and madness.

And slammed the Gate in its face.

I pulled myself up as Ameline fell, my magic returning to me in a rush so powerful I staggered, light headed and body on fire. Watched and felt as Gram's magic woke the demon Ameline ripped from its rightful place, his amber flames scorching her. Ameline screamed, blisters forming on her skin, smoke rising from her even as Liam's portion of Cian woke and shook her from the inside, more blood flowing from her ears, her eyes, her nose, out of the pores of her skin, bursting blisters made by demon fire. The vampire taint devoured her as she had devoured others, sucking at her witch power, drinking it like cheap wine. And her sorcery died, her own blossom withering, the petals of it falling into dust beneath her as she screamed one last time and collapsed.

But not done. Not yet. She reached out with one clawed hand for my son.

Power still around his heart.

In the same instant Alison darted forward and scooped Gabriel into her arms. Spun as she turned them ghostly.

And Ameline's remaining control slipped through and away from them both.

Grim but herself, Alison nodded to me and stayed where she was, still insubstantial, my now silent child watching as I turned back to Ameline.

I felt the wall behind me collapse, a shudder of fear the world was about to do the same. That would suck, wouldn't it? We finally won only to be crushed by the falling house above. But Max's tired sigh and push of positive feeling told me we weren't done yet.

Awesome. Because I wanted to be the one to squash Ameline like a bug. Not some random chunk of ceiling.

That was, if she yet lived.

The familiar touch of Enforcer magic hit me in the back, joined by the rush of wild Sidhe as I strode forward to stand over Ameline. I was amazed to see life still in her eyes. Was glad.

So glad.

Crouched over her as she blinked at me slowly, choking on her own blood, her flawless face covered in it.

I gave her a little power, cleared her throat. She turned her head, spit out the crimson flow. Tried to use it, blood magic, only to have it reject her as her stolen magicks rejected her. They were as powerful as ever, hovering, waiting. Keeping her alive.

For me.

How thoughtful.

I'd have to buy them flowers or something.

"We could have been so much together." She coughed, barely whispering, coughed again. "You and I were destined, Sydlynn Hayle."

"I told you before," I said, "I will never care about you. No one does. Or ever will. Because you picked the wrong side, Ameline. Maybe we could have worked things out. But you just couldn't let him love me." Tears formed in my eyes, trickled down my face. "You could have taken any Sidhe soul. But you wanted Cian."

267

She nodded, hardly moving, breathing labored. "Because he loved you," she said.

One of my tears splashed on her cheek.

"For doing so I will never forgive you," I said. "But for taking my son, for making me think he was dead... Ameline, for that I'm going to kill you."

She stared at me, blank and empty.

As I gathered my power.

"Syd." Quaid crouched beside me, turning me toward him, desperation on his face, mixed in with a large smudge of ash and a trail of blood from a cut on his cheekbone, signs the fighting had been fierce and more dangerous than I'd let myself believe in my need to be here, now, in a position to do what I had needed to for a long time. "Let me do it."

Was he cracked? "Let me go."

"Syd." He hugged me over her dying body. "You've never killed before." Hadn't we had this exact conversation once? Also over Ameline. "You don't know how it will change you."

And he did? "Quaid," I hugged him back before pushing him away, seeing the fear in his eyes, the need to protect me. Touched his cheek with my fingertips. Showed him I wasn't afraid. And that he had exactly two seconds to back the hell off before I made him.

Quaid retreated, though it took him longer than I'd like, my warning ignored.

But he did leave me at last, to turn back to Ameline.

Found her smiling at me, cynical and full of spite.

"I've taken him from you, too," she whispered.

What?

She coughed one last time before falling still, eyes burning gems of ice blue. "I hope your heart never finds happiness."

I smiled down at her. "Oh," I said, "but it's about to."

And slipped my power around her heart. As I'd done to Maurice. To Rosetta.

As Ameline had done to Gabriel.

Paused, suddenly afraid after all. Now understanding why Quaid was so concerned.

Point of no return. Doing to Ameline what she'd tried to do to my son. Justified or not, had it coming to her or not, I was about to take her life.

So be it.

Power shimmered beside us. I looked up, saw Iepa and Trinol watching, waiting.

"It's time," Iepa said. "This must end so Fate can finally move on."

Ameline twitched, hand reaching for Trinol. He turned his back on her.

And she sighed. Looked up at me.

"You need me," she whispered.

"I don't," I said. "But you needed me. Sucks to be you."

Her own tear escaped, cut a track through her blood as she gave in at last, releasing herself as I crushed her heart.

And she died.

chapter thirty four

All of her stolen power rushed at me, slamming into me, Gram butting up against the family magic, her Sidhe soul, Lady Rionach, scrunching in next to Shaylee. The taint tried to shoulder aside my vampire essence while the male demon's power growled and snapped at mine even as Cian danced unhappily around the two female Sidhe. The remains of the Brotherhood magic was the only one to go quietly, absorbing into mine, though I could feel the separation remained.

Shud. Der.

I almost missed Ameline's echo rising as I fought to control the magicks suddenly taking up residence inside me like they planned to stay awhile. Unlike the broken and bloody mass at my feet, her echo was as perfect and beautiful as she'd ever been. And, from the snarling hate on her face, just as evil.

I stood quickly, still fighting for control, only to have someone grab my shoulder. Turn me around.

Press a warm and wriggling body into my arms as Alison dropped Gabriel on me.

Her blue eyes met mine, now solid and real, while my son locked his arms around my neck.

"This is my task," she said. And spun on Ameline's hovering echo.

I shouldn't have been surprised the bitch didn't need to be called to stay here and haunt me. Or that she had enough magic behind her to attack.

Alison stepped in front of me, absorbed the thin and pathetic attempt. Raised her hand to Ameline's hateful shade.

Gestured at the air beside her, tearing at the veil much like I did. But not between planes. Between levels of existence.

Ameline's echo shrieked, kicked, fought. Threw more power at Alison who absorbed it, too. Pushed her firmly toward the blackness waiting. A blackness I knew, had dove into to save Charlotte's life, to try to save Liam's, to retrieve Sebastian. But Alison had tools I didn't, was, herself, an echo.

Master of ghosts.

"Curse you, Sydlynn Hayle," Ameline's echo shrieked at me as she clung to the edges of the rift. "Curse you forever!" And, with a wet, tearing sound, pulled free, sucked into the black as she screamed.

Cut off abruptly as the hole snapped shut behind her.

Alison staggered, caught her breath. Smiled at me.

"That was harder than I thought it was going to be," she said.

I laughed, hugged my son who snuggled into my neck, his weight so much more than I remembered, but welcome, so very welcome as my heart healed at last with him in my arms.

"Isn't it always?" She laughed with me, nodded.

And we both turned to find our friends watching us.

"I take it the mansion is in a bit of a state," I said. "Made a mess, did you?"

Charlotte flashed her teeth around a large bruise on one cheek and an eye swollen shut. Her leather jacket was torn at the shoulder and I knew she'd be pissed about it later. For now, she seemed too happy to care. "A bit," she said.

"It'll buff out," Piers said. Limped to the side, longcoat covered in soot, hair charred on the ends.

I laughed again, couldn't help it. Even as the powers inside me grumbled and shoved against each other. I wriggled a bit in discomfort before Gabriel's little hands gripped my cheeks, hazel eyes smiling.

"Momma," he said. "Love you."

Oh. My. Freaking. Swearword.

And then, his power slid inside me and very carefully

mended the places between magicks. A Gateway indeed. They all settled at last, in balance, happy and content while Gabriel giggled and kissed my cheek.

"You're funny, Momma," he said.

I stared at him in wonder, the flood of magic now at my disposal so huge I felt like I was going to explode from it. Caught Iepa smiling at me, tears on her cheeks, hands clasped under her chin even as Trinol bowed to me and vanished.

"Sydlynn," my maji guide said. "It is done. You are in balance, as it was always meant to be."

Um. What?

"This was your fate," she said. "To carry both halves of the whole. Only one of you could carry the weight. I always knew it would be you." She sighed softly, looked down at the mess that had been Ameline, still leaking blood onto the floor. "She would have crumbled under it, destroyed us all by allowing the Creator's dark brother entry into our Universe. But you," her shining eyes lifted to mine, "you are our salvation."

Total what the hell moment.

"Sorry?" I looked down at Gabriel who frowned with me. All the powers inside me, aside from my own, had other homes. Gram, the demon. The taint needed to be destroyed or healed. Even the Brotherhood power that I could pass on to Demetrius. Make up for years of being tortured and broken.

"You must carry both in harmony," Iepa said. "With you in balance, Light and Dark will finally be at peace."

"You can promise me that?" Holy crap. Could I make that choice?

Iepa's sudden hesitation told me what I needed to know. "You are our champion," she said, now looking and sounding a little desperate as she clearly read the unhappiness in my face. "Please, this was Fated all along. Don't turn your back on your destiny when we need you the most."

Max, I sent. *Tell me the truth.*

She speaks it, he sent. *And yet, she doesn't know everything.*

If I do this, if I keep these magicks, will we really be safe forever? Hard to believe. But maybe—just maybe—worth the sacrifice?

Gram.

Sob.

His vast mind fell silent a moment before he spoke again. *Forever is a very long time*, Syd, he sent. *And there is darkness, outside that of the Creator's Fate, I fear now knows we are vulnerable.*

I shivered at the memory of the gaping maw of fire, the glowing eyes. The roar.

Will having this power make it easier to fight? I had to stop thinking about the creature behind the Gate Gabriel opened.

No, Max sighed. *I believe your power—as does Light*

Fate—will attract his attention more than ever. And create a new danger, one we may not be able to destroy.

Gulp. *A fight I can't win?*

A fight we will all be forced to wage, he said. And his voice slowly shifted, became feminine and I knew then, it was Light Fate speaking through him. *And, I fear in the murk of my visions, we will lose.*

Great.

And if I give up the power? What then?

I could hear her smile in her voice as she faded, Max's taking over again.

Then the tasks I spoke of, she said through him, *the future I see, will unravel as it will. And your challenges will continue.*

I nodded physically. Hugged her through him with my magic.

No brainer, then, I sent.

Max laughed, diamond eyes sparkling as I turned to look up at him.

Indeed, he sent.

Little fingers touched my cheek, drew my attention. Gabriel's eyes, so sweet, young and innocent, but filled with enough knowledge to make me nervous, nodded once. Kissed my cheek again. Laid his head on my shoulder.

"Good, Momma," he said.

And made my decision for me.

Returned my attention to Iepa.

"You may think all this balance crap is important," I said. "But if keeping this power means what Fate seems to think it does, I don't want it."

chapter thirty five

Iepa's concern grew to fear as she reached for me, but I turned my back on her. Focused on my friends, waiting, watching. Max bowed to me.

"I will see you soon, Syd," he said. And stepped through the veil, vanishing from sight.

I felt Iepa leave, didn't care.

Let trouble come. Better than some unknown darkness I might or might not be able to survive. We'd faced difficulty before and if my constant state of alertness meant my friends and family—and the planes— would be safe from that creature from another Universe, I'd do it.

Time to divvy up the power.

I smiled down at my son. Opened my Sidhe magic to him. And felt Cian sigh and slip inside Gabriel, joining the soul my son already had. Two peas in a pod, Liam's and Gabriel's two magicks coming together as though meant for each other.

Gabriel giggled and hugged me.

So. Amazing.

I then looked up and found Demetrius watching me. Smiled at him. He nodded and smiled back.

Detached the Brotherhood's power from my sorcery and handed it over. The small sorcerer bowed backward, body shuddering as the magic joined his and, for a moment, as blackness floated over his eyes, I worried I'd ruined him all over again. But when it cleared and he drew a breath, his beaming smile told me this was exactly the right thing to do.

I reached out with my demon and guest, flew across miles to the west coast. Felt the empty shell, the fearful family. Released him into his statue where he flared into life again.

Keranitheronius, he sent. *Demon Lord of the Sixth Plane. My Ruler will hear of your bravery, maji. My thanks.*

Say hello to Dad for me. I laughed as he started and let him go.

Trill was next, though she hung back, almost hiding behind Owen and Apollo. I gently pulled her forward with magic until she stood before me, hands wringing in front of her.

"I don't want it," she said.

"I know," I said, feeling sorry for her, now

understanding the pressure of the dark maji. The need of it, almost as hungry as sorcery, but with its own power to sustain it. "I don't either. And I have no one else I trust to give it to."

Trill nodded, miserable and, though I felt terrible for her, I also knew in a flash of intuition, this was exactly how things were meant to be.

Separated the maji creation magic, the blood power, from my own and slipped it inside her.

She didn't react beyond a shiver, rubbing her arms. Backed away.

I'd talk to her about it later. Help her reconcile it.

For now, I had one more to deliver here.

Before the last one.

Alison watched, again apart from the group, as though doubting she was welcome even yet. I smiled at her, shook my head.

"I thought I lost you," I said.

She grinned. "The taint, yeah. Well." Ran her hand over her ponytail. "I have a little experience with that, don't you know." She winked and laughed. "And an extra kick of power to help me clean it and use it. I guess Ameline didn't know that."

I glanced at Sebastian. "I can split it," I said. "The two of you can share it."

But he shook his head, speculation on his face before he smiled at Alison and bowed to her.

"The lady has earned it," he said.

"Has she ever." Tears welled all over again as I kissed Gabriel's soft hair. He should have been getting heavy by now.

Wasn't.

The taint went to Alison almost eagerly, as though wanting to devour her. I watched her flare with my magic, the blackness shuddering over her until it burned off, brighter and more shining than ever.

And when she smiled, I knew everything was going to be okay.

Because I still had Ameline's power. But I also had a group of amazing people behind that power.

Bad guys had better watch the hell out.

One to go. And though I knew I could do it from here, I wanted to deliver Gram's magic back to her in person.

Bounced my son who giggled and clapped his delight.

"Home, Momma," he said.

Home.

chapter Thirty six

The maji chamber said goodbye as I left, not through the veil, but on foot.

I just had to see what kind of disaster my friends had wreaked.

And yes, I was expecting a mess, especially knowing it took the power of the drach to keep the house from falling in. Was leaving a particularly gory disaster behind myself, one I'd get around to cleaning up eventually.

Eventually.

Even though I had a picture in my mind of what the destruction would look like, I still winced at the giant chunks of rock littering the round room above, the blackened holes in the walls and groaning, fallen sorcerers and dark maji who struggled to rise as I exited into the corridor, my son in my arms.

"I take it I don't have to warn you lot not to get into

any trouble," I said. "Or try to leave." Flaring blue magic erupted above ground, the touch of Enforcers arriving in droves, probably thanks to Mom after our little tête-à-tête during my near fail with Ameline.

The cavalry were more than welcome to mop up the damage and take care of the mess.

I was going home.

Trill and her brothers dashed up the stairs ahead of us, she pausing just before I reached the steps to meet my eyes.

"We're going to help in the cleanup," she said. "See you at the house." And ran up out of sight.

Okay then.

I found Pender at the top of the stairs, beginning his own run down toward me. He stopped, stared, bowed to Gabriel who smiled back his beaming little smile.

"There's a few down there," I said. "Shouldn't give you too much trouble." Paused. "Oh, and if you want to gather Ameline's bones and crush them to a powder, I'd be all for that."

Pender snarled an eager smile. "She's dead then?"

"As a door knob." I bounced Gabriel and smiled. "Isn't she, sweetie?"

He giggled. "Yes, Momma," he said.

I would never, ever, ever grow tired of hearing him say that.

Never.

Sebastian paused just outside the door. I looked up and into his troubled eyes.

"Stewart," he said.

I followed him down the corridor, stopped at the door to the basement—the real one—where I'd found Sebastian dying, where Batsheva trapped the vampires while Mom was on trial. Followed him down into the dank, lit only by a few pale bulbs.

Found the trusted butler dead, drained of blood, stacked like a log of discarded wood on top of the other human servants.

Alison moved forward, reached out with her power. Whispered to them, soft and hopeful. And they rose, all of them, their echoes forming ranks before us, smiling at Sebastian who wept and smiled back.

Stewart raised is hand in salute. "Master," he said.

And was gone.

The hall rang empty with their echoes moved on. I choked on more tears, knew they probably wouldn't be my last tonight, but hoped the ones to come could be happy.

Happy would be a very nice change.

Sebastian hugged Alison suddenly and she embraced him back after the shock on her face wore off.

"Thank you." His deep voice whispered into her hair.

"You're welcome," she said.

When he released her, Sebastian's tears dried up as his

expression settled into grim anger. Without a word, he strode forward two steps, pulled out a plain wooden coffin, the lid sealed shut with large iron spikes and rainbow magic.

Eagerness woke in my heart. I'd killed Ameline and felt none the worse for wear, no matter Quaid's fears about it. Would I suffer over it later? Maybe. Probably. But it was still worth it. Looking at that coffin, knowing there had to be only one vampire Sebastian would save for me in such a way, I figured adding Celeste's death to my tally wouldn't hurt my soul either.

"You wanted her alive," Sebastian snarled. "She is. Barely."

My need to kill faded as Gabriel's sad face pulled me back.

"Let the Enforcers know," I said, turning my back on Celeste Oberman. "Mom and the Council will be happy to burn her. I have better things to do."

Did I. I could taste the anticipation in Gram's power, the need to return home. And I was more than happy to oblige.

One last pause, to hug Alison. "Thank you for everything."

She hugged me back with great enthusiasm. "Thank you," she whispered. "I wouldn't be here without you."

Time to go. I smiled at Quaid, wiped at the smudge of ash on his face, only then noticing he could barely tear his eyes from Gabriel who smiled shyly at him before opening his arms to the startled Enforcer.

Who opened his arms back.

"No way." I clung to Gabriel who giggled and sighed. "Mine."

Quaid laughed.

It was a nice sound.

Charlotte stuck to my side, tickling Gabriel, whispering to him in Ukrainian and, to my shock, he whispered a word or two of her language back. As long as she wasn't teaching him swears, we'd be fine.

Galleytrot panted beside me, hopping up now and then, a little whine in his voice until I stopped almost to the foyer and bent. Gabriel dug his little hands into Galleytrot's fur and pressed his forehead to the dog's.

"'Alleytot," he said.

"My Gatekeeper," Galleytrot said, voice heavy with emotion, the air around us smelling of a fresh spring rain.

Gabriel giggled and let the dog go. "Gate," he said, clear as a bell. And the air beside him shimmered.

Oh boy.

"No, sweetie." I shut him down gently, feeling my concern turn to fear at the vastness of his power. Had I done that, giving him Liam's Cian? In a way, but not as I expected. There was an undercurrent to him, and it was all me.

Gabriel sighed deeply, head on my shoulder. Yawned

and closed his eyes like opening a Gate to who knew where was no big deal.

I was going to have to do something about that.

The mansion was a disaster, though Max's magic kept it from falling in completely. Most of the foyer was filled with the top four floors of the house. The dust had pretty much settled, but I still formed a protective bubble around us to keep the air breathable, glad Gabriel was asleep so he wouldn't see the bodies, the blood and gore.

Like he hadn't just watched his mother kill someone.

Yeah.

I walked out the front door to the musical sound of Enforcers arriving and leaving on flares of blue flame, down the steps and to the wide front lawn before turning and looking back.

And up.

Three quarters of the mansion was on the ground, debris spread down the drive, trees knocked over and smoldering as Enforcers flew overhead to contain the flames. I gaped a bit despite myself, then turned on my friends.

Quaid grinned, shrugged while Piers punched him in the shoulder with a laugh.

"Told you she'd be pissed," he said.

Quaid rubbed his arm, hit Piers back, so hard the sorcerer staggered.

"Worth it," he said.

Boys.

I laughed. Opened the veil. Gabriel woke, eyes glowing as Ahbi reached for him.

"Ahbi," he said.

Gabriel. I could feel her love from my contact with him.

"Home, Ahbi," he said.

She opened the way, adding me her embrace.

"Syd." I turned, saw Quaid glance up at the hovering Enforcers.

Why did my heart fall so hard? Of course he had to stay.

"Thank you," I said. "For being there for me."

His jaw worked. Head bobbed. And he spun on his heel and left.

I sighed as Gabriel watched him go, eyes full of tears, lower lip trembling.

"Momma," he said, grasping after the Enforcer.

Weird. "Don't you want to go home, sweets?"

He nodded, rubbed his eyes with his little fists. "Wanna."

How would I ever survive his cute? Or say no to anything he wanted?

I was so screwed.

"Guess I should stay, too," Piers said. "Can't let the Enforcers have all the fun."

"Piers." I was already choked up.

He shook his head, dipped toward me to kiss my cheek. "You're amazing," he said. And turned and strode off.

Sebastian smiled as I sighed and looked away. Met his blue eyes.

Knew our little crew was shrinking by another member.

"This was my home," he said. Turned to survey the damage. "And with help and time, it will be again."

I nodded, smiled. "You know where to find me," I said.

"That help." Alison's voice vibrated with nerves. "Could you use mine?"

Sebastian's eyes widened before he reached out his hand for her. She took it, fingers trembling.

Wait. Was she blushing?

Oh. My. Swearword.

The pair stepped back, still holding hands, Alison looking a little embarrassed, but smiling nonetheless. The handsome former vampire waved to me as I turned at last.

Ahbi was waiting. And I was ready for this to be over.

With Charlotte on one side, Galleytrot on the other, Demetrius behind me, and Alison and Sebastian waving us on, I walked through the veil and headed for home.

chapter thirty seven

Exit stage left. Enter the triumphant heroes.

I landed in the kitchen with a massive smile on my face, already heading for the back hall and Gram's room. Almost ran right into Shenka. Who sobbed once and raced for me, hugging me and Gabriel both. I hugged her back, one armed, before pulling away, expecting a smile through her tears.

Seeing only terror.

"Syd," she whispered.

And then, I felt it. Or didn't. And I knew then what Gram had really given up. Raced past my second, spun around the bottom of the stairs, burst through my grandmother's door. Saw Lula and Phon, both collapsed in the corner, eyes glazed, energy depleted. Sassafras perched on the pillow, silver fur mingling with wispy hair.

Mom kneeling beside her bed, Gram's limp hand

between hers, sobbing.

Sobbing.

Everything froze: time, breath, life, death. There was only this snapshot of a moment.

My mother. My grandmother. Emptiness and darkness.

A purr broke through, unraveling time, waking me from the moment. Amber eyes caught mine, the rattling sound of Sassafras's magic through his voice surrounding Gram.

"She's alive," he grated through his purr. "But you'd better damned well hurry."

Exhausted, his power. I fed him some of mine even as I set Gabriel down at last, on the side of the bed. My son crawled immediately to Gram, cuddled against her as Mom looked up. Spotted him. Cried harder.

"Syd," she choked. "Oh, Syd."

So much sadness and happiness. How could we bear it? I fell next to Gram, felt her eager power ready and able. Dove inside her, felt her heartbeat, slow and steady. Alive thanks to Sassafras.

I would so kiss him later. If I'd only known, I would have rushed home. Or never let her do it—

Stupid girl, her power snapped. *You needed me.*

I did, I sent. *But it's time for you to go home.*

Demetrius crouched next to me, gentle face streaked in tears. But he smiled up at me and nodded as I thrust

Gram's power back into her body. Felt it wriggle around, like a kid in a car seat trying to get comfortable. And sigh as Gram's body rejected it.

Lula's voice broke through my shock.

"She's too weak," the young healer whispered, dragging herself to my side. "Her body too broken."

No. No, I brought her power back. I tried again, coaxing, as Gram's magic did the same, begging, fighting, struggling.

Failing.

"Syd." Sassafras's hiss came with a stutter of power as he began to falter again. "Do something."

But there was nothing. Nothing I could do. Gram's power wept over her and returned to me even as I covered my face in my hands and cried.

No. Not after all we'd been through. No one deserved a happy ending as much as Gram.

I felt Gabriel stir, watched him kiss her cheek.

"Ethie," he said.

She stirred, but didn't wake, her heartbeat failing further as Sassafras finally stopped purring.

And let her go.

Gabriel's power flared, a soft shimmer around my grandmother. I understood then, what he offered. The Gateway to death, without strife, sweet and gentle. A gift to the great-grandmother he'd never get to know.

I couldn't stand it. Couldn't breathe. It would NOT

end like this. Would *NOT*.

Demetrius sighed beside me, leaned in and kissed Gram's cheek. "You have a choice, my love," he said. "You always have. But you need to take it, now." He brushed his fingers over her hair. "I don't want to lose you again."

Da-dum.

I turned to him, desperate hope in my heart. "You can fix her?" Like she was a broken clock or a fussy engine.

He nodded. "If she'll finally accept what she really is," he said.

What?

Da-dum.

"Gram." I grasped her hand as Mom choked on tears, both of us pouring power into her, her magic trying one more time. "Please, don't leave me. I need you." Sob. "I can't let you go."

Da-dum.

Da—

Silence.

I held my breath. Listened for another beat. Hugged her heart with my power where I'd crushed Ameline's life from hers. Begged it to start up again. Saw the flicker of glow and knew what it meant as Gram's soul began to rise, slowly from her body.

Demetrius leaned back. Nodded. "You leave me no

choice," he said. Opened his power. Detached the magic I'd given him in the maji chamber. And drove it directly into Gram's heart.

She gasped, her spirit slamming back inside her. Gabriel sat up as my grandmother choked on air, the black swarming her. I almost screamed at Demetrius, demanded to know what he'd done.

Only to catch my breath as she collapsed back onto the bed. Breathing. Blue eyes no longer faded, but crisp and bright, wispy white hair now deep, thick black. Glaring at Demetrius like she was going to kick his ass.

"How dare you." She shook where she lay, looking more like Mom and me than her old self. Gone was the thin old lady I knew. This woman was forty if she was a day, skin glowing with good health. If it weren't for the fuzzy socks on her feet and the thin, flowered dress hugging her body, I would have sworn this wasn't my grandmother.

What the hell?

"I dare," Demetrius said. Smiled and took her hand from me. She tried to pull it away, but he didn't let her, his power brushing mine on the way to her.

To hers.

"You're a sorcerer." I gasped the words as Mom stared, Sassafras stared. And Gabriel laughed. Hugged her around the neck. Her face softened as he did, her tension easing. Gram met my eyes.

"And you wondered where you got it from," she said.

A thought crossed my mind. "Gram," I said, "were you supposed to be the Light One?"

She stilled then shook her head. "I don't know," she said. "I don't think so. But all of the power I had bypassed Miriam and went to you." She smiled at Mom. "Sorry, Mir."

Mom laughed, kissed Gram's cheek, still crying. "I think we both did a good job on Syd," she said. "So I'm okay with that."

Gram shuddered as her sorcery settled. Sat up after stroking Sassafras's fur and kissing his head. Hugged Gabriel to her who kissed her firmly on the cheek.

"Ethie," he said.

"Gabriel," she said.

"Good, Ethie." And hugged her back.

Gram glared at Demetrius again. "You've carried my secret for years," she said.

"There's nothing to be ashamed of." Demetrius's blue eyes shone. "And you're not an Enforcer anymore."

"Or a coven leader," she whispered.

"Is that why you hid it?" I looked back and forth between them while Mom pulled herself together.

"Mother," she said. "Why?"

"Because Enforcers aren't sorcerers," Gram said, a bit of her old self showing through in her tart reply. "There was a time it was frowned on." She met Mom's eyes. "I had to hide it or I would have been kicked out of the order."

"Is that how you two met?" Curiosity burned as much as my poor eyes. So the tears had been sad at first. But now the happy had shown up.

Wicked.

"That's a long story," Gram said while Demetrius said, "In a way." The pair exchanged a look, his soft and loving, hers irritated.

And then they laughed.

"So when you became coven leader…" I could only imagine.

"This family was in a disaster," Gram said. "And I couldn't afford any doubts." She hesitated, turned to Demetrius. "Nor could I choose the person I really wanted to marry."

Gape. Ing.

"Sorry?" I shook myself. "What?"

Mom stared, too. "Mother!"

Gram shrugged even as Demetrius kissed the palm of her hand.

"I understood," he said, soft, focused on her as though we weren't in the room. "Though I worried Ivan wasn't the right man for you." He sighed. "You broke my heart, Ethpeal Hayle."

Tears stood in her eyes, anger flashing. "That's why you went undercover in the Brotherhood." She freed her hand and smacked his shoulder. "When I found out..." she trailed off, voice choking. "I would have kicked your ass if I'd known."

He nodded. "I had nothing to look forward to," he said. "My heart was lost. And so, I did the only thing I could. I dedicated my life to my work."

And we all saw where that got him.

Then again... I was kind of glad, in a way. Because I wouldn't be sitting here without him.

Gram met my eyes and I felt her power, the witch power she'd given up, sigh inside me. I could still feel my grandmother, but it was different, through the emptiness of sorcery.

"I'm not a Hayle witch anymore," she said. "Imagine."

"You will always be a Hayle." I surprised myself with the intensity of my tone. Saw her lips twitch into a smile.

She might not be part of the coven anymore, but I had my grandmother back. I could live with that.

chapter thirty eight

I'd sat here before, on a bench in the Council chamber, watching a trial unfold before me, Shenka at my side. But this one was far different. I had no regrets, no old grief—at least not for the creature about to stand before my mother.

Any sorrow I felt around Celeste Oberman centered on the Hayle family members she'd killed. Martin and Louisa Vega, the darling couple who loved and cared about me when there were times no one else in the coven seemed to. Sandra Crossman, leaving her husband, James, alone to raise their daughter.

Old wounds long since healed over, but never, ever forgotten.

Worse, Gabriel wasn't with me. Antsy pants wriggled my butt in my velvet skirt as I fidgeted and held him tight with my magic while he laughed at something and ignored me.

My own son, a traitor.

Sigh.

Shenka squeezed my hand, smiled a little. "He's fine," she said.

"I know," I whispered back. Not needing to. We weren't the only ones chattering. The gathering for Mia's burning—it seemed so long ago, now—had been packed. But this trial conclave was stuffed so full it looked like the room would burst from the pressure of so much magic—and animosity.

Witches loved to point fingers. And found a perfect target in Celeste.

Like with Mia, the Council moved swiftly, barely giving the withered witch-turned-vampire enough time to recover after feeding to understand she was on trial before leveling accusations against her. Celeste refused to defend herself, stone-faced and cold, glaring at Mom every chance she got.

And at me.

A lot of good it did her. I just grinned and waved back. Held up the bag of marshmallows I'd brought with me before giving her a thumbs up.

Heh. Yeah.

No judging. She earned it.

Without a defense, because she had none, Celeste's

trial was short and sweet. Guilty, hands down.

I should have felt relieved now as morning crept close. Knowing she was going out into the sun, would die and never return, did make me feel all fuzzy inside.

But I just couldn't stop thinking about Gabriel. I hadn't let him out of my sight once since our return from the vampire mansion. Okay, except to shower. But Charlotte sat on the toilet bouncing him on her knee the whole time and though it was awkward to towel off and pull on my robe behind the curtain, I could hear him the entire duration of my very fast scrubbing.

Knew he was safe.

Did now, too. Recognized the power holding his interest as a quick image flashed from him to me.

Of Quaid smiling down at him. And felt Cian, the part that belonged to Liam, whisper something to my son I didn't quite catch.

My breath exhaled in a rush before I managed to draw another. I'd left Gabriel in an anteroom a few doors down, surrounded by Enforcers—Mom insisted—guarded by Charlotte, Demetrius. Galleytrot refused to leave his side, Sassafras, too. Uncle Frank stayed behind while Sunny joined the proceedings with Sebastian.

So my son had more than enough protection, I knew that.

Still.

Old fears died hard.

Gram grasped my other hand, her sorcery pressing against mine. Mom's decision to open Celeste's trial to all magic races harmed by the witch-turned-vampire-turned-Brotherhood ally meant I could have my grandmother at my side despite her new shift in magic. She felt powerful, calm. More in harmony than I'd ever known her to be. When her blue eyes met mine, I relaxed a little.

I understand, she sent, the taste of her power so different though her voice was the same. *But there will come a time you will have to let go.*

I know. I shivered. *But it's only been three days and I just can't bring myself to forget yet.*

Not his abduction. Not Ameline. Not Liam's loss.

Yes, I'd let go of Liam. But the linked memories were too comingled to just discard them out of hand.

We will, as a family, destroy anyone who comes near him. Gram's whole being had shifted, changed. But I liked it, how fresh and young she felt, invigorated where once she'd carried the weight of her madness with her even after she'd returned to us with the recovery of her witch magic. And while I still missed her fuzzy socks, her hilarious dancing around the kitchen while making pancakes, I realized this was the woman who led the Hayle Coven. The real Ethpeal I'd only known through magic.

When she released me, her old power stirred within me, but only a moment. The family magic welcomed

Gram's stolen power—now inside me— home to the collective. And Gram's witch magic, safe and sound at last, seemed content to remain, to be absorbed, no longer fighting to return to my grandmother. I hoped I'd never lose the sense of the old her, that it would linger even when her power flowed and combined with mine, her personality ebbing under the pressure of my dominant power. Though I knew eventually my magic would swallow hers and make it indistinguishable from my own.

I'd miss the old Ethpeal, even though I loved who she was now more than ever.

I perked when Sebastian strode into the room, Sunny at his side. The flow of conversation stilled, all eyes following them as they approached Mom together, bowed their heads to her. So like them to dress to impress. Sunny's court gown and the sparkling tiara in her hair made her every inch a queen while Sebastian's crisp white stockings and puffy shirt under his tail coat, long hair tied back into a jet velvet ribbon almost made me swoon again.

Dee. Lish.

He didn't wear his own crown, but Pannera's loss just yesterday led to a change in his status. I'd taken Gabriel with me to sit at the old queen's side at her request.

I worried my son might react with fear, especially considering how horrible Pannera looked at the end, as though the fire had finally burned through her, the leaves of her life so frail every movement made her crumble further.

But Gabriel simply smiled at her, eyes sparkling. Then looked at me. "Home, Momma."

I thought he wanted me to take him back to Wilding Springs.

Was I wrong.

Her gray eyes wide, the only living part of her remaining, Pannera stared at my son as he leaned down and touched the tip of her nose with one finger.

"Home, Nera," he said.

She gasped. And her soul rose from her remains as they crumbled into dust.

Hovered beside me, smiling, stunning once again.

"Thank you," she said in her musical voice.

Alison stepped forward, bowed to Pannera. "Your Majesty," she said. "It would be my honor to show you the way."

The former queen smiled, nodded. And Alison opened the door to the other side.

Pannera met Sebastian's eyes one more time. And flashed into light, vanishing forever.

Sebastian sank to his knees beside the dead queen, weeping. Even as the gathered vampires came to mourn. To surround him.

Anastasia laid one hand on his shoulder.

"It was her wish," she said, "that you be our king."

Holy. What?

Sebastian seemed as shocked as me, head jerking upward.

"She wished that our family be free," Anastasia said, weeping and smiling as the rest of Clan Sthol pressed closer, mirroring her expression. "And knew you would be the one to free us."

He bowed his head, still weeping. Gabriel watched with a pinched look of hurt before turning to me.

"Crying," he said.

"Yes, sweets," I said. "He's sad."

"Nera home," Gabriel said as if that should make everything all right again.

Sebastian looked up. Smiled at my son.

"She is," he said. "And I accept."

And the first vampire king ever rose to accept the throne of his clan.

I wasn't sure what he had in mind to link himself to the others, considering he didn't drink blood anymore, but when he held out his hand to me, I knew I was part of the plan.

Did my best as I understood what he needed. Reached inside him.

Felt his new life, the changes in him. The vampire energy still living in every cell of his body. And had an idea.

Sent my own vampire through him, outward to those

his power came from, led to. Touched the clan with a breath of life. Retreated.

They glowed a moment, sighed. Though not alive as he was, as I hoped they might be, I felt their connection to him once again. And knew they were on the right track.

That they now had the tools to figure it out for themselves.

Sebastian kissed me. Hugged me tight, my son between us. And released me with a beautiful smile on his face.

I left him, Alison still hovering, watching him as he turned to speak with his now-excited clan. Took one moment to hug her, too.

"He needs me," she whispered. "I think I can help where you left off." Hesitation pulled her to a stop. "And I have nowhere else to go."

"You always have somewhere to go," I said, kissing her cheek. "The Hayle coven is your home whenever you need us."

Alison's eyes sparkled with tears. "I think I'll stay," she said. "But you have no idea how much that means to me."

Another hug and I left her there, knowing for as long as Sebastian lived, she was home, too.

The Sebastian who stood before Mom was different than the one I'd left in Pannera's chambers. His giddiness at being alive again was gone, a deep and powerful calm living in his magic, in the set of his shoulders, the gracious smile on his face.

"Council Leader," he said in his deep voice, velvet over spice, "we ask you grant us the right to complete the sentence on Celeste Oberman, formerly of Clan Wilhelm."

"I have lost my sister queen," Sunny said, voice carrying as well as his, bright but sharp. "Both my predecessor, Yvette Wilhelm," no mention of Batsheva, "and now Queen Pannera Sthol."

Mom bowed her head, didn't look surprised.

Cooked this up on the side, did you? I focused the thought at her, felt her amusement.

Are we so obvious?

To me. I hugged her and let her go. *Only because it's what I would have done.*

Mom's eyes flickered to me, only for an instant.

Great minds, she sent. "We understand and accept your claim on Celeste Oberman," she said. Looked to her right and the hall leading to the courtyard where Mia had burned. "Bring the accused."

Six Enforcers escorted Celeste into the chamber. She'd lost most of the beauty vampirism granted her. With only a single infusion of blood to bring her back from her drained state, she looked more frumpy and horse-like, as though she'd reverted back to her previous appearance. But worse. Disheveled and beaten, her most prized possession, her long, thick hair, chopped off at the nape of her neck in ragged strands.

But she was not broken. She glared in defiance at Mom who glared back.

"Celeste Oberman," Mom said, "while your crimes are too numerous to repeat, your greatest was the betrayal of all races to the influence of the Brotherhood. Not through thrall, but by choice. You have offered no defense until now. Do you have one to offer?"

Celeste spit on the floor at her feet, thin gown pulling across her lumpy hips, her sagging breasts. "What's the use?" She barked a laugh. "You're going to kill me anyway."

"We are," Mom said, grim and full of scorn. "Celeste Oberman, you have been found guilty." The crowd murmured, but not in surprise. In anticipation. I have to admit, I was almost on the edge of my seat myself, plastic bag of marshmallows crinkling in my grip.

Just freaking get it over with already.

"For the crime of treason against all magic races, you are condemned to be put into the sunlight until it devours you and you are fully dead."

Since she was already undead, I understood the specific wording Mom chose.

And felt a deep measure of satisfaction from the hate and flash of desperation on Celeste's face.

Mom, she must have something planned. Fear flared as the Enforcers turned and marched her toward the door. Sunny bowed her head to Sebastian who kissed the back of her hand. She turned then and blew me a kiss before flickering into shadow and vanishing.

Morning was coming. I felt Uncle Frank leave too, with a spirit hug for me, as Mom answered.

We've done everything we can, she sent. Sighed. *If she escapes this, Syd, it will be a miracle.*

Or a setup. I quickly followed, pushing through the crowd, almost to Sebastian when the big doors at the far end swung open and the courtyard was revealed. A flash of memory, of a lovely girl rising from the ashes, blue eyes smiling at me, at her brother as she flared with light, almost choked me as I stepped into the wide open space. Eyes locked on the scorched ground where Mia's stake had been.

Where who knew how many witches were burned over the years.

Sebastian paused. Drew a breath. Turned to smile down on me.

And stepped out into the approaching dawn.

I almost screamed at him, grabbed for him. But he turned and shrugged like it was no big deal.

Lunged at Celeste and pulled her into his hands.

Stepped out into the light and let her go just before her eyes rolled back, the forced sleep of morning taking her.

But that sleep couldn't save her from the agony of her punishment. She woke as quickly as she'd passed out, screaming in the early light, hands stretched to the sky and the sunny death beaming down on her.

I'd watched one other vampire die this way. But the Firbolg magician, Cesard, went willingly, grateful for his release, surrounded by Sebastian's blood clan.

Celeste fought for what seemed like far too long for someone on fire, eyes bubbling in the flames, the right one bursting at last, trickling fluid into the hissing coals of her cheek. She withered and collapsed, thin white sticks of her bones charring instantly as her surface burned and flared and smoked, the last of her wail finally dying as her chest sank in on itself. The stench rolled over me, my gorge rising at pace with her death.

I was so grossed out, I almost missed it when her spirit magic escaped her body, flashing upward.

To be caught by Alison. Grim and solemn, she held tight, trapping Celeste's wriggling soul in her grasp. Every other spirit I'd seen rise—echoes not included—was clean and beautiful, the tie to their ego cut, leaving them pure again.

Not so Celeste. She spit and fought, her fury as alive and well as ever. This soul was filthy beyond redemption.

"You will not go on," Alison said, voice sharp, firm. "This spirit is not meant to continue."

Sebastian nodded. Mom.

Me.

And with a flare of light, Alison flashed into ghostly and devoured Celeste's soul.

If I wasn't already borderline pukies from the whole burning thing, I was so close now I had to hold my breath.

Count to ten.

Even as my friend solidified and burped softly.

"Excuse me," she said.

chapter chirty nine

I was already turning and moving back inside by the time Mom began her little speech to wrap up the trial. I had no desire to listen, moving on from it though Celeste's foul stench remained on me. A quick push of magic cleared my nose, clothes and hair of the stink, even as I strode with ever-increasing speed toward the back of the now-emptying chamber and the hall beyond.

A startled Enforcer was the lucky recipient of the bag of marshmallows, slapped against his chest on the way by.

I seemed to have lost my appetite.

Was so focused on my final target I almost ran right into Payten when she dodged out of the shadows of an archway and stepped in front of me.

My first instinct was to hit her so hard with magic they wouldn't find her body.

Ever.

Second instinct was to flatten her into a Paytensquish and smear her all over the floor with my shoes.

Yum.

Third impulse won, partially because I was a sucker for a sobbing girl, Enforcer or not.

Hated enemy or not.

She radiated grief, hands clutching in front of her chest, eyes red and swollen. Had she been crying since I saw her in the tower at stronghold? Wow, she had some serious faucet issues. Should go get a drink of water or something before she dried up and blew away.

But she had something else in mind.

"Coven Leader." She hiccupped softly, impressive chest heaving under her robe as her golden hair fell forward over her wet cheeks. "I know you hate me and I'm the last person you want to see right now. But please, may I speak to you?"

Sigh. My son was waiting for me.

This had better be good and not a lot of gushing over Quaid.

"Two minutes," I growled, joining her under the shadowed arch.

She wiped at her tears with her sleeve, gulping air in an attempt to get herself under control.

I crossed my arms over my chest. "Clock's ticking," I said.

Payten nodded abruptly. Drew one more breath. "I've

ruined everything with him."

This was about Quaid.

Whatever.

But before I could leave, she rushed on. "I owe you a huge apology," she said.

Okay. I was listening.

"I lied to you," she whispered. Caught her breath. Spoke up. "I lied to you."

"About?" A terrible and aching sadness broke over me as I suddenly had a bad feeling about what she was going to say. That I'd believed a jealous and needy girl over the one person who understood my heart better than anyone else.

"Quaid," she wailed.

Damn it.

"I wanted him so much." She sniffled into the cuff of her sleeve. "When I met him at camp that first summer, I loved him at first sight." She coughed a soft laugh. "I was willing to do anything to have him. But then he told me about you." Payten's face crumpled into more grief. "And the way he talked about you…"

My chest felt so tight I didn't think I could breathe. Tears wanted to come. For a lost chance at something I knew now was long gone.

"I seduced him." Her head bobbed, chin on her chest. "One night. Got him drunk, slept with him." She sobbed once, shook her head so hard her hair whipped around her. "It wasn't his fault and he was so upset. Didn't blame me. Blamed himself."

Of course he did.

Oh, Quaid. How long had I misjudged him?

"When we got to Harvard," Payten said, "and I saw you for the first time, I was so jealous." Of me? "You were as beautiful as he said you were and I was all clumsy and pathetic." Wow. Um. Wow. Talk about role reversal. "I didn't know what to do. I knew I was going to lose him to you and I just..." She stilled at last, met my eyes, hers full of misery. "I was at a party. Was drinking a lot. Met this girl who seemed sympathetic."

Gut punch.

No. It couldn't be.

"I told her everything." Payten's face paled, nose and the rims of her eyes bright pink in contrast. "She was so beautiful and kind. Told me if I wanted him, if he was worth it, I should do everything to keep him."

"Ameline," I said, voice detached, emotionless even as my heart screamed her name one last time in hate and grief.

Payten began sobbing all over again. "I didn't know it was her," she said, "I swear it, until she was captured and taken to the stronghold. It was only then I understood. But it was too late, I was in so deep and I loved him."

I reached inside Payten's mind, felt her lack of resistance, her openness. And the final trace of Ameline's control on her magic. On her very soul.

"She thralled you." I felt suddenly dull and hollow even as memory surfaced.

"I've taken him from you, too," Ameline whispered in my memory. Her last black gift.

Payten gasped, hands over her lips. "She did?" Horror crossed her features. "I have to… Leader Tremere will have to be told."

I nodded, now impatient. "So it was all lies." All of it. The show she put on, rubbing up against him when I could see, the kissing, Quaid's anger.

Not aimed at me.

Aimed at Payten.

And his insistence they weren't together—

Because they weren't.

"He would have left the Enforcers long ago," she whispered, "that first summer, would have gone back to you, if I hadn't worked so hard to convince him to stay." She flushed suddenly. "Very hard."

She was asking for me to punch her in the face.

Just. Asking. For. It.

"I've wanted to hate you," she said, more tears flowing. "But I can't. You're so amazing and beautiful and powerful. But you act so casual about it, so confident." Payten snuffled. "The only hate I feel is for myself. Because I wish I was more like you."

Didn't make up for it even a little. But saved her an

uppercut.

"Get your ass to Pender," I snarled, detachment gone as my whole body crawled with the need to pace, to scream and throw things, to wail myself my sorrow.

Payten bobbed her head. "Yes, Coven Leader," she said. Turned to go. Looked back. "I know you'll never forgive me," she said. "And neither will he. But from the bottom of my heart, I'm sorry."

I refused to acknowledge her apology. But I had one question for her.

"Why bother?" For the torment? Just to torture me? "Why tell me this now, when it's too late?"

Payten choked. "When I felt her die, her control leave me…" She shivered. "I guess I finally knew just what I'd become. And that I couldn't live with myself anymore."

I watched her face fall, her body turn away as she slunk down the hall in search of her leader.

Wanted to go after her and pound her a good one anyway.

Didn't. Because the one person I really wanted to punish was already dead.

Ameline had her wish. I was alone. Quaid was an Enforcer. Too late, chance lost.

But the one thing she failed to remember in her need to curse my heart was I happened to be surrounded by love.

And I would never, ever be alone.

I'd blamed Quaid for so much. Told myself he was the jerktard, the one who was at fault in everything. Chose his family over me, to be an Enforcer over us. And yet, I hadn't trusted him really, had I? Not once. The fear remained no matter how he tried to convince me otherwise. Sure, he made bad choices. But so did I. And not believing him over some random girl with big boobs and determination to ruin us was the least of my sins.

I wondered, standing there in the quiet hall, how different things would have been if I'd just trusted Quaid.

My alter egos hugged me, demon still grumbling torture possibilities for Payten as I sighed deeply, shook off my sadness and moved down the hall. Toward the door where my heart waited for his mother to come get him.

Quaid might be lost to me. But Gabriel? He Ameline could never take away from me. Not ever again.

Two giant Enforcers bowed to me before releasing the magic seal around the entry to the antechamber as I approached, not missing a beat allowing me to pass.

Mom wasn't screwing around when it came to Gabriel's protection. The whole room hummed with magic, the long walls lined with dark-robed figures. They all snapped to attention as I entered, Charlotte and Demetrius turning from a head-down conversation they'd been having, Galleytrot lifting his big noggin from the floor beside Quaid.

Who sat on a stool in the middle of the room with giggling Gabriel in his arms.

The sob built in my chest, begged for release as Quaid looked up, chocolate eyes full of wonder and laughter as they met mine. Gabriel reached out and grasped Quaid's face, turning him back toward my son's smile.

He then leaned forward and kissed Quaid on the corner of his mouth.

"Love you," he said.

Choke.

Quaid stared at the boy as I rushed forward and held out my arms. Gabriel frowned up at me, wriggling when I scooped him free of the Enforcer's embrace.

Yes. Exactly.

Quaid the Enforcer.

End of story.

"Thank you for watching him." The words came out in a rush as Quaid stood, the scent of him washing over me, the touch of his magic almost pushing me over the edge. I had to look down, couldn't meet his eyes.

Not now.

Not knowing what I did. That I could have had him, that we could have—

"Syd." Quaid touched my arm, same supportive feeling to his magic almost undoing my resolve. "Are you all right?"

I couldn't answer him. Not when grief held my

tongue, sealed my throat. Maybe if we'd been alone in this moment, I could have collapsed into his arms, told him about Payten, begged him to try to find a way to make us work.

But we were surrounded and my damned pride wouldn't let me break over this last hurt left behind by Ameline.

I was already turning when Gabriel burst into tears. Reached over my shoulder at Quaid.

"Daddy!" Gabriel's voice quavered. "Home, Daddy."

I froze, did sob this time. And fled.

Tore the veil and ran for home. Stepped out while Ahbi's power flared with concern, bounced Gabriel as he continued to cry.

Cried myself in the dark kitchen.

Kissed my son's cheek and shushed him even as I pulled myself under control.

"Sweets," I said through my tears, "Quaid isn't your Daddy."

Gabriel locked eyes with me, shock on his face. "Cian said."

Cian what?

"No, Gabriel," I said. "Cian was wrong." Why would Liam's Sidhe soul tell my son Quaid was his father?

Made no sense.

My son's face paled to white as he absorbed what I said.

Before he burst into tears and bawled like I'd never heard him.

It was hours before he fell asleep, still softly whining as I sat, drained and broken at last, in the chair beside his crib. Sassafras perched in my lap, sadly purring and supporting me as I told him the story.

"With Liam gone," Sass said, "Gabriel must feel the continuing connection between you and Quaid. Though the Cian comment is most puzzling."

Unless, in the pure kindness of his heart, the part of Liam that remained wanted our son to have a father.

Misplaced choice, unfortunately. And really terrible timing. Quaid had already chosen to be an Enforcer.

Damn the stupid magical tie between Quaid and I. I had to break it. I just couldn't bear it anymore.

Lifted my demon cat to my chest and sobbed into his soft fur.

chapter forty

I glared at my reflection in the mirror. "I'm not going."

"You are." Sassafras growled softly at me before sighing heavily. "And so am I, remember?"

"They're not going to make you wear a ridiculous outfit and parade around like you're their property." More glaring.

I. Was. Not. Going.

Sass hopped down from the bed and waddled to my side, tail quivering. "You can't let Meira down," he said, leaping into my lap. I stroked his fur absently. "It would be a terrible thing for her to have to sit through Harry's marriage alone."

"So maybe he shouldn't get married." Whiny much? But there was the crux, wasn't it?

Today was my father's wedding day.

And the last place I wanted to be was Demonicon. In fact, a hole somewhere deep and far away would have been preferable. Anything other than having to endure my father marrying a demon.

That would be the end for Mom and Dad. The real end. And I didn't think I could handle it.

"Harry has made his choice," Sassafras said, meeting my eyes in the mirror. "And perhaps his marriage will at last allow Miriam to move on and find someone to make her happy."

That was true. I hadn't thought of it like that before. Was Mom holding on until Dad got hitched before she'd let him go?

Made sense to me, considering my own shattered love life.

"Fine," I grumped. Set him down on the floor. "Smartass cat."

"Stubborn girl." Sass thrashed his tail. "I'll meet you downstairs."

Sigh.

I let him go, sat there another minute. Felt for Gabriel who was already down the hall in my old room. With Charlotte.

Drew a breath and stood, ignoring my jeans and t-shirt, knowing Pagomaris would be dressing me anyway.

Such bliss to look forward to for the next several

hours.

The feeling of emptiness rushing into the kitchen sped my steps. But when I entered the sun-lit room, it wasn't Gram and Demetrius arriving home from who knew where. I'd grown used to them popping out of nowhere, giggling and tickling each other only to straighten up when I appeared.

Cutest thing ever. And almost made losing Liam and Quaid worth it.

The tall, handsome sorcerer standing in the sunbeam was nothing of the sort. He tilted his head, long, blonde hair bleached almost white by the sun recovered from its singeing at the mansion, gray eyes transparent as he smiled at me.

"You look beautiful," he said.

Made me grin. "Thanks." Total sarcasm. "What's with the visit?" Not that I minded the distraction from my duty as I sank into a chair and kicked one out for him.

Sassafras could wait.

Piers took a seat, though slowly, dark jeans glowing indigo in the sunbeam falling between us.

"I wanted you to know." He sat back, smirk fading. "I've decided to take Clover's place here with the North American Council. She can handle back home just fine with Femke."

I grinned. "Oh, because we Americans are so much more trouble, is that it?"

He kicked my chair with the toe of his boot, but his gray eyes laughed. "Something like that." Piers hesitated. "And I've been meaning to talk to you," he said. "But the timing has been so bad all along." Piers shrugged, eyes sparkling. "When isn't it, really?"

I grinned. "Word."

"You amaze me." He shook his head, eyes distant. "And I know this is bad timing. And that you really probably don't care." Piers sighed a deep, long breath. "I know it's just my arrogance talking, the part of me that thought maybe you and I could…" The handsome sorcerer leaned forward suddenly. "You were pretty clear about how you feel," he said. "That you didn't love me. Yet, I still told myself I had a chance." He winked. "Vanity, right?"

I reached up and stroked his cheek. "You can dream," I said.

Piers laughed again. "I was dreaming," he said. "I know that now. Syd, you're awesome and gorgeous and the most incredible woman I've ever met."

"But," I said, hearing it in his voice, that word.

"But." Piers sat back again. "I wanted to tell you, you were right about me." Pause. "About us."

Huh?

"You scare the crap out of me." More laughter, edged with a tremor. "All that power, so casual. So natural." He ran one hand through his hair, pieces of it clinging to his

324

longcoat. "You'd eat me for breakfast and spit me out."

Ah.

Sigh.

"No," I said, leaning forward to pat his knee. "That's not it."

"It's not?" Pier's arched brows shot up. "Then tell me, oh wise one."

"That mouth will get you into trouble," I said, still grinning.

He leered. "Promise?" And laughed again. "I know we're not right for each other," he said. "But you're a hell of a lot of fun."

"And far too much like you," I said.

Piers stilled. Met my eyes. Smiled slowly.

Nodded.

He stood then, hugged me. And I hugged him back.

"If you need an adventure," Piers said, "give me a holler."

"I have a feeling I'll be fishing you out of trouble in the near future." I kissed him softly. "Thanks, Piers. For being honest. But we both know we're better as friends."

He nodded and backed away. Smirked, opened the way in a black, gaping hole behind him.

"See you, gorgeous," he said.

And stepped through, the dark snapping shut behind him.

While I'd known all along I didn't love Piers, that he

wasn't the right choice for me, I still had a "just great" moment.

Quaid wasn't an option. Poor Liam was… Ram had a thing for my sister. Sebastian was out.

Now Piers.

Looked like I'd run out of boyfriend material. And I didn't know if I had the energy to go looking for another one.

Not like I had much of a choice, though, did I? The coven needed daughters.

Later.

First, I had to go to my father's wedding.

Grumble, mumble.

I had just turned to go down the stairs and join Sassafras in the basement when I felt Gabriel moving toward me, the sound of footsteps and giggling.

Watched as Mom came around the end of the staircase and down the hall to join me in the kitchen.

Oh. My. Swear—

"I wanted to be here," she said. Kissed my cheek. Bounced Gabriel who wasn't giggling anymore, one hand stuffed in his mouth as he watched us.

"Mom." What could I say? She had to know where I was going—why—or else there was no reason for her to take Charlotte's place today.

"Kiss your sister for me," Mom said. And burst into tears.

I hugged her, Gabriel between us, hating how hard this was for her.

Pulled away and nodded.

"Double date it is," I said. "But I pick the boys."

Mom laughed though her sadness, eyes sparkling. "I love you, Syd," she said.

"Love you." Gabriel stroked Mom's cheek.

I wrapped my son in power, sealed the house behind me, feeling the hovering Enforcers waiting at Mom's beck and call. The touch of Galleytrot in the back yard. Knowing Charlotte had to be somewhere, probably on patrol.

Drew a breath.

And left my mother and son behind to attend my father's wedding.

chapter forty one

The sparkling kneepads attached to my heavy leather pants caught the light of the triple suns overhead as I shifted for the millionth time, foot bobbing on the end of my crossed leg. Sassafras hissed at me. The bobbing stopped.

For the moment. The longer we sat here, the more agitated I felt. Didn't help it took Pagomaris an age and a half to dress me while Meira was being man-handled in her bedroom.

"Your demon form would be so much easier to dress, Your Highness." Hopefulness lit the aide's eyes as she smiled and scrunched her shoulders like talking to me as if I were a child would endear her.

"Not." I scowled at her. "Work with this or nothing." I gestured down at my human form.

And she sighed.

Gestured for her minions to come forward.

Left me to them as though I was no longer worth her effort, returning to my sister who grinned at me through the open door of her bedroom.

Argh.

I did concede to shifting my size, remembering how small I felt next to Meira when she was in demon form at the betrothal. But my skin remained softly pink, eyes blue, hornless and nails as clear as they'd ever been, not a hit of scaly blackness to them. Which meant the dressers were saved the trouble of altering the clothing on my body to fit my smaller size.

No way Meira was towering over me this time.

Platform boots presented themselves on the arm of a weakly smiling demon girl.

I stuck out one foot, just hoping I could remember how to walk in the damned things and not fall on my ass.

Magic, Meira sent, as though knowing exactly what I was thinking.

Splutter. *Sorry?*

Syd, she laughed in my head. *Have you really learned nothing in all these years?* Showed me an image of the two of us, her just a little girl, both robed in black.

Holding candles.

Mine leaking smoke into my eyes while hers formed a perfect plume.

She'd taken pity on me that night, so long ago.

Showed me how to control the wisp back when I still refused to use my power.

And winked one amber eye at me. *Always magic,* she said.

Okay then.

I stood slowly, pushing down with my earth power, feeling Shaylee latch onto the ground beneath me.

Keeping me upright.

Allow me, my vampire sent, spirit power releasing some of my weight, making it easier to balance.

And me, my demon growled, her fire blazing around me a moment before forming a column of power supporting me in the air.

Hell yeah.

Meira laughed in my head.

And I couldn't help but laugh, too.

Magic. You betcha.

Sydlynn. Sassy's voice hissed in my head.

I stopped my knee from bobbing as I jerked my attention back to the throne room. *Shouldn't this damned thing get going already?*

Sass swatted my leg with his claws just as the gathered family fell silent.

I stood abruptly beside my sister as Dad strode down the aisle toward us.

Toward his throne.

Our grandfather walked behind him, looking angry.

So did Dad, for that matter, face darker red than normal, power crackling outward. When he saw us, he faltered a step, then marched the rest of the way to our side.

His bride stood to the side, her elaborate gown, consisting of so many layers of fabric and fur and what looked like plate mail weighing her down as much as the four-foot tall headpiece her hair had been piled into, watched with bated breath from the sidelines, managing to dip a curtsy without falling over.

Even with magic, that took skill.

Personally, I wished she'd fall on her face and never get up.

Dad stomped past Meira and me, stopping at the top, spinning to face us all. I half turned, Meira too, breaking protocol as Dad's voice boomed through the whispers of the gathered court.

"I have served you as Ruler for only a short time," he said, hands clenched into fists as Henemordonin stared him down with a deathly glare from behind my sister. A glare so intense it drew my attention before I returned my eyes to Dad. "In that time, I have come to understand I am not the demon for this throne."

Um.

What?

"I am abdicating my Seat," he said. Gestured at Meira while our grandfather ground his teeth, his own face turning a brilliant shade of crimson, "in favor of my heir,

Hathenemeira." She gaped up at him.

Dad.

What the—

Meira bowed to Dad, barely missing a beat while I continued to stare like he'd punched me in the stomach.

"I accept," she said in a clear and ringing voice.

Holy crap, she sent to me as Dad's tension eased.

I'm sorry, girls, he sent to both of us. *Mostly for you, Meira. I never wanted this.*

But I was made for it, Meems sent. *Let it go, Dad. I'm ready.*

Was she? I had no say in the matter. Not when Dad was already opening himself, the power of Demonicon surging above him as the court gasped and shrieked in shock.

It hovered a moment, a column of twisting amber fire, as Dad shuddered. Met Meira's waiting eyes.

"Senne Hathenemeira," he said. "I make you First Seat, Ruler of all Demonicon."

The power descended on my sister in a rush, hitting her with the sound of a barreling freight train, the very air cracking as the sound barrier snapped in half.

She didn't sway. Took it full in the chest, her eyes lighting with the flames of this plane as the power of Demonicon claimed her as its own.

Before anyone could react, the veil parted and, with a suctioning sound almost as loud as the boom just prior,

Ahbi's essence pulled free of the veil. Smiled at Meira who spun to smile back at her. Turned her motherly happiness on Dad.

Brilliant, she sent.

Scowled at Henemordonin.

Idiot.

And flew at my sister.

Hit her as hard as the first power had.

This time Meira did sway, but only for an instant. And I'm sure no one besides Dad, Sass and our grandfather saw it, because we were so close to her.

When Meira's eyes snapped open, Ahbi shone behind her gaze. Only for a moment, but long enough.

My sister was in for a hell of a ride. But at least I knew she wasn't alone.

Meira tensed, power crackling over the uproar of the court as the massed family tried to protest, yelling and throwing magic around. She crushed them instantly, Ruler's force coming to bear as though she were born with it.

"Silence." She didn't have to roar. They listened instantly, suddenly trembling, quiet. "We will always be grateful for the service of Teris Haralthazar." How had I not known Dad had a second name added when he became Ruler? Way to pay attention and stuff, Syd. "And we name him Prince of the Second Plane." They gasped. "Though he will never again be asked to take the Seat."

Whether they liked it or not, Meira didn't seem to give a crap.

"Now," she said, voice louder, backed by power, and I wondered how much of this moment was courtesy of Ahbi, "bow before your Ruler."

And they did, to a demon.

All but Dad's bride. No one could blame her, not even my sister, when the sobbing Zinniaperimote bobbed a fast curtsey before running from the room, her massive train thudding and banging along behind her.

I locked eyes with my grandfather and grinned.

"Good luck with the two of them," I said.

And laughed in his face.

chapter forty two

Meira grinned at me like it was funny. And it was, in a way. She sat behind Dad's old desk—Ahbi's, too—and bounced a little in the chair.

"Comfy," she said. Winked.

Oh. My. Swearword.

Dad laughed, hugged me abruptly. "Meems, pumpkin," loved his pet name for her, though I liked cupcake better despite years of protest, "I'm sorry to do this to you."

"You've already apologized, Dad," she said, looking quite pleased with herself. Hard to remember she was only fourteen with that evil grin, hands rubbing together in expectation. "I'm going to do some housecleaning first. Then the real fun will start."

I shook my head, giggling. "Just leave a few of the

planes standing."

She shrugged, inspected her nails. "We'll see."

"I take it the Node is fine?" It felt fine, Demonicon still intact at least.

"It was in balance long before Ahbi took up residence," Meira said. "She was only just hitchhiking anyway."

I looked up at Dad who sighed deeply, lines of anxiety leaving his face.

"You're crazy," I said. "You just had to do that out in the open, all public like."

Dad shrugged. "It's a demon thing," he said.

Mine grumbled her happy agreement.

"Girls, I was never the right one for the job." Dad met Meira's eyes. "Your grandmother must know it by now."

My sister nodded, sobering, rising to join us. "I think she did all along," Meems said, frowning. "But you were the only one she could trust."

"So no problems with Meems being part witch?" She'd made it as far as heir, but Rulers lasted centuries, longer. Which meant the demon court was at least placated knowing with Dad firmly ensconced as Ruler my sister may never have survived to take the throne.

Guess that little lie died a sparkly death.

Dad smiled, wry and sparkling. "Too late now," he said.

Was it ever.

"Besides, Meira is already a better Ruler than I ever was," he said. "I wasn't comfortable with the power. But she is. Aren't you, pumpkin?"

She wrinkled her nose at him. "Don't call me that."

I just had to laugh.

And so did Dad.

"I've finally figured out what's important." Dad sighed. "Took me long enough." His sad eyes met mine. "I should have just stayed, Syd. I could have. And now… well, now I get a second chance." He bit his lower lip, forehead wrinkling as he frowned in concern. "That is, if your mother will have my fool hide back."

My insides shivered with so much joy I thought I'd shake apart. Why were my cheeks aching?

Oh. I was smiling.

Smiling so wide it hurt.

Awesome.

Meira hugged us both, the three of us sharing our power, our love even as the door to my sister's office banged open and Henemordonin stalked through.

Sassafras trailed behind him, sashaying his fat cat way down the two steps and into the sunken living room area as my grandfather huffed and puffed.

No way he was blowing this house down.

Before he had a chance to lose his freaking mind, Sass leaped onto Meira's desk and wrapped his tail around his paws.

"Ruler," he said. "I believe your Second Seat would like a word with you." He paused, heavy and long for effect. Because Sass loved a good show, didn't he? "When you have time for such things."

Oh, snap.

Meira pulled away from Dad and me, face settling into a mask that looked so much like Ahbi I choked on a laugh.

"Indeed," she said.

"I demand—" That was as far as Henemordonin's huff went as he stepped toward my sister, looming over her.

She grew, quickly, until she towered over him.

"YOU DEMAND NOTHING." My whole body trembled from the volume of her voice. "But," she shrank again, cool and collected until she was her normal size, "you may *ask*." Paused. "And I shall consider your thoughts." Poked him in the chest with a giant fist of amber power. "But never forget, I am Ruler here. And you are Second Seat because I suffer it be so."

Snickersnort.

From the furious look on my grandfather's face, Meira had years of battle ahead of her.

"Father." Dad's soft smile was the gentlest expression I'd ever seen him wear. "She's the perfect choice, and you know it."

"Too young," Henemordonin grumbled.

"Perhaps." Dad turned, same expression aimed at my sister who smiled back. "But she has the finest Ruler who ever lived in her heart now. And I have no doubt the pair of them will lead Demonicon with honor and a passion I lacked."

My grandfather eased up. Nodded.

"And she has me," he said.

Like that mattered. But whatever made him feel better.

We said goodbye quickly, Dad's need to leave apparent in his sudden anxiety. I hugged my sister, sent her and Ahbi love even as I used magic to unlace the damned boots from my feet and kicked them free. Shrank to my human size, now a runt before her in clothes far too big.

"Those are my favorite jeans in your closet," I said. "Tell Pagomaris I want them back."

Meira grinned. "We'll see," she said.

I tore open the veil, Ahbi's absence making me sad a moment. Just a moment.

And then Dad and I were stepping through, into the basement, Sassafras at our feet.

I'd never seen my father so excited. He was actually trembling. Held one finger over his lips as he pointed at me, then the stairs.

Sassafras sighed heavily. "Oh, for the sake of the

elements," he said. "Children." And bounded off, tail straight up even as I understood what Dad wanted.

I went upstairs, forcing myself to take the steps one at a time, schooling my features to calm though I had to force the grin from my lips about every two seconds.

I knew what was coming, even as the demon clothes bagged around me, dragging on the floor, the sparkling knee pads scraping over the tile floor as I entered the kitchen.

Found her touch, waiting in the living room with Gabriel.

Went to her, Dad hiding behind me as I walked into the sunlight and tried my best to act casual while my whole being begged me to just step aside.

Refused to ruin the moment for my parents.

"Hey, Mom," I said, waving a little, sleeve flapping and ringing as the spikes embedded in elbows knocked together.

She looked up, eyes rimmed in red, smiled a little. "Syd," she said. "You look silly, sweetheart."

I glanced down at myself, grinned. "Yeah," I said. "No time to change. I had to get home right away."

"How was the…" Mom didn't finish, eyes locked on Gabriel's sleeping face. He stirred as a tear drop hit his cheek. She wiped it away quickly, kissed the spot.

"It hasn't happened yet." Dad's deep voice broke the stillness and my eager tension.

Mom's head whipped up, eyes huge.

"But if you'll forgive me for being a thoughtless ass," Dad said, slipping around me with a quick hug of power in thanks, going to one knee at Mom's side where she sat on the couch, "the wedding can happen any time you want."

Choke.

Mom sobbed, deep and wrenching, a thin wail escaping her. I rushed forward, slipped Gabriel from her arms as she lunged for Dad, arms locking around his neck.

"Harry," she whispered. "What are you doing here?"

Dad leaned away, kissed her cheeks, her mouth, so intimate I was almost embarrassed, but refused to look away, beaming, my whole soul full of their joy. "I never should have left you, my love," he said. "And now, I swear, I never will."

Mom's sobbing started all over again as she clung to him. I left them then, Dad crooning to her, rocking her as he joined her on the couch, the pair of them curled into each other as though they longed to be one person.

I caught sight of Gram and Demetrius peeking out of their room, the sparkle in Gram's eye as she gave me a thumbs up. Closed the door with a wicked giggle.

I kissed my son who smiled at me, now awake and beaming.

"Momma," he said. "They're happy."

Even if I never met anyone again, my family was back together.

I could live with that.

chapter forty three

I looked down into my son's sleeping face before sinking into the rocking chair beside his crib and releasing of the last of my stress. He was really too big for the thing now, but I needed to do some thinking about a bed and a room for him and just didn't have the energy to deal.

A soft, furry body landed in my lap, Sassafras purring as he kneaded my leg a few times before turning in a circle and settling himself.

"Nice to see them together again," he said.

I knew exactly who he meant. Mom and Dad wasted no time taking off for Harvard for some private time. I blushed at the thought of my parents and what they were probably doing right now.

Shudder.

Gallcytrot groaned from the end of the crib, eyes flaring with red fire as he looked up.

"What about you, Syd?" His rumbling voice shifted my shudder to a shiver. "Have you thought about a new mate?"

Not going there. "I've been thinking," I said, totally changing the subject. Yes, on purpose. No judging. "About Gabriel and his power." My eyes went right to my son, the cat and dog's with me as though we were all drawn to watch him like iron to a magnet.

"We don't know what being a Gateway really means," Sassafras said. "From what you've shown me of his ability, it could be anything."

I really had to find out. But later.

Right now I had another task ahead of me.

"I think," I said, heart weighing heavy, "in light of everything that's happened, we should seal the Gate."

Neither of them protested.

"I was thinking the same thing," Galleytrot said, ears drooping, chin hitting his paws again.

"And me," Sassafras said. Sighed. "Gabriel may be a Gatekeeper, but this Gateway power of his—do we know or can we guess if it might affect the Sidhe Gate?"

"Not a freaking clue," I said. "But it doesn't matter. It's not like I need a Gate to visit the Sidhe anymore. And not having to drag him to the cavern to answer the knock every year would be a bonus." As much as I'd miss it.

All of it.

Because sealing the Gate meant saying goodbye to

Liam.

Forever.

"It's a huge responsibility to put on one so young," Galleytrot said. "And I have a feeling our boy is going to have other things to focus on as he grows without the weight of the Gate holding him back."

Permission from the one person I needed to hear it.

"Thank you," I whispered.

He nodded, head still down. "It's time we all said goodbye."

Gabriel chose that exact moment to wake. His beautiful eyes met mine as he yawned, stretched. Smiled.

I scooped him up, hugged him, kissed his soft cheek.

"Up for an adventure, little man?" Yes, it was late. I was tired.

But there was no time like the present.

I bundled him in his new jacket and slipped shoes onto his feet. But when I tried to pick him up, he slid from the edge of my bed and wobbled. Stood. Held out his hand.

How much of his development had I missed?

No. Not going there.

I would enjoy every second I had from now on. End of grieving.

"Let's go, sweets," I said, laughing at myself for giving him a nickname I only now realized I had.

Like parents, like daughter.

Sassafras purred, pressing against Gabriel's legs. The smiling boy took a soft hold of the Persian's tail even as Galleytrot rose to his feet, shook.

Not a moment of fear passed over my son's face as the giant dog came to tower over him and ever so gently nudged his cheek with his big, black nose.

"'Alleytot," Gabriel said. "'Assfras."

Snort. Chuckle.

So. Freaking. Funny.

"Not a word," Sass snarled. "You should have heard what you used to call me."

No comment.

Giggle.

The veil parted easily, though I still missed Ahbi's welcome as we entered, stepping through into the Gate room, the cavern rejoicing immediately at Gabriel's arrival. He laughed out loud, squeezed my hand before letting me go, running forward to press himself against the Gate.

As though hugging it hello.

And the Gate sang to him, its love and joy pulling him close, cutting us off as the two became one, Cian's power, doubled in Gabriel, called to the magic of the Gate.

The seal flared with green power, Gabriel tottering back as it opened under his touch. I rushed forward, catching him before he fell, looking up into the endless green of the realm into two familiar faces.

Thalion's smile was as real as the warmth in his eyes. He'd evolved past any Sidhe I'd known, his empathy growing, it seemed, by the day. And while I knew it was a wonderful thing, I wondered how he would survive his people, now his heart was open.

"Lord Gabriel," Thalion said, bowing so his long, white hair slid over the ground. "It is a great joy to see you again."

Gabriel clung to my hand, suddenly shy. But he wasn't looking at Thalion.

He was staring at Fergus, one hand in his little mouth, eyes huge.

Liam looked back from his grandfather's face. It didn't hurt so much to see him, this time. I smiled, waved. "Gabriel," I said as I pointed. "That's Fergus. Your great-grandfather."

Gabriel suddenly smiled. Laughed his sparkling laugh. And ran right for the open Gate.

Passed through before I could stop him, slippery as an eel as I lunged to catch him. Hugged Fergus as the old Gatekeeper knelt and swung my son into his arms.

Smiled at me.

"He looks just like us," he said in Liam's voice.

I thought I'd be okay.

The tears on my cheeks told me, yeah. Not so much.

Gabriel kissed Fergus on the cheek before wriggling.

His grandfather let him go. My son paused long enough to wiggle his fingers at the smiling Thalion before dashing back through the Gate and into my arms.

"I think we both know why you're here," Thalion said as I smoothed Gabriel's hair back from his cheeks. "You wish to seal the Gate."

"It makes the most sense to us, as well," Fergus said. "Now that you can cross to the planes of your choosing, this Gate is no longer necessary."

I let out my breath, glad to hear my furred companions and I weren't the only ones who thought this was a good idea. Knowing Fergus felt the same took a huge weight from my shoulders.

The weight of my guilt over abandoning Liam and the place he loved so much.

"What about Wilding Springs?" It was really my last concern, the only question I had left. "Will the town revert right away?" To the ordinary, the hum of Sidhe power that had been a part of every tree, flower, rock and building cut off with the loss of the Gate.

"I don't think so," Fergus said. "At least, not right away. Over time, maybe. But I think having you and your extraordinary family in residence will more than make up for the loss. As will the continued slumber of the Wild Hunt here on your plane."

Good to know.

I didn't get a chance to say so. My son was already

trying to get down. I set him on his feet, watched him go back to the Gate. Wave at Thalion and Fergus who waved back.

"See you," he said. And the Gate sang.

Swung closed for the last time.

I tried to step forward, wanting to help, but the gentle pressure of the Sidhe magic asked me not to.

He must do this alone, Shaylee sent.

He's just a baby. And I was his mom.

He is more than that, my vampire sent. *And you know it.*

Just let the boy be, my demon snapped.

Fine.

Bossy bunch.

The Gate must have known what Gabriel needed, though how my son understood I have no idea. For the moment it sealed, the flare grew in power. Instead of dying in a flicker of flame as it usually did, it roared to life, forming a wall of green flames.

And rushed at Gabriel.

I know I screamed. I could hear the after echo of it bouncing around the cavern. But I was too late.

And it didn't matter.

Gabriel absorbed the magic, drew it into his little body until he glowed like a Christmas tree bulb, shimmering and sparkling. The magic rushed from the cavern itself, the energy sustaining this place pouring into my son.

When it was over, it snapped like a rubber band. I could feel traces of power still left behind. Sleepy and dreamy magic, yawning and ready to rest.

Gabriel's glow snapped off like a light-switch was thrown and he giggled, hands over his mouth.

"Momma," he said. "That tickles."

Oh. My. Swearword.

I choked out a laugh, half terrified, half in awe, and opened my arms. He ran to me, snuggling close when I scooped him up.

"Well now," Sassafras said. "That was…"

"Something else." Galleytrot shook his great mane. "I think it's time to go."

Gabriel looked around. Nodded like he'd made a choice. "Home, pweese."

He felt fine. And his beaming smile told me he was okay.

So I released the last of my fear. Turned in a slow circle. Headed for the exit.

Felt the last bits of Liam leave me as I walked past the archive, his room—our room—and into the entry. Stopped one more moment to look back.

And walked out through the wards.

We all stood in the dark basement of town hall and watched as the Sidhe shielding protecting the cavern flickered out.

And vanished.

Taking the Gate with it.

And Liam.

Gabriel's little face pinched a moment, in a frown, lips quivering. And then he sighed and bobbed his head in a nod.

"'Bye," he said.

chapter forty four

I sat on the side of my bed, looking out the window into the quiet street, the buzzing streetlight below me oddly comforting. I'd tried to sleep after returning home, put Gabriel to bed with Charlotte who met me at the front door after Sass, Galleytrot and I strolled home in the sharpening night air. Her massive scowl told me I was in horrible trouble as she took my son from me.

Okay, so I didn't exactly put him to bed.

Snort.

Galleytrot and Sassafras naturally abandoned me for her room, leaving me alone. Which was fine, it really was. I had a hot shower, pulled on my favorite robe. Had a little cry. Not much. Just a pathetic little spill of tears I held over from the Gate.

From Liam.

And felt my heart ease at last.

Wrapped myself in the love in my house, the people sleeping there. Shenka and Charlotte, Galleytrot and Sass. Gram and Demetrius. All of us, happy just to be home.

But sleep wouldn't come. My mind struggled with belief. That Ameline was really dead. That Gabriel was safe. That I'd won.

I'd actually won.

Imagine that.

Even the Brotherhood were crippled, Liander Belaisle on the run. And with the help of the Steam Union, I hoped they would never be a threat again.

I'd be ready, waiting and able to take them out the moment they were stupid enough to try it.

But my disbelief ran deeper than that. My family was whole, Mom and Dad, Gram and Demetrius. Meira was Ruler. Sebastian and Alison safe. Uncle Frank, Sunny. With the possibility they could be healed as Sebastian was healed as his clan built on what I'd supplied them. I was holding out on doing the same for Sunny's family, if only to see where Sebastian's ended up before risking the vampires I loved.

Just in case I'd screwed up after all.

Despite that reservation, the future was so bright I didn't know if I could stand it.

Now that the Gate was sealed, I felt like the last thread was tied up. My fate was fulfilled—okay, for now—and the coven was safe.

I should have been jumping for joy.

So why did I feel so empty?

Longing ached inside me, despair. The phrase, "No fair," echoed in my head.

Why did I have to win, but lose all at the same time?

We feel it too, my vampire sent, soft and mournful.

Shaylee wept quietly, though her strength rose and hugged me.

We know what we're missing, my demon snarled. *And we're never going to have him.*

I felt the thread between Quaid and I. The one I'd seen, the day Liam died. The tie keeping the two of us together.

Reached for it. *We need to be free*, I sent. *And so does he.*

They sighed and grumbled and wept. But agreed.

Heart trembling, I reached out to sever the connection.

The very moment I felt him in the backyard.

We don't have to go, my vampire sent.

Yes, my demon sent. *We do.*

Agreed. Shaylee's crying stopped. *If only to say goodbye.*

I went to my door, opened it. Drifted through the hall, down the stairs. To the back hall.

My hand hesitated on the handle to the door, pushed it open.

The grass was cool on my feet, damp with dew in the first of September night, the motion sensitive light over the door already on. Illuminating the back yard.

Casting a cool, bluish glow over Quaid. He stood waiting for me, hands in his jean pockets, leather jacket creaking over his shoulders. His dark waves fell across his cheeks, hiding his eyes from view as my body cast a shadow between him and the light.

It wasn't until I stopped and actually reached for him with my power I felt it.

Quaid.

Not Enforcer Tinder.

Just. Quaid.

And my heart.

My heart leaped.

"What did you do?" The words breathed out of me as I tried to inhale and exhale all at the same time.

Quaid ran one hand through his hair, head down, power pulsing softly, quietly around him. "I saw Miriam," he said, deep voice full of light. "And Harry. They looked so happy, Syd."

I nodded, stupidly, mouth open.

"I'd already made my choice. But they sealed it for me." Quaid's shoulder's shifted, as though he bore some uncomfortable burden. "I resigned."

Duh.

"I should never have joined the order in the first place." Quaid's anger finally showed through, poking out of his magic.

With a face attached.

"Quaid," I said. "You love being an Enforcer. Don't let her ruin that for you."

Payten.

How could I live with this agony? And why, oh why, was I trying to send him away again?

Because, if he had any doubt, I would sever the connection. Still held it carefully in my magic. Ready to let him go.

Listened.

"She lied to me," he said. "Tried to convince me you thought you were better than me. That you didn't love me." He shook his head. "I shouldn't have listened. But, Syd, I was so proud. And I have so much of my life to make up for." He finally met my eyes. "Or I thought I did. That the sins of the people who raised me were my responsibility. And that I had to redeem myself before I could be worthy of you."

I was going to sob. Held it in with sheer will.

"I let myself believe you didn't need me," he said. "That you were better off without me. Only to have my love for you punch me in the gut over and over again." Quaid's voice stuttered, fell quiet before he rushed on. "It's not Payten's fault. I didn't lie to you, we weren't a couple. But I did... Syd, I did sleep with her, that first summer."

"I know," I said, somehow managing to sound calm

despite my magic quivering around the thread of power keeping us together and my need to run to him. To hug him and never let him go. "Payten told me everything. Including about Ameline."

Quaid's surprise was sharp, painful. And then, sadness took over.

"Pender is putting her on trial," he said. "For treason."

"I'm sorry." And I really was. I could at last feel sympathy for the girl. Knowing how much I loved Quaid myself.

And would, I now understood, do anything to have him.

Released the thread, let it live. Wanted it to.

No matter how tonight ended.

"I've been looking for a family," he said. "But I needed to grow the hell up enough to know I already had one. That I threw it away." He choked. "Threw you away. Because I couldn't believe I could ever make amends for Batsheva and Dominic. Odette. Clare and David." All the hurt, all the weight, I saw it now, the burden he carried from the people who were supposed to love him. Who used him instead.

The heart and soul of an honorable man, crippled by his need to prove he wasn't them.

"And Mia." Quaid finally sobbed himself, but just once, abrupt and harsh. "I couldn't even save my own sister."

"Quaid," I whispered. "No one could have. She didn't want to be saved."

He shook his head, but not to deny my words. "That was the moment I realized I couldn't be an Enforcer anymore. Because the very order I wanted to be my family killed my only sibling."

Oh, Quaid.

He looked up again, chocolate eyes brimming with tears, tracking down his face, into his stubble, dripping onto the dark fabric of his t-shirt. "I just didn't know how to leave them. Where to go. Because you married Liam and then he died… and I knew you wouldn't want me. Not after everything."

We had the worst timing ever.

"Quaid," I said, "this isn't just your fault, you know." My hands fisted, thumped against my thighs in agitation. "I didn't believe you. Never trusted you, not completely. And I'll always regret the fact I chose to listen to someone else's truth instead of yours." He didn't say anything as I let my hands fall open, shook the cramping from them as I went on. "This is the hardest part," I said, tightening chest squeezing the words from me. "Knowing Fate manipulated us." I shook my head. "I'm not excusing what I did. But if I hadn't married Liam, I wouldn't have Gabriel. And I think, despite the fact I love his little self so much I would choose to die than have him leave me again, he is necessary for another reason."

Damned Fate and her meddling.

Quaid nodded slowly. Ran one hand over his face. "I do understand that now," he said. "As hard as it is to swallow. We had to come to this place, like this."

We did, didn't we? Almost made me feel better.

"I thought I'd be alone forever," he said. "It was keeping me from acting. From taking the step I needed to. Until I saw your mom and dad." His lips smiled, cheeks still wet. "And how happy they were. I knew, if there was even a chance, I had to try." He lifted one hand. Dropped it to his side with a thud. "Try to find happy." He let out a long, shaking breath. "I know I've been an ass, no matter what Fate's intentions," he said. Laughed through his sorrow. "I'm amazed you haven't kicked my butt before now."

I choked out my own laugh.

Didn't answer.

Held my breath and my tongue for fear of breaking the spell of the quiet dark and his need to speak.

"Coven Leader Hayle," he said. "I find myself without a family. I am a powerful witch of all elements in good standing with the High Council." Breathe, Syd. "I would humbly ask to be allowed to return to the Hayle coven where I wish to remain all the days of my life."

Syd. Breathe.

He hesitated as I tried to draw air.

"Even if that means we can only ever be friends," he said in the space of my silence. "All I want is to be with you, Syd. Because, you're my happy."

Exhale.

Inhale.

I crossed to him, floating on air, my alter egos sighing, stretching outward, their power wrapping around him, pulling him to us. His mouth was hungry, his lips hot, tongue desperate as he breathed into my lungs and pinned me tightly against his broad chest, our power mingling, tying together more tightly than ever.

As I pulled free, panting for breath even as I longed for his again, I filled him with the family magic, its power going eagerly to him, as though it missed him as much as I had.

"Third time's the charm." He chuckled, shrugged. Kissed my cheeks, my forehead, my lips, gently. Oh, so gently. "Syd."

"Quaid." There were no words as the thread tying us together since we were born, set ablaze the day we met, the power binding us sealed forever.

I stepped back, taking his hand, calm and at peace for the first time since I could remember. Smiled up at him, tugged a little.

"Come inside," I said. "We have daughters to make."

The light in the back yard flickered off as the door swung softly shut behind us.

chapter forty five

Another mirror. Another dress. Totally different experience.

I stood on what amounted to a pedestal as at least a dozen or so giggling vampires tugged, pushed and laced me into the biggest, heaviest mass of fabric and jewels I'd ever seen in my entire life. The thing weighed so much I had to have my alter egos help me carry it so it wouldn't drive me to my knees.

This was the punishment I got for picking out my first wedding dress alone.

This one was, at least, the pale ivory I'd requested. White would have felt disrespectful to Liam's memory. And Mom happily acquiesced before losing her freaking mind.

And when I appealed to Sunny for assistance in my

mother's sudden loss of sanity?

Yeah.

I was surrounded by vampires, wasn't I?

Shenka hovered, her ball gown sparkling, covered in as many gems as could possibly be stuck to her. Again Mom went with the jewel tones. I guess she figured a good idea was a terrible thing to waste.

And considering only a handful of people had seen the last wedding party…

Did I mention I wasn't in my room? Yeah. The vampire mansion. Put back together with massive help from all sides. I was shocked to discover when Sebastian sent out a request for assistance, almost every single race came to his rescue. I forgave the Sidhe, considering they were now trapped on the other side of the Gate in their own realm.

Good excuse.

I shifted to one side as Sunny prodded me. "Foot," she said.

And held out what amounted to a glass slipper.

Sigh.

She wasn't even being nice about it anymore, all grumpy and snapping at her people like they were failing her somehow. Only her human servant, Chambrelle Strait, seemed amused by the whole thing. Winked one of her pale green eyes over Sunny's shoulder at me, thick, red hair tied back, dark suit impeccable.

Nice to know someone found this funny.

I really wanted to get married in a quiet, private ceremony. To me, my first one had been big enough. The coven was there, my choice friends and family. They were all I needed.

Just made it worse when, the morning after Quaid rejoined the coven, Mom and Dad showed up at the house.

Dressed up. Dad was in a suit, for goodness sakes. Looked like a model for Armani. And Mom in a blue dress showing all the right skin and curves.

Yowza.

I was so floored by their appearance, I missed the fact Varity came in behind them.

Grinning.

"We need a favor." Mom grasped my hands, kissed my cheek before hugging Quaid. Without a word.

"Um." I glanced at my love—no melting—and back at Mom. Beaming Dad. "Okay."

They grabbed us both, Dad muttering, "If you hurt her again, boy, I'll kill you," even as they ushered us out to the back yard.

My father suddenly pulled to a halt. Pointed at Mom and Quaid. "You two, stay put," he said. "You," grasped my hand, "come with me."

Dragged me down into the basement.

Stood in the middle of the pentagram. And pulled

free of his statue.

I gaped as he staggered out of it, turned his mortal body to look back at the diamond effigy, smiling at us both.

"Cupcake," he said. "Here's what I need you to do."

Showed me.

I gasped even as Sassafras pounded down the stairs, skidding to a halt. Looked at Dad. The statue. And growled.

"Don't tell me," he said. "After I *died* and *everything*."

Dad laughed. And looked at me with hope and expectation.

And I did as he asked.

Wrapped his effigy in a cocoon of power. Searched for weakness. Found it, buried in his feet, where the boy Sassafras was bled his life away to save my father.

"You're sure?"

Dad's grin was boyish, joyful. "Do it," he said.

Sass hissed. Sighed. "Just do it, Syd," he said. "I'm done saving his ass."

I laughed. And shattered Dad's statue into a million pieces.

The shield caught them all, sparkling and spinning inside the wards. I let them drop with a musical, tinkling sound, all of them. All but two pieces. The ones he'd asked for. Floated the pure diamond bands to his hand and let them go.

Dad's eyes sparkled with tears as he kissed me. Then dragged me back upstairs with Sassafras following behind.

Charlotte stood on the edge of the flagstone walk bouncing Gabriel and grinning, Quaid and Mom talking quietly with Varity. But my mother's attention instantly broke when Dad and I appeared.

Who was I kidding. When Dad appeared.

"Lovesick puppies," Sassafras grumbled. "Nothing's changed."

Dad laughed. "You really expected it to?"

Sass waddled across the grass to Mom. "I warned you about him."

She bent and kissed him as he rose to rest one paw on her knee. "You did, silly cat," she said. "And I love him more than I ever did."

Sniffle.

Charlotte stood with us as I took Gabriel from her, my son grinning and staring as Varity hurried through the quick ceremony. Not because she wanted to. But because Mom and Dad, both giggling, kept telling her to hurry up.

Hilarious and sweet. I stood next to Mom, smiling between them and Quaid who grinned like a little kid as Varity finally, huffing in frustration, said, "Give her the damned ring then, Harry, if you're in such a rush."

We laughed, Gabriel's a sweet birdsong. And, after a second, so did Varity.

When Mom saw the rings, she gasped, hand over her

mouth.

"Harry…"

He slipped hers onto her finger, pressed his into her shaking hand.

"Forever, Miriam," he said. "For as long as we have. My love."

I was going to collapse in a little heap of helpless tears if they didn't hurry the hell up.

Varity wrapped it up with, "Just kiss her already then. I'll tell everyone I finished."

Dad swept Mom into his arms, dipped her. Breathless, Mom gazed with adoration into his eyes.

There was a time their open affection made me all ewie.

Not anymore.

I let my tears fall on Gabriel's shoulder as Dad kissed Mom.

What could be more awesome?

Someone cleared their throat and we all turned, Dad pulling Mom back up so she could look, too.

My jaw dropped at the sight of Demetrius, dressed in a tuxedo, and my grandmother, her dark hair pinned up in an elaborate 'do, draped in a white lace dress.

"Excuse us," she said, stepping past Mom and Dad who beamed and bowed their way to one side. Gram winked at me. Grasped my hand. "Next," she said. Glared at her friend as Varity sighed. "And make it snappy."

"Gram." I reached out to her. "There's no hurry." She was leaving me again, I could feel it, though this time physically. Moving away from me, moving on. With Demetrius.

She snorted at me, swatted with her flowers. "Girl," she said, "I've been waiting my whole life to marry this man. Don't you dare get in my way." Her face softened. "I'll leave the fuss and waiting for you."

I loved my family.

More tears. Holy. But they were the happy ones at last.

I'd cry as much as I wanted.

When it came time for their rings, Gram and Demetrius drew on their power. Pulled energy from each other, instead of the world around them. And made two shining circles of light from darkness. When the rings settled into their hands, they glowed, platinum and powerful.

Varity set her fists on her hips. "Yada, yada, married," she said. "Kiss her."

Demetrius laughed. Leaned in to peck Gram on the lips.

She grabbed him. And I honestly had to look away.

Or laugh.

Whoa.

When she released Demetrius, he looked dazed and very, very happy.

As Varity hugged her old friend, I met Quaid's eyes. *Wanna?*

He grinned. *Marry me.*

But the moment we stepped in front of Varity, Mom put her foot down.

And continued to.

All the way to this moment. This giant dress.

My wedding night. My circus. Because, wouldn't you know, the minute everyone found out Quaid and I were getting married, they all suffered from collective madness.

Half the paranormal population of this plane wanted to show up. Not to mention a bunch from others. The wrangling of people was massive, scary and, thank goodness, left to Mom, Sunny and Shenka. I think Mom's experience with the world conclave served her well.

I sighed and tolerated it, and the three weeks it took to put the wedding together.

I really wasn't complaining. It meant I got to see everyone again.

And I was totally okay with that.

"She's ready." The vampires backed away, Sunny's grim expression suddenly bright and beaming.

I turned, the massive dress floating under my power, endless diamonds and ropes of pearls, studs of tiny rubies, emeralds, sapphires, black diamonds and amber flashing from the bodice, trailing down into the frothy layers of poof.

Endless, endless poof.

Sunny chased her minions out, paused to help me down from the pedestal as the glass heels, now warmed to my body temperature, slipped firmly into place.

I was shocked. They were actually comfortable.

"I love you." Sunny kissed me on the cheek, dodged my hug. "Don't muss," she snapped. Laughed. "Oh, dear," she said, touching her perfectly updone hair, her pale silver dress a match for Shenka's blue shimmering as she giggled. "Syd, I'm sorry." Then shrugged. "Muss and I'll bite you."

The door opened as I giggled, the dress bouncing with my laughter. Mom and Dad swept inside, Meira behind them, Trill and Charlotte again wrapping up the group.

Though one more beautiful face joined us. Gabriel ran for me. Stopped before he could touch me. Looked up with huge eyes.

"Momma," he said, awe in his little voice. "'Parkles."

Snort. I bent, ignoring Sunny's hiss of worry, and kissed my son's cheek. Straightened his little bow tie, brushed one hand over his tailcoat. "So handsome," I said.

He giggled. Showed me his basket full of flower petals. "Pretties."

"They are," I said. Stood up. Drew as deep a breath as the dress would allow. "Showtime?"

Mom nodded, held out her hand as the girls lined up. Sunny fussed a bit, only to have Meira and Shenka drag her away. Held her in place while she bit her bottom lip and eyed me for faults.

And then, the sound of music reached us, the din I barely heard in my excitement dying down in the distance.

I hooked my arm through Dad's, the other through Mom's. Nodded to Trill who led the way with Gabriel at her side.

"Let's go," I said. "I have my true love to marry and I don't want to keep him waiting."

chapter forty six

How was this for a happy ending?

Bittersweet, this walk down the halls of the newly restored mansion. I'd been through this before, but I knew this time, I didn't have anything hanging over my head.

I loved Liam. But I was finally marrying the man I was meant to be with.

The pressure was off this time too, our battles won. I could enjoy my wedding without worrying about Fate or the Brotherhood or Ameline looming in the near future.

Awesome.

I even found Wilding Springs was fine without the influence of the Gate, just as Fergus said. That it still felt like magic. Probably a combination of the century or so of the Gate's influence deeply mired in the whole town.

Not to mention the presence of the Wild Hunt still snoozing in my back yard.

And the coven.

I didn't worry we'd have to move anytime soon. Good thing. I kind of liked being in one place for once.

Made me think of Sonja, of Liam again. His mother disappeared after the night she met Gabriel. I tried to look for her, feeling badly, wanting her to know her grandson, if he was willing. But I couldn't find her. Mom told me Sonja had been seen with Hortense Spaft, my old Vice Principal and co-conspirator to steal the Gate power with Venner, the Unseelie lordling I'd returned to the realm. But according to my mother, the horrid woman fell on hard times, being carefully watched by Enforcers regardless.

I strode down the hall, my parent's love for each other and for me joining in the middle, hugging me and making me smile through my thoughts. I glanced to the right, into one of the vast rooms, thought of the giant pre-wedding party held here just last night. Of talking with Sebastian, our gracious host, who kindly allowed Sunny's insanity to bully his new servants. He was making headway, Alison hovering at his side always. Which made me happy.

I'd asked her to join the wedding party. She cried but declined.

I wished she'd said yes.

All I could do was hope Sebastian gave her what she was looking for. He certainly seemed to treat her with great affection.

They both needed more of that in their lives.

I sighed as we passed the door, excitement forcing the air from my lungs. Was it worth it? Yes. All the pain, the suffering, the loss. It was. Because it had to be this way. I accepted that when Max showed earlier in the evening, came to see me before the frenzy of dressing began.

Handed me a paper flower, intricately folded.

"From Fate," he said. Smiled.

I kissed him, hugged him.

"Thank you," I said.

Forgave him.

And Max wept.

Seeing him did make me worry a little. About the future. His mention of Fate, no matter her sweet gift, so personal, clearly made by her hands, reminded me there was more to come.

But someday. Not today. And, hopefully, not in this lifetime.

I had many more to live. And we'd earned a little peace and quiet.

Trill's dark hair bobbed to the left as she rounded the corner. I thought of her and the new power she possessed, power I'd forced on her. She admitted at last she feared it would change her, though assured me it did nothing of the sort. I took her word for it. And I choked on a laugh at the memory of her brother, Apollo, hitting on every female vampire he could catch. Trill spent the whole party last night chasing him around, giving him a hard time.

When he came to me, kissed me full on the mouth while Quaid watched with a raised eyebrow, I laughed and hugged him.

Apollo winked at Quaid, shot him with his thumb and index finger. "That's how you kiss a woman like her," he said.

To which Quaid's answer was, naturally, to sweep me off my feet and, well.

Showed Apollo Zornov what a real kiss was.

Smartass fiancé.

Not that I was complaining.

The biggest shock was to see Tippy, Nicci, Donalda and Josie show up. I actually squealed and jumped up and down at the sight of my college friends, hugged them and Shenka at least a million times.

It was Tippy who begged me to let them join our coven. Shenka just grinned.

Her sister, Tallah, was just going to have to get used to losing witches to me.

I was amused to find Shenka distracted by Piers at the party, caught myself grinning and forced my eyes away. If Piers thought he could smooth talk Shenka, he was in for a shocker.

Yeah, good luck with that.

Since she seemed to be enjoying the attention, I didn't bother warning him off.

She'd give him the boot when she was tired of him.

We rounded the corner with Meira just ahead, caught sight of the girls walking down the length of the foyer toward the back of the house.

I'd thought it rather inappropriate to be married in the same room where Mom stood trial. But Sunny thought it was funny.

And it was the biggest room in the mansion, turned out.

Like I had a say in the matter.

The music swelled louder as we approached. Changed just as Trill reached the door.

She turned and met my eyes. Waved. Sighed. I grinned and blew her a kiss.

And the march began.

I floated down the aisle behind the girls, Mom and Dad at my side. The room was packed, the strains of music drifting from the front of the long room. Sunny clearly had control over the renovations because it seemed much larger than it was when Mom's life was in danger. Didn't matter now.

So many smiling faces turned toward me. I glanced around Meira to check on Gabriel, saw a fluffy silver tail at his side. Knew he was in good paws.

I'd spent a quiet few hours with my demon cat that very morning. Talking. Laughing. Crying into his fur. Curled up on my bed, listening as he told me stories of the witches he knew, the ones who came before. Wept himself for their loss.

Told me he now needed daughters, as much as he loved Gabriel. Since Galleytrot was hogging the boy and all.

We stayed there, cuddling, me stroking his fur while he purred in my ear, until Mom came to get me.

Best wedding morning ever.

The memory pulled away my remaining tension. Relaxed and beamed around me as we walked slowly past the people who came to see me marry Quaid.

And to celebrate our success. Our triumph over evil.

Charlotte's blonde hair caught the light as she passed under a floating ball of glowing power illuminating the room. She'd told me she had decided to return home. To take up her responsibilities as heir to the werenation. And, to find a husband.

I could only wish her as much happiness as I now felt.

It would be sad, not having her with me. But, if there was anything I'd learned from this experience, it was that family came first. And I would never, ever let the people I loved—blood related or kin of the heart—fall to the wayside or off my radar ever again.

They were too important to me to lose.

I drew a breath, smiled and waved at Erica. Still in shock about the shuffle in the Council. Only one day after marrying Dad, Mom resigned as Council Leader, to the dismay and fear of the rest of the Council. I was in a bit of shock myself, but understood.

Had to take a moment to process they chose Erica to replace her. Even Mom was surprised. But Gram rolled her eyes and told us of course they did. After all the terrible things that happened, they wanted another Hayle witch at the helm.

I just hoped Erica's weaknesses wouldn't be an issue. She was born to be a second. Not a leader. Time would tell.

At least we had that time.

Past her were the other Council Leaders, so nice of them to come. Femke beamed at me, waved, eyes sparkling with tears. Bindi Braylen, Australia's cheerful Leader, waved with great enthusiasm while Asia's Sumiko Himura bowed her head to me.

I turned my head at the feeling of Sidhe power, smiled at King Odhran and Queen Niamh. I'd taken a moment earlier to allow them and their Sidhe entourage across, knowing they'd be hurt if I didn't invite them to the wedding. I even nodded to Queen Aoilainn as Shaylee sighed over her mother's extravagant dress.

No match for mine.

So that was what Sunny was up to with my gown.

Giggling.

Eva Southway stood with her family, Felix with his hand on Clover's shoulder, Piers grinning at me. I wrinkled my nose at him, rolled my eyes.

As we neared the front, I spotted Lula and Phon Kennecott, sent them love through my power, felt their steady return. Beside them stood Esther and Estelle Lawrence who bounced with barely-contained excitement in matching pink dresses, these clearly new for the occasion. I paused and kissed them both, feeling the love of the family flow through them and into me as the coven, all of them packed in on the right, flooded me with love.

If I tried to fit any more inside me, I was going to explode.

I spotted Gram near the front, Demetrius leaning around her to see. They were too freaking cute, that pair. Gone to live at the stronghold, of all places, recruited by Pender Tremere to start training Enforcers with buried sorcery to access their power.

I'd say one thing for Pender. He might have thought he'd failed us all, but he was the best Enforcer leader I could have conceived of and exactly what we needed. With no word from Belaisle or his people, it made total sense to give the Enforcers the tools they needed to fight back just in case.

I hadn't heard a word on Payten's case.

Probably should have cared.

Mom squeezed my arm as we stopped, waiting for the girls to get in line at the front. She and Dad were happily ensconced at Harvard, planned to teaching in the winter, taking the fall to be together. Giggly and so joyful I could barely stand them sometimes without laughing.

The scent of smoke reached me, the giant candles at up ahead releasing enough I caught a whiff. Thought briefly of Maurice's burning the week before.

I didn't attend.

I heard Gabriel's giggle, the sound snapping me out of the moment of melancholy and into joy again. Everyone loved my son—me included, naturally—and he adored Quaid. Followed him around everywhere, called him Daddy ever since that day at Celeste's trial. Because of Cian and Liam and the most generous of souls. I felt tears rise as I remembered overhearing Quaid talking to Gabriel just yesterday. Telling my son he would be the very best Daddy ever.

Choke.

Quaid had to be feeling terrible about Liam. I was just grateful he loved my son like his own.

It was a hard decision to block off Gabriel's power of the Gateway. I left his magic intact, of course. I didn't want another Mia on my hands and really thought hard about doing anything to keep him bottled up. But when I found him sitting on his new bed, calmly pitching stuffed animals through a portal he'd made, I decided, in the best interest of all planes, my son would have to grow up a little before I'd let him explore further.

And winced at the thought of just where those bears ended up.

Galleytrot's giant form appeared as I passed the last of the onlookers. He'd been a little lost lately, but Gabriel was his focus, followed the boy everywhere. Who followed Quaid everywhere. Which meant the three of them were inseparable.

I could understand why Sassafras wanted some daughters to manipulate and maul.

And love.

I hadn't told him yet. Or Quaid, either. But his wish.

My command.

As my eyes lifted and met Quaid's, his face so full of love, his magic embracing me, I felt the hot power stir in the base of my belly, funneling both of our magicks to feed the tiny seed.

The soul just growing there would fit the bill perfectly.

Ethpeal is a great name for a girl, don't you think?

my very dear reader:

I can't tell you how much it means to me, knowing you've taken this journey with Syd over her incredible twenty volumes. I've had so much fun writing her story—laughing out loud, crying so many tears I'm sure I've decimated the tissue stocks of the world, wanting to be right there with her, battling the bad guys even as I've needed to just shake her at times for being so stubborn.

I know you know what I mean.

It's so hard to say goodbye. I feel like this is the end of something truly incredible—and you've made it that way as much as Syd has. Thank you, thank you, thank you so much for your enthusiasm and love and for buying these books. It means the world to me you've come all this way for Syd's happy ending.

Never fear. There is more of Syd available for you to dive into. But first, you'll be seeing her from new points of view. From Meira's and Charlotte's. From Zoe Helios's. **The Hayle Coven Novels** might be complete, but there are many stories remaining to be told in Syd's universe—including a full series from her starting with *The Outcast*, book one of the **Hayle Coven Destinies**.

The full list of the **Hayle Coven Universe** (and recommended reading) is here:

The First Plane Trilogy

The Planeless

Second Seat

Ruler

The Lychos Cycle

Weregirl

Revenant

Lychos

The Helios Oracles

Foresight

(*Sanctuary* and *Phoenix* are pending thanks to spoilers for the **Hayle Coven Destinies**)

The Hayle Coven Destinies

The Outcast

Steam Union

The Brotherhood

Lord of the Drach

Gateway

The Order

Dark Brother

Blood of the Maji

Also, in case you missed it, **Sassafras** has his own history:

Sassafras

And explore the beginnings of the Hayle coven with Syd's great-great-great grandmother, Auburdeen Hayle in the **Blood and Gold Trilogy**:

Smoke and Magic
Fire and Illusion
Steam and Sorcery

Not to mention the **Hayle Coven Inheritance**
Rite of Passage
The Forsaken
Ashes to Ashes
Daughter of Witches

There is so much more of the **Hayle Coven Universe** to explore!

I'm leave you now with this letter. And my gratitude.
Sydlynn Hayle Forever.
With love,
Patti Larsen

About the Author

Everything you need to know about me is in this one statement: I've wanted to be a writer since I was a little girl, and now I'm doing it. How cool is that, being able to follow your dream and make it reality? I've tried everything from university to college, graduating the second with a journalism diploma (I sucked at telling real stories), am part of an all-girl improv troupe (if you've never tried it, I highly recommend making things up as you go along as often as possible). I've even been in a Celtic girl band (some of our stuff is on YouTube!) and was an independent film maker. My life has been one creative thing after another—all leading me here, to writing books for a living.

Now with multiple series in happy publication, I live on beautiful and magical Prince Edward Island (I know you've heard of Anne of Green Gables) with my very patient husband and multitude of pets.

I love-love-love hearing from you! You can reach me (and I promise I'll message back) at patti@pattilarsen.com. And if you're eager for your next dose of Patti Larsen books (usually about one release a month) come join my mailing list! All the best up and coming, giveaways, contests and, of course, my observations on the world (aren't you just dying to know what I think about everything?) all in one place: http://smarturl.it/PattiLarsenEmail.

Last—but not least!—I hope you enjoyed what you read! Your happiness is my happiness. And I'd love to hear just what you thought. A review where you found this book would mean the world to me—reviews feed writers more than you will ever know. So, loved it (or not so much), **your honest review would make my day**. Thank you!